PROTECTED SECRETS
A Whispering Pines Mystery, Book Ten

Shawn McGuire

OTHER BOOKS BY SHAWN MCGUIRE

WHISPERING PINES Series
Missing & Gone (prequel novella)
Family Secrets, book 1
Kept Secrets, book 2
Original Secrets, book 3
Hidden Secrets, book 4
Rival Secrets, book 5
Veiled Secrets, book 6
Silent Secrets, book 7
Merciful Secrets, book 8
Justified Secrets, book 9
Secret of Her Own (novella)
Protected Secrets, book 10
Burning Secrets, book 11
Secret of the Season (novella)
Blind Secrets, book 12
Secret of the Yuletide Crafter (novella)
Wayward Secrets, book 13

HEARTH & CAULDRON Series
Hearth & Cauldron, book 1

GEMI KITTREDGE Series
One of Her Own, book 1
Out of Her League, book 2

THE WISH MAKERS Series
Sticks and Stones, book 1
Break My Bones, book 2
Never Hurt Me, book 3
Had a Great Fall, book 4
Back Together Again, book 5

PROTECTED SECRETS
A Whispering Pines Mystery, Book Ten

Shawn McGuire

Brown Bag Books

Copyright © 2020 Shawn McGuire
Published by Brown Bag Books
ISBN-13: 9798643597766

For information visit:
www.Shawn-McGuire.com

First Edition/First Printing May 2020

For anyone looking for an escape.

Chapter 1

SCOOP. LIFT. DUMP. REPEAT.

After only five minutes of this, I had worked up a sweat and needed to peel off my fleece jacket.

Scoop. Lift. Dump.

Scoop. Lift. Dump.

After another five minutes, it was clear I would regret volunteering for this job tomorrow. This stuff was heavy. My arms were already yelling at me.

Still, I continued lifting, dropping shovelfuls of snow over the side where they landed on the thawing lake with a solid wet *thump.* This was good for me. Not only the physical exertion of pushing and removing snow from the boathouse deck but also the emotional exertion of preparing the small boathouse apartment for someone else to stay in it. I was being a bit dramatic about this. I knew that. It's just, this was the first place I'd ever lived by myself. I'd gone from my parents' home to sharing a dorm room with my college roommate to an apartment with my then boyfriend. This apartment, approximately the length of a school bus and twice the width, was the place where I'd become independent. Emotionally, at least.

Once I'd completed my task, except for a couple stubborn stuck-on spots that would have to melt on their own, I leaned against the railing and took in the sight before me. The first warm day of the year in Whispering Pines was glorious. According to the calendar, and the even more reliable local Wiccan population, it wouldn't officially be spring for three more days, but it sure didn't look like winter to me. I breathed in the smell of wet sun-warmed pine and smiled. Across the vast forest that surrounded both the lake and the village, any snow left from the storm that hit two days ago was melting quickly, dripping like rain from the boughs. Little *plip, plop, plip* sounds came from everywhere as the drips formed small puddles on the ground. Any animals wandering through the woods today were in for a shower.

"Here you are."

I turned to see my boyfriend and business partner, Tripp Bennett, cresting the stairs along the side of the boathouse. I pointed at the dozen or so fishing huts dotting the lake.

"Don't you think the owners should pull those in now? Look at all the puddles forming on the surface." As if backing me up, sunbeams glinted off a few. "Isn't that a sign that it's time?"

"The villagers know the lake pretty well. I wouldn't worry about it."

"It's been warm for March, though. If it was me, I'd haul them in."

"What are you doing up here? Other than worrying about fishing shanties."

"I came to help Holly clean the apartment."

He took in my leaning against the railing stance and teased, "You appear to be doing a fine job."

"She kicked me out." I flexed my hands up and pressed them against the rail to stretch my tight forearms. "I shoveled the snow off the stairs and deck instead."

Our housekeepers understood full well why Tripp and I had hired them to keep our bed-and-breakfast, Pine Time, clean and tidy. Tripp was constantly busy with food preparation or attending to our guests' needs, and I was born without a tidying gene.

Tripp chuckled at me. "How are you feeling about renting out the apartment?"

The worst part, as it had been from the start, was not having this deck to sit on anymore. Tripp and I had spent countless nights out here taking in the sights, sounds, and smells of the lake and the towering pine trees. Not to mention wishing on the billions of stars above. Even over the winter months, the deck occasionally served as the perfect spot for soothing my wounds after a bad day. No more. People paying us for the privilege to stay in the apartment would probably object to the owner hanging out in their space.

I shrugged. "It's time."

"That doesn't answer my question."

Grabbing his arm, I pulled it tight around me like a security blanket and leaned against him. "You built us the most comfortable, coziest apartment imaginable. No place could be better."

The most embarrassing part of my ridiculous attachment was that I hadn't lived in the apartment since October. It had been sitting empty for five months.

"You still didn't answer me."

"It's like ripping off a bandage. After the initial sting of seeing other people in it, I'll be fine." I pulled him to the side where we could see the grand white house across the yard. I pointed up at the top floor, which held our apartment. "I was thinking we should put a deck up there. We could take out a few windows and put in French doors off the living room. A small one big enough for a couple chairs, a little table, and maybe a grill. The only thing that's missing with that apartment is a private place for us to sit outside at the end of the day and take in the lake and trees."

Tripp frowned as he tried to envision what I was proposing. "I don't think so. I mean, it could be done, pretty much anything can be done. It would really mess with the aesthetics of the house, though." His head tilted to the side. An idea was forming. "What about a rooftop deck?"

The house's roofline formed a pyramid shape, but instead of coming to a point at the top, it had a flat surface that was about sixteen feet square. A tingle started in my toes and traveled all the way up my body.

"That would be awesome," I whispered. "Can we do it?"

"I'll climb up there and check it out. We'd need to install a trap door and ladder, but that should be an easy enough conversion."

"I like easy."

He placed a kiss on my temple. "Which is why you like me."

From the middle of the sundeck, we heard someone clearing their throat and turned to see Holly grinning at us. "You two are so sappy."

"You mean in love," I corrected, and Tripp nodded in agreement.

She rolled her eyes. "Wait until you've got a toddler running around."

Holly was the twenty-two-year-old mother of a high-energy toddler named Ash. We hadn't had much business over the winter, but whenever she came to clean, she told us how grateful she was for a little time to herself. She was also the reason we paid our housekeepers by the room. Holly took twice as long to clean a room than our other helper, Arden, but didn't seem to be in it for the money. In fact, she claimed almost everything she earned went to pay her sitter.

"It's not that I don't love Ash," she insisted once. "I adore my little man. But everyone should have time to themselves now and then."

"Kids aren't on the radar," I told her now and shivered at the thought. Tripp stiffened slightly and removed his arm from my shoulders. We were not on the same page when it came to children. Then again, we'd only been dating for six months. And it hadn't even been a year since we'd met. To ease his mind and my sudden pinch of guilt, I added, "Not yet, anyway."

"I'll go see if Arden needs help in the house." Holly pulled the apartment door shut and gave it a firm tug. "You'll need me the rest of this week?"

"Yes, we're booked solid," Tripp acknowledged. "We're taking overflow from The Inn, which is why we have to open the boathouse."

"Is everything working properly in there?" I asked. We turned off the water over the winter so there'd be no worry of burst pipes and left the heat on the lowest possible setting.

"The water sputtered at first," Holly confirmed, "but it's good now. The heater is heating. Lights are illuminating."

"You and Arden decide on your schedule for the week," Tripp instructed. "The house and rooms will need touching up each morning. Full cleanings once everyone has left. We should also plan a spring cleaning soon."

This perked her up. More time to herself. "I'll talk to Arden."

Holly headed for the stairs and let out a little screech when she got there. A second later, Meeka appeared at the top.

"You're soaking wet," Tripp scolded the Westie. She turned away as though ashamed, but her tail was still wagging. "Found some puddles to play in, hey?"

"Great," I groaned. "Now she needs a bath." I shook a finger at her. "The last thing we need is the smell of wet dog stinking up the clean house."

Tripp chuckled at her. "I actually came up here for a reason. I'm going over to Sundry to pick up a ton of food. Good thing they were prepared for this weekend. I sure wasn't ready for a full house."

"At least we had a little notice."

As in twenty-four hours. Laurel called yesterday, wondering if we could take eight guests because The Inn was at capacity. I told her we had four rooms and the apartment available so some would have to share. She confirmed that wouldn't be a problem, so we took them all. Then we scrambled to put together a menu and clear a path through the snow-covered yard from the B&B to the boathouse.

"Want to come with me?" Tripp asked.

"Sure. Food is the last item on our to-do list."

"And you want to stay busy."

"Well, yeah. I'll pace the house and drive Arden and Holly nuts otherwise."

"Do you know when they're supposed to get here?"

"Rosalyn called earlier. They're running late."

He took my hand and led me down the stairs. "What does late mean?"

"I'm not sure. They'd originally planned on three. So maybe five?"

"Let's go shopping and after we put all the food away, I'll take you out for an early dinner. Triple G?"

It was the equivalent of a verbal pat on the head to keep me calm. A welcome one, though. It had been months since we'd seen each other, and I'd been mentally preparing for their visit for weeks. Still, I tossed and turned last night. Sometimes guests showing up later than originally planned was a relief. It created a little breathing room so the host could make sure everything was ready for them. This time, it only meant my nerves would be on edge longer.

"Dinner out sounds fine." Even I could hear the tension in

my voice. I gestured at Meeka who was running laps around the backyard. "Let me dry her off and we can go."

Tripp gave me a sad smile. "Everything will be fine, babe."

I laughed. "You've only talked with her on the phone. You haven't had to deal with my mother face to face."

"This is the chance you've been waiting for. Right? You'll finally get to resolve the issues between you."

"That's the plan." Problem was, trying to stick to a plan around here was like trying to predict the exact location of a terrorist attack. Not that I was comparing my mother to a terrorist. Exactly.

Chapter 2

BOTH TRIPP AND I WERE happily surprised when my ailing Jeep Cherokee turned over. It hadn't liked the deep freeze of January and February at all. Neither had Meeka. The Westie loved car rides, but unlike most dogs she preferred the security of her cage to hanging her head out the window. A hard stomp on the brakes years ago during rush hour sent her flying to the floor, and she'd been skittish ever since. Because we couldn't fit her cage in the backseat of Tripp's F-350, she roamed free back there but never seemed completely comfortable. Now, as I tucked her into her cage in the SUV's cargo area, her tail wagged triple time.

"Maybe it's the battery," I suggested. "We could try popping a new one in."

"Why do you keep putting this off?" Tripp asked. "You don't love this old thing that much do you?"

"No. I love not having car payments that much."

Thankfully, we got through the winter sharing one vehicle without a problem. However, with the weather warming and the tourist population starting to pick up, sharing wouldn't work for much longer. He'd make almost daily trips to Sundry during tourist season since there was always some ingredient or household item we'd run out of. And I'd need to start keeping regular hours at the station again soon.

Honestly, I was a little excited to get back to work and be busy again. After five solid months of tourists taking over the village, the long winter's rest was nice, but everyone was ready for spring and all that it brought with it.

"All right," I agreed when we were halfway to Sundry and the Cherokee nearly sputtered to a stop every time I slowed down. "I've put this off long enough. I promise I'll start searching for a new vehicle. If Dad would've left the Forester here, I could use that."

"He's heading overseas again soon, isn't he? Maybe he'll bring it back. Or we can make a road trip down to Madison and pick it up."

"I'll ask Mom. She'll know his schedule and whether he wants to keep the thing." My grandmother left the Subaru to him in her will. Along with the house and the two thousand acres that comprised the village.

I turned on the blinker to enter Sundry's lot and had to wait for a cluster of people crossing the two-lane highway. Most were dressed in head-to-toe black and had long, flowing hair in shades of blonde, black, red, or purple.

"The witches are in town," Tripp noted with amusement. "What are we celebrating this time?"

With one foot on the brake and the other on the gas to keep the thing from dying, I stated, "Ostara. Morgan will have to give us the full explanation, but this one is about budding plants and more daylight or something like that. Otherwise known as the spring equinox."

"Vernal."

"Excuse me?"

"Vernal equinox. I always remember that one because it sounds like the name of a goofy neighbor or crazy uncle."

"Crazy Uncle Vernal?"

He gave a crisp nod. "Yep."

I chuckled and studied the group of ten or twelve people before us. They all appeared to be in their mid to late twenties. By the time they had cleared the highway and I could enter the lot and park, a second group was coming out of the store. There were similarities, many of these women were also dressed in all black, but the biggest difference between the groups was their ages. Those in the second one looked to be in their thirties to sixties or older. As the two crossed paths, one of the older ladies pulled one of the younger ones to the side. Just that fast, my instincts started to tingle.

"What are you thinking?" Tripp asked. "And don't tell me nothing. I know that look."

I kept my eyes on the exchange between the two women. "Not nothing. There's something going on with those two." They were just talking, so why had they caught my attention? Mostly to myself, I murmured, "I think it's their body language."

"What about their body language?" Tripp leaned closer to me and followed my line of sight, as though he'd see the scene differently from my angle. "What am I looking at?"

"I'm not sure. The younger woman doesn't appear threatened, but look at how she's turned away, not just her head but her whole body. And her arms are crossed tight. It looks to me like she isn't at all interested in what the other one is saying. The older woman looks like an authority figure. See how she's standing? Confident and tall with her shoulders back, feet planted in a wide stance, hands steepled in front of her abdomen."

Tripp made a humming sound, agreeing with my assessment. "Wonder what the older one is saying."

"How many guests can The Inn accommodate?"

"Why would they be talking about that?"

"No." I laughed and shook my head. "Sorry. Different topic."

"Oh. Thirty, I think. Why?"

A quick, rough estimate put two dozen women in front of Sundry. "I thought Laurel said only one coven was coming. Including the overflow staying with us, that means thirty-eight members. I thought covens capped at thirteen."

He shrugged. "You're asking the wrong guy."

I turned my attention back to the group.

"It's probably nothing," Tripp stated after a minute. "Just you, expecting trouble. And yes, I know that's part of the job." He observed the loosely assembled but definitely divided group. "You know what they look like? Mother and daughter. And mom is embarrassing her kid in front of her friends."

Funny what a shift in perspective could reveal. As I looked again, it simply seemed the older woman was scolding the younger one. My tingles relaxed. "You could be right. They do look like a big group of mothers and daughters."

"They probably caught your attention because your mom will be here soon. You see trouble where there most likely isn't any because you're on high alert and want everything to be perfect for her."

He tossed his hands in the air like he'd solved the world's most complicated riddle. That being me.

"You're right. I would prefer the village stay trouble-free for the next few days. Guess that's hoping for the impossible."

"That's pretty much impossible anywhere people are gathered together." He placed a finger to my chin and turned my face away from the group. "Relax, babe."

I sighed. "Okay. Let's go shopping. I also want to stop in at the station before we go home."

"No problem."

The shopping carts in Sundry were the stubby, double-decker kinds with a smaller basket on top and a larger one on the bottom. Tripp had so many things on his list, we needed two of them. I placed Meeka in the top basket of mine. As we roamed the aisles, she happily accepted ear scratches from fellow shoppers and hung her head over the side to inspect every item Tripp put in the bottom basket.

I, on the other hand, was distracted by the coven members and bumped into Tripp twice.

"Sorry."

The older group had left, so this was the younger one. They had gathered snack foods and bottles of wine and were checking out the cosmetics and jewelry sections along the far wall. The selection was half commercial items and half handmade by various villagers. The girls didn't seem happy with the well-made but somewhat ordinary inventory.

I couldn't stop myself. Leaving Meeka with Tripp, I went to them. "Let me guess, you're looking for something more metaphysical."

"We are," a young woman with hair the coppery-orange shade of fall leaves agreed as others nodded.

Gesturing vaguely at the food in their cart, I said, "You can't go wrong with the snacks here. For cosmetics and jewelry, however, Shoppe Mystique will have things more suited to your taste."

"And how could you possibly know what our tastes are?"

Five foot one, maybe one hundred pounds, medium-brown skin, wavy shoulder-length black hair in a slight triangular shape, black-brown eyes.

This was the same woman who had gotten a talking-to outside a few minutes earlier. At her confrontational response, Sheriff Jayne came out. "No need to snap at me. I'm only trying to be welcoming."

She pursed her lips in a bored pout and crossed her arms. "Is that what you were doing? Or were you making an assumption about us because we're witches?"

Looked like the body language I'd witnessed earlier might be her normal posture.

"Maewyn Barnes," a patient voice from within the group chided gently, "it's not a big deal. She's just offering a little help."

A long and lanky young woman who looked to be in her early twenties stepped forward. *Five foot eight, one hundred ten pounds, lavender-gray hair straight to her waist, pale skin.*

"I'm Ariel Birdsong." She looked at me with a sparkle in her heavily lined pale-blue eyes. A five-inch-wide black belt dotted with silver studs drew attention to her tiny waist. "We had a long drive from Chicago and when we got here, they told us there isn't enough room for all of our coven at The Inn."

"Some of you must be staying with me, then. I'm Jayne O'Shea, owner of Pine Time Bed-and-Breakfast." I pointed to Tripp at the end of the aisle. "That's my partner and boyfriend, Tripp Bennett. I'm also the sheriff of Whispering Pines."

"Is that supposed to impress us?" Maewyn asked.

Unsure of which title she was referring to, I replied, "If you'd like it to." To the rest of the group, I said, "Welcome to the village. Shoppe Mystique, the store I was trying to tell you about, is run by Morgan Barlow."

"Should we know her?" asked a young woman with dark-brown skin and long frizzy black hair partially covered with a black headwrap.

"You should, actually. Morgan is the most talented green witch in Whispering Pines. You'll know who she is by the time you leave. Which of you are staying with us at the B&B? Laurel told me there'd be two parties of four."

Ariel raised her hand and pointed around the group. "Me, Maewyn, Selina Flores, and Kegan Cleareye. Also, our high priestess and other higher-ups in the coven. They're not here. In the store, I mean. They left a few minutes ago."

Selina had a flawless olive complexion and gleaming

deep-brown hair. Kegan was as pale as Ariel but had thick dark hair like Selina's and eyes so unnaturally icy blue that she had to be wearing colored contacts.

"Nice to meet you all," I greeted.

"Wait," Maewyn interrupted, "Rosemary and Wanda are staying at the B&B?"

Ariel nodded.

"I can't stay in the same place as them. Especially with Wanda." Maewyn jutted her chin at Amaya, the one with the headwrap. "Switch with me. I'll stay with Iris in your room at The Inn."

Amaya laughed, incredulous. "I'm not switching."

"Then Iris can stay at the B&B and I'll stay at The Inn with you."

Laughing harder, Amaya replied, "Iris and I have been excited to room together for weeks. You can handle a couple nights in the same building as Wanda."

Maewyn leaned forward and said something in her ear the rest of us couldn't hear.

Amaya crossed her arms and rolled her eyes. "Whatever. Doesn't really matter where I sleep."

"Who's Wanda?" I asked. "Is she someone I need to be worried about?"

Ariel held her hand an inch above her own head. "Big woman. Really wide hair. She's intense but not dangerous if that's what you mean."

She had to be the one talking to Maewyn when we got here. So I was right. There was some tension between them. Of course, now that I'd come face to face with Maewyn, I saw tension between her and everyone.

"Look," I told them, "it doesn't matter to us who stays at Pine Time. Make sure you tell Laurel about the change, though. And if after you're checked in you want to change again, please let us know. Tripp and I will be back at Pine

Time soon. Check-in is at three. I recommend you visit Morgan's shop while you're waiting or maybe stop in at Treat Me Sweetly and grab a scone or cookie. I believe they've got lemon blueberry and mocha chip scones right now. Trust me, you won't be disappointed."

"What's the verdict?" Tripp asked when I returned to his side.

"I feel old."

He chuckled while inspecting bananas and settled on one yellow and one green bunch. "They're not that much younger than us."

I sighed. "Yes, but they seem so carefree."

"They're here on vacation. Remember how carefree we were on Maui?"

Ten glorious days in River's Kahului condo with Tripp's Aunt Addie and Uncle Jim. The only worry we had was whether we'd applied enough sunscreen. A real challenge for pasty-white Wisconsinites. There was one minor crime that I helped River's neighbor Gemi Kittredge solve. Not that I wanted to be a cop on vacation, but she was so desperate I couldn't say no to her. It was my fault. I told her I was a sheriff. Won't make that mistake again.

"Sun, sand, and plenty of water." I sighed again. "Let's go back."

"We have guests to take care of." He placed an armful of baking supplies in my basket. He'd decided that leaving a plate of cookies on the sideboard in the dining room along with thermoses of coffee and hot water for tea in the afternoon was a nice idea. This would be in addition to our occasional wine and cheese gatherings.

"What kind of cookies are you starting with?"

"White chocolate macadamia."

"See?" I gently jabbed a finger into his chest. "You miss the tropics too."

"Sure I do. But you can't miss something if you're there all the time. River promised we could use the condo again and that next time he and Morgan will go with us."

Which meant their baby too. In two short months, Whispering Pines would welcome a new villager.

Tripp had filled his cart to almost overflowing with breakfast items and needed both of my baskets as well. I took Meeka out, snapped her leash onto her collar, and kept her close. The last time I let the leash out too far, we ended up having to pay for a pack of Twinkies and a chocolate cream snack pie she pulled off the end cap and devoured.

At the checkout counter, a case of different wines and a selection of cheeses were waiting for us. Tripp had become very particular about his wine and cheese pairings and ordered them ahead of time.

"I forgot the coconut," Tripp announced as he took six loaves of French bread out of one of the carts.

"I'll get it. Anything else?"

"Coconut milk. The light version. Six cans if they have that many. And the boxes from the truck, but I'll get those."

I passed by three aisles of five-foot-tall rustic wooden shelves—breads and cereals, canned goods, various beverages—and then came to the baking aisle. There I found LaVonne LeBeau chatting with Lorena Maxwell.

"You two seem excited about something," I noted while scanning for shredded coconut. Tripp didn't say how many bags, but he had six loaves of bread and asked for six cans of milk. That seemed to be the magic number. "What's going on?"

"You must know that there's a large coven visiting the village." Lorena pulled Meeka out of the hole I'd left at the front of the shelf and slid the bags of coconut forward from the back.

"Sorry. Meeka, sit. I know about the coven. That's exciting?"

Whispering Pines had the largest percentage of Wiccans per capita of any town possibly anywhere but definitely in Wisconsin. Witches were no big deal here. Why would this group be different from any other group of tourists? Maybe it was more the season than the visitors. Ostara and the start of spring reminded everyone that tourist season was only two months away. Time to start preparing.

"Of course it's exciting," LaVonne chided in a voice too deep for her short body. "To have so many other witches in town to share sisterhood and ideas with? It's like going to a conference and being around the energy of like-minded geeks."

LaVonne worked from home as a computer programmer. She baked and decorated her cottage when not writing code or cracking codes or whatever it was a programmer did.

"I thought you followed Christianity," I murmured while looking for the coconut milk.

"I do," LaVonne agreed, "but my husband is Wiccan, remember? You should hear him going on and on about the different topics he plans to discuss with the witches. Tarot and runes. Candle and crystal magic. Moon magic."

"What are you looking for, Jayne?" Lorena asked.

"Light coconut milk. Tripp needs six cans."

"I've got some in back. Go on up to the checkout. I'll grab a box and bring it up."

I watched as LaVonne added a bag of flour to the yeast, currants, dried fruit, and powdered sugar in the willow basket hanging off her arm. "What are you making?"

"Hot cross buns." The plump woman gave a happy wiggle. "It's been interesting to me, over nearly thirty years with my husband, to learn that most Christian traditions are Pagan in origin. For example, to Christians, the cross on the buns represents the crucifix. To Wiccans, it represents the balance between lightness and darkness."

She motioned that she was done, and I walked with her to the checkout.

"Your husband is one of the few men that follow Wicca. There aren't many."

"It's a little more balanced here, but in general no, there don't seem to be as many men as women. Not because they aren't welcome. The concept appeals to women more, I guess."

I handed the bags of coconut to the waiting checker. "Lorena is getting the milk." To LaVonne, I stated, "I can hardly wait to see what this week will bring. Hopefully everyone will play nicely together."

"Why shouldn't they?" LaVonne set her basket on the checkout counter across from ours. "They all believe the same thing, right?"

A shiver ran through me as I thought of the group outside when we got here. Not a good sign.

"You would think so, but how many wars have been waged in the name of religion?"

LaVonne frowned at me. "No talk of wars. Wars mean death. We don't need any more of that around here. Let's be positive."

"Good plan," Tripp agreed even though he didn't know what we were talking about.

My paranoid sheriff persona was coming out, and it had nothing to do with wanting things under control for my mother's visit. Over the last ten months, every time there was a special celebration or a larger gathering of some kind here, someone died or was critically injured.

I held a hand in the air as though taking an oath. "All right, no talk of wars. Only positive thoughts of warmer weather and good times to come."

"There you go." LaVonne patted me on the shoulder, paid for her items, and took her re-filled basket from the counter.

"Happy equinox, you two."

"You don't believe what you just said about good times," Tripp murmured so only I could hear. "Do you?"

"I want to. Does that count?" When I let my guard down around here, though, bad stuff happened. No matter where I was, if people were gathered, Sheriff Jayne was on alert. Which meant Sheriff Jayne rarely had downtime. There was the glorious string of days while we were on vacation where I didn't have to think about law enforcement. Someday, I'd be able to permanently turn off that part of me. Until then, guess I needed to take more vacations.

Lorena set our box of coconut milk on the counter, gave a wave, and then scurried off to help another customer. Tripp handed over the B&B's credit card to pay for the purchase as the bell over the door jingled. Two older women walked in—a white woman with gray-blonde dreadlocks to her shoulder blades, and a black woman with shoulder-length curly-frizzy hair that puffed out to twice the width of her head. I didn't know the woman with the dreadlocks, but the other woman was the one who'd been out front earlier talking to Maewyn. She had to be Wanda. Ariel had been right about the wide hair. My instincts tingled again, as though I'd had some sort of premonition. There wasn't anything I could do with the feeling other than take note of it, but one thing I knew for sure was that, regardless of what I'd just said about good times, this was not the day to ignore my gut.

Chapter 3

THE STATION'S VAN WAS IN the parking lot when we got there. That meant my deputy, Martin Reed, was on duty. He'd been studying at the police academy in Green Bay for sixteen weeks and graduated shortly before we left on vacation. It eased my mind to have him back full time. Figuring nothing big would happen while we were in Maui, especially since February was the quietest month in Whispering Pines, I let him manage things. Maybe a villager would have a beer too many at the pub and get a little vocal. Or some cabin-fever-inflicted neighbors would get into a scuffle. In other words, incidents he was more than qualified to deal with.

I held the back door open for Tripp and Meeka. The Westie took a sharp right at the end of the short hall and headed for her favorite cell. In particular, the cot bolted to the wall where she preferred to nap.

"We'll only be here long enough for me to check in," I told her.

She shot a look over her shoulder that said, *And your point is?*

"Hey, Sheriff," Reed's voice called from my office on the

far front corner of the building. "Everything's under control."

I glanced at Tripp. "What's he doing in there?"

The only problem with Reed's new knowledge base, or maybe it was leaving him in charge for ten days, was that his self-esteem had become a bit overinflated.

"Probably rearranging your desk," Tripp replied straight-faced. "You know he's trying to steal your job, right?"

"As Gran would say, you're stuffed full of sass today, aren't you?"

He gave me a big, cheesy grin and pointed at Reed's desk in the center of the rectangular building. "His desk light is on and so is his computer. My finely tuned detective skills, acquired by living with my sheriff girlfriend, tell me he was working and needed to check on something."

I blinked at him and repeated, "Finely tuned detective skills? Maybe I should take over running the B&B and you can work with Reed."

Tripp gave a sharp inhale like he was excited. "Did you suddenly learn how to cook?"

Sassiness.

We entered my office to find Reed standing in front of the four-foot-square map of Whispering Pines on the wall next to my desk.

"What's going on?" I asked while pulling off my fleece jacket and hitting the power button on my computer.

"I've been thinking of ways to make patrol more efficient during the tourist season." He circled a finger around the northeast quadrant of the map. That section of the two thousand acres was home to the Whispering Pines Circus. "I was thinking that we should enlist a small team of carnies to be on alert for any goings-on up there."

Once a week through the winter, Reed and I had meetings to touch base on both office and village issues. Even while he was at school, we'd have a brief phone call. The further into his training he went, the faster ideas for "operational improvements and efficiency" started coming to him. By the time I returned from vacation, he had filled one entire side of our six-foot by four-foot whiteboard with ideas.

Procedures in the law enforcement world were always changing. While I was willing to listen to what he'd learned at the academy, most of his ideas were better suited to a large department rather than a two-person station. Enlisting civilian help, though? In certain situations, like large gatherings, that could be helpful. But having volunteer carnies take over part of our daily tasks? He'd have to convince me on this one.

"You're not suggesting that we stop patrolling the area altogether."

"No, not altogether. Our presence is important." Reed practically vibrated with his seemingly never-ending stream of ideas. "The point is, they rarely have issues up there."

I stiffened at that. "Two people were murdered on circus grounds a month after I arrived here."

"Yes, but that was eight months ago. It's never happened before, and it's been quiet up there ever since."

"They've been closed since Samhain. Other than the animals, the only beings up there for the last four months have been Creed, Janessa, Igor, and Britta."

He shook his head like I didn't understand his vision. I did, though. I remembered being fresh out of the academy, ready to take on the world and solve all its woes. Not that I didn't still screw up occasionally, but time, experience, and a few embarrassing mistakes had shown me that while sky-high visions were exciting, they weren't always practical.

Reed took a half-step back and snorted. "You always expect the worst."

"I understand what you're trying to do, Deputy. You're trying to make life easier on us, and I appreciate that. But being prepared for the worst is the biggest part of our job.

If they didn't teach you that at the academy, you need to ask for a refund."

"Think about it this way," he pushed, animating again. "Right now, we patrol the grounds once a day. Twice if they ask us to. The chance of us being there when an incident occurs is remote. Doesn't it make sense to have trained personnel there when we're not?"

He had me on that point. In the spirit of keeping an open mind, maybe this was the perfect time to try tempering some of that exuberance. I wanted him to think this way, to keep moving us forward, but practically and in ways that wouldn't risk citizen safety. He was right about things being calm at the circus most of the time. The circus was sort of a village unto itself, and the carnies rarely needed our help.

"Tell you what."

His eyes sparkled with hope. "Yes?"

"We'll give your idea a try. Talk to Creed and Janessa. They may not be on board with this. If they are, ask them who their most reliable, qualified carnies are and then interview them like you're hiring for a security squad."

He gave a sharp nod, and his mouth fought with a smile.

"This is your project, so I expect you to manage it. Start by going up every day to check on them. Ask and answer questions. Then go every other day until we know for sure it will work. And report to me on how things are going."

He stood with his shoulders back and head high. "Yes, ma'am."

"You know there's a coven visiting the village for a few days. The Inn is filled to capacity, and Laurel asked if we had room for eight more at Pine Time. Capacity for The Inn is thirty people. Add in those that we're taking means there are thirty-eight members in this coven. At least that's how many are visiting the village." Reed grew up Wiccan. He'd know this answer. "Is that a lot for a coven?"

He shrugged. "I've heard of covens with as few as three and as many as sixty members. This one is near the middle."

"Interesting. I figured covens were cozy, smaller groups. Anyway, that amount is nothing compared to what it's like around here during tourist season. So effective immediately and for the next five days, you're taking the lead."

"Taking the lead?"

I nodded, amused by the panic-laced confusion suddenly creasing his brow. *Be careful what you wish for, Deputy.* "You'll take care of patrol and monitor any issues. You'll also be the main contact for all village businesses. I'll be a walkie talkie call away from backing you up should you need it."

"All right. You're sure?"

An involuntary sigh escaped from somewhere near my knees. "My mother is coming to visit."

"I heard. Rosalyn called and told me she'd be here too."

Reed knew about the feud between my parents and grandparents. All of Whispering Pines knew about that. Rosalyn had also filled him in on how much Mom hated the village, which was a big part of why I was so freaked out about her coming. The last time she and I spoke, she said something about wishing she'd come for my birthday in January. We were going on vacation during the part of February that would've worked best for her, so she said she'd come with Roz during her spring break. Why was she suddenly so determined to come up here? She never left Madison except for work-related reasons. If she just wanted to see me, she'd insist I come to her. No, my gut was telling me she was coming to inspect the village.

On the other hand, as Tripp had pointed out numerous times, her timing was perfect. My mother was the last person left on my list of unresolved issues that Morgan and Briar had me create during Samhain. I'd been wondering when I'd ever get this chance, and it seemed now was the time to take care of our problems. And if, while spending time with my mother working on our relationship, I could get her to see the village the way Tripp and I saw it, maybe she'd finally agree to let us keep the B&B open permanently.

"Boss?"

I blinked, and my deputy's concerned face came into view. "Hmm?"

"I asked if you were sure you wanted me to be acting sheriff during Ostara. You okay?"

"Sorry. Yes, I'm sure. There should only be minor tourist problems over the next few days. You deal with those, and I'll deal with my personal issues."

"All right. And you'll be available in case—"

"I'll be a call away. I need to spend time with my mom, but I won't shirk my responsibilities to you or the village."

He visibly relaxed with that statement. "Okay. Let's do it. I'll go up and talk to Creed now. The carnies who left for the winter should start returning over the next week or so. They can make a list of who they think will be the most qualified, and I'll do interviews after that."

I nodded my approval of his plan. "We won't be here when you get back. I only stopped in to do a quick email check. I'll have my walkie talkie on my belt, so give a shout if you need me."

Once Reed had left the building, Tripp asked, "Split-second decision to hand him the reins?"

"Absolutely. Never even thought of it until it was coming out of my mouth."

"How do you think that will go?"

"He'll do fine. He's been around the villagers and visitors longer than I have."

"But?"

"No buts. He'll be fine as long as everyone behaves. And by behaves, I mean as long as no one kills anyone."

In this village, that was a literal concern. So maybe there was a *but* or two.

There were three emails I needed to reply to, and then we were free to leave. It was a little after two when we got back to Pine Time, check-in was at three, so we were surprised to find four vehicles in our driveway. One was River's gleaming black Bentley SUV. We were used to that one. We didn't, however, recognize the white Prius, the silver Audi, or the oxidized red Explorer that looked older than my Cherokee.

Tripp grabbed one of the eight boxes of food from the bed of the truck and handed it to me. "Seems our guests are ready to check in."

"I told them three o'clock. River must have let them in."

We'd gone back and forth over whether we should leave the front door locked or unlocked during the day. This was our home, but we were also a service similar to The Inn. Their doors were always open, but they had a fulltime front desk person to keep an eye on things. River's company, Blackbird Industries, had the perfect solution for us. A programmable smart home security system. We set it to unlock the doors every day during the check-in window of three to five.

"Each registered guest," River explained, "will receive a computer-generated passcode via text at noon on the day they are to arrive. That code will open the front door should they arrive outside your stated three-to-five window. Once checked in, their room keycard will let them into the premises for the duration of their visit."

So far, it had worked perfectly.

We entered the foyer to find Ariel, Amaya, Selina, and Kegan lounging in the sitting room to the right of the front door.

"We got here a little early," Ariel announced. "Hope that's okay. The others were coming over, so we came too."

"The others?" I asked.

"They're in another room." Kegan waved toward the back of the house and held up her cell phone. "Your B&B is beautiful. Is it okay if I take pictures? I'll post them everywhere. I'm sort of an influencer and have tons of followers, so it'll be great exposure for you. Smile, I'll take your picture too."

"Take all you want of the house. We love social media exposure." I held out the box in my arms. "How about you wait until we can pose somewhere and look more professional for ours?"

"Okay." She sighed. "My followers like candid shots better but whatever."

The front hallway led to the great room. There we found four of the older women from the coven. I recognized the two we'd passed as we left Sundry—the woman with gray-blonde dreadlocks and the one with the wide hair who I assumed was Wanda. The two others we hadn't seen yet.

"Hi," Tripp greeted. "We're the owners. Sorry we weren't here to greet you."

"Looks like you've got the fixings for our breakfast tomorrow," one of the unfamiliar women noted with a slight Jamaican accent.

Five foot nine, lean build, very dark-brown skin, black hair to the waist woven into dozens and dozens of small braids.

"I'm Marie Nurse. This is Rosemary Chauderon." She pointed to the woman with the dreadlocks. Next, she touched the knee of a Latina woman with dramatic and haphazardly applied makeup sitting next to her. "Calliope Jones."

"I'm Wanda Bishop," the woman with wide hair announced, confirming my suspicion.

"He's Tripp and I'm Jayne."

"Nice to meet you." Wanda's voice was filled with impatience. "We're ready to check in."

Along with all that hair, Wanda was tall at about five foot

nine, had a neutral expression that verged on angry, and intense dark eyes rimmed with thick black liner. She didn't blink much. Even her clothes had attitude. The long black caftan coat with gold tribal embroidery was striking. As was the coordinating gold scarf with black embroidery. From head to toe, Wanda was very intense.

"Give me a few minutes to help Tripp bring in the groceries and I'll be right with you."

"Not the best first impression," Wanda grumbled to the other ladies. "We should have stayed at The Inn."

I turned back to her with a smile. "Laurel, The Inn's owner, called us yesterday and asked if we had room for a few guests. We're happy to have you, but Tripp and I had to scramble because we'd only expected my mother, my sister, and our long-term renter, River, to be with us this week."

"River," Calliope repeated, waggled her eyebrows, and growled.

My smile warmed. "You met him?"

"*He* was here when we arrived," Wanda informed, not even trying to disguise her displeasure over our absence.

"Laurel surely told you check-in is at three o'clock at The Inn," I continued in my Jayne the Gracious B&B Host voice. "Same time here. It's only ten after two, so if you can be patient for a few more minutes, I'll be happy to check you in early. If you're unsure of the accommodations here, I'm sure Laurel would be willing to make a swap."

Shooting Wanda a less than pleased look, Rosemary, the woman with the dreadlocks, rose from the sofa. Her mannerisms reminded me of Morgan. She had the same effortless way about her, and when she stood, it was like invisible strings pulled her to her feet. Rosemary even dressed like Morgan in her flowing mid-shin dress and shawl wrapped around her shoulders. But where Morgan always wore head-to-toe black, Rosemary wore all ivory. And while this woman's softly lined face didn't hold a trace of makeup, Morgan was always fully made up.

"Alternate accommodations won't be necessary," Rosemary assured. "Forgive Wanda's rudeness, please. The coven drove up from Chicago together, and one of the cars in our caravan had minor problems along the way. We're all a bit tired and hungry."

"I'm sorry to hear about your troubles," I replied. "Mr. Powell runs our village services group and can help if the car needs work. Let me help Tripp with one more load and I'll start on your paperwork."

Rosemary placed her palms together and lowered her head in a bow. "Don't rush. As you always should, complete your task with intention."

My smile went from slightly forced to warm and genuine. "You sound like my friend Morgan Barlow. She's a green witch here."

"I know the Barlows." Marie clasped her hands and looked around at her group. "We all do. We met them when we came last year."

While they reminisced about last year's Ostara gathering, I followed Tripp back out to the truck.

"You diffused that nicely."

I gave a little curtsy. "Years of practice working with drunk, injured, angry, or otherwise unhappy citizens. Seems Wanda doesn't deal well with being tired and hungry. The rest of the group is fine."

"River just left for the Barlows'." Tripp slammed the tailgate shut. "He assured me he would never let guests into the house without keeping an eye on them and checked on this group every few minutes."

"He's more attentive than we are," I joked. "We should train him on check-in procedures."

With all eight boxes inside, Tripp lined them up on the

counter with the frozen items at one end, refrigerated foods in the middle, and pantry items last. Then he'd unpack starting with the frozen things. He had a process and was so particular about what he wanted in each box, the folks at Sundry let him pack his own groceries now.

"Thanks for your help. I can handle things from here if you want to get them settled into their rooms."

"In other words," I teased, "don't mess with your process?"

He shrugged in response.

"The problem with checking them in now is that I took a stance with Wanda." Like a parent with a child. If I backed down now and gave in to her attitude, she'd expect us to give in to her for the entire visit. "I have an idea."

I returned to the great room where Meeka was busy entertaining the ladies, and herself, by going from one to the other to get a belly rub or an ear scratch. Even stern Wanda had softened a bit in her presence. More important than their reactions was Meeka's. She liked them. She wouldn't still be in the room if she didn't.

After gathering all eight women together, I began, "Rosemary commented that you're all hungry. I thought you might want to go into the village and get something to eat. The Inn's restaurant should be serving today, and there's also Grapes, Grains, and Grub on the west side of the Pentacle Garden. Since we're between the lunch and dinner hours, Ye Olde Bean Grinder serves coffee and pastries if you want something lighter. Or there's a bigger variety of pastries and other goodies at Treat Me Sweetly. They're all right there in the commons along with plenty of shops to explore. You can bring in your bags, and if you give me your names and credit card information, I'll take care of the paperwork while you're gone. Your rooms and keycards will be ready when you return."

They glanced around at each other, had a short discussion, and decided that was a good plan. The older ladies preferred their own rooms, so I'd divide them among the Jack and Jill rooms, The Side, and The Treehouse. Our younger guests were fine doubling up on the bed and pullout sofa in The Boathouse. We helped them bring in their luggage, which we piled in the great room for the moment, and they were off.

"You're sure I can't help with the groceries?" I confirmed with Tripp after the witches left.

"I'm sure. You put things in the wrong places."

I made a face at him and then reached up for a kiss. "I'll go take care of their paperwork. Then we should go grab something to eat. I'm starving."

Before he could respond, a familiar voice demanded, "What on earth is going on in here?"

Chapter 4

I STOOD ON MY TIPTOES to peek over Tripp's shoulder and found my mother and sister standing a few feet away. Mom looked fabulous. My mother always looked fabulous. Her makeup was done to perfection, and despite the five-hour drive from Madison, there wasn't a single wrinkle on her outfit. Speaking of which, she looked very stylish in slim khaki pants tucked into knee-length dark-chocolate-brown boots. She wore a scoop neck ivory sweater beneath a brown, rust, and tan tweed plaid blazer that hit at mid-hip. Her entire outfit was almost certainly made of merino wool, her cool-weather fabric of choice.

I sidestepped to stand next to Tripp. "You changed your hair." Gone was the simple medium-brown bob. The color was the same, but she'd added layers and long bangs that framed and softened her features. It made her look younger, not that I'd tell her that. And, of course, not a strand was out of place.

She crossed her arms tightly, and a frown darkened her face. "There are suitcases all over in here." She looked around the corner into the kitchen. "Groceries are everywhere in there. And you two are in the middle of the chaos putting on a public display of affection."

Rosalyn, standing behind Mom, rolled her eyes at that last bit. I was only marginally successful at fighting off a laugh and reminded myself that the house never looked like this. It was a fluke. A badly timed one, but still a fluke.

How are you going to handle this? Jayne in my head challenged.

Good question. Trusting my gut, because my logical brain had abandoned me, I threw my arms wide, strode over to my mother, and wrapped her in a hug. Startled by my response, she patted me awkwardly on the back in return. As we "embraced," I shot my sister an evil eye glare. "You're early. We weren't expecting you until after dinner."

Rosalyn held her hand in the air. "That's my fault."

I glanced at the large clock on the wall. "It's quarter to three. You drove, didn't you?" Rosalyn nodded. My sister had a speeding problem. "How fast were you going?"

"Not that fast, I swear." She stared blankly at Mom. "We ended up leaving at our originally planned time, and I was so excited to get here I forgot to call back. Ask Mom. She only let me go five miles over the limit."

"I have one of those apps on my phone," Mom stated. "It tracks how fast the car travels, and I get a rebate check for driving responsibly."

Roz let her head drop back, indicating she'd had enough of our mother for one day, and trudged toward me like her legs weighed two hundred pounds each. She was being dramatic, but after five hours in the car with our mother, she was entitled. Draping herself over me, she let out a happy sigh. "Hi, sis. I missed you."

A light as air feeling took over my heart, and I squeezed her tight. "I missed you too."

This seemed to confuse our mother. The last time she'd seen us together, we barely spoke three words to each other.

That was before Rosalyn came up for the Samhain celebration in October. We spent a lot of time together during that visit and worked through our old issues. Since then, not only did we text or talk multiple times per week, she'd come back for Christmas and stayed for her entire winter break, which meant almost all of January. She also had a thing going with my deputy, so I wasn't her only reason for visits. She'd come to love the village so much, I wouldn't be surprised if she decided to move up here after she graduated in May. As long as she could pay her way, I was all for it. Come tourist season, we'd lose a ton of money if we let her take over a room here.

"Told you," Rosalyn said over her shoulder to Mom. "We like each other again."

Mom stepped forward and extended her hand to Tripp. "You must be Tripper Bennett."

"And you must be Georgia. Great to finally meet you face to face."

Tripp took her hand, and she leaned in so they could exchange air kisses. I'd never seen Tripp do that to anyone before. Who knew my guy had such a cosmopolitan side?

"Sorry about the mess. We had last-minute guests check in. Long story." He went to my sister, wrapped her in a hug, and gave her an actual kiss on the cheek. "Welcome back. Your room has been wondering where you've been."

Rosalyn bounced on the balls of her feet and clapped her hands. *Her* room was the one off the kitchen and the only bedroom on the main level. "Can't wait to sleep in my bed again."

She was always welcome, but I'd seriously charge her rent if she stayed here this summer.

"Can I get you anything?" Tripp asked them.

"A glass of water would be lovely," Mom said. "With a lemon wedge, please."

Rosalyn nodded that she'd have the same.

Mom sat on one of the sofas in the great room. "Are these the ones you had recovered?"

There had been three leather sofas in the room when I got here in May. Whoever had broken in and trashed the place had taken a knife to all of them. One had been slashed everywhere—back, arms, cushion. They must've gotten tired after that and only cut the cushions of the other two. To save money, we recovered the slashed cushions with a fabric that coordinated with the leather. Then we kept the two sofas and added some armchairs in here. I loved how it all turned out.

"Ruby McLaughlin, who owns The Twisty Skein, the village hobby shop, helped me choose the fabric and recommended one of the local women to do the upholstering."

Mom ran her hand over the medium-blue and beige tapestry and gave a brief hum. Did that mean she approved or not?

Rosalyn had just dropped onto the other end of the couch when Meeka came racing down the stairs and leapt into her lap. The K-9 must have been patrolling the second floor and heard her voice. Her wagging tail was a blur as she covered Aunty Roz in kisses.

"I missed you too, sweetie." Rosalyn turned her to face Mom. "Do you remember Grandma?"

Mom shot her a withering look. "Don't call me that." She held the back of her hand to the Westie, and when Meeka gave it a sniff followed by a quick lick, the barest hint of a smile turned her mouth. Not even my mother could resist Meeka's charms.

Tripp brought three glasses of water and handed one to each of us. "I'm going to finish putting away the groceries."

As he returned to that task, I explained why the main level was such a mess.

"You're sold out in March?" Mom replied, looking ever so slightly impressed.

"We're not at capacity," I explained. "We could fit more people in the rooms, but all the rooms are booked. And we opened up the boathouse apartment to accommodate four of the coven members."

She made a sour face at the Wiccan reference. "I'd like to see this apartment. I've heard so much about it."

"No one is in there yet, right?" Rosalyn asked. "We could take a quick peek."

"Tell you what," I began, "I still need to take care of the paperwork for our guests. They went into the village, and I promised their rooms would be ready when they got back. Since their luggage isn't in there yet, you can take a peek. It's spotless right now, so kick your shoes off. Holly dusted, tidied up the bathroom, and scrubbed the floor this morning."

"Holly is your housekeeper?" Mom asked. Like a stakeholder inspecting her investment, she was taking stock of everything.

"One of them. She's a little younger than Rosalyn. Arden is our other one and is about your age." I almost mentioned that she was a green witch who supplied the flower bouquets for Pine Time in the summer, but figured it was best to ease Mom into the whole Wiccan scene.

"They're both fantastic." Rosalyn kissed Meeka's head and set her down. "After a while, I could tell which of them had cleaned my room. Arden leaves the hand towel folded with the washcloth laying on top next to the sink in the bathroom. Holly does some sort of origami folding thing and tucks the fanned-out washcloth into this little pocket she forms with the towel."

"Really?" I asked. "I didn't know that."

"That's because you don't have them clean your apartment." She raised her chin importantly.

"Maybe I should." When Mom arched a judgmental eyebrow at the comment, the equivalent of a demerit on my record, I sighed. "No, then I'd have to pay them more."

Tripp appeared with his treasured grocery boxes. It had taken him three months of saving boxes from deliveries, but he finally collected eight of them, two of each size which fit together to make two neat bundles. The set provided ample storage for even large shopping trips like today's. This thrilled him more than seemed reasonable. He was on the way to put them back in his truck, paused, and asked, "Did Jayne explain why things are a little chaotic?"

Mom nodded once. "She did. Sounds like there's never a dull moment around here."

"No, never dull," he confirmed. "Especially during tourist season. January and February got a little long. Good thing we both picked up some hobbies."

"And took a trip to Hawaii." There was the eyebrow again. "I'd like to meet this River Carr as well. Is he here?"

Even River was on the inspection list. She was being thorough.

"He was," I answered. "He left shortly before you two got here. Went over to the Barlows'."

She pursed her lips, tiny lines forming around her mouth, and all the warmth Tripp had inspired disappeared like popping soap bubbles. "Another time, then." She turned to Rosalyn. "You were going to show me the boathouse."

I met Tripp's gaze. He frowned, as confused about the sudden change in demeanor as I was.

"Right." I stood. "I'll get the key. Then you can get settled into your rooms. Tripp and I were planning to go into the village for dinner tonight. If we knew you'd be here, we would've made something instead. Well, Tripp would have made something."

"We'll join you," Rosalyn piped up. "Where are we going?"

When I said Triple G, she clapped her hands again.

She really had missed this place. I understood. As much as I loved being on Maui, I was missing the village a lot by the time we boarded our return flight. Not the cold and snow, but everyone and everything else.

"Triple G," Mom repeated. "Is that the grub place?" She emphasized the word *grub* and wrinkled her nose.

"Bar food," Rosalyn confirmed, "but the good kind."

"I remember eating there years ago." Mom wasn't anywhere near as excited as Roz about that fact. "I don't recall my *grub* being 'the good kind.' Has anything in this village changed?"

Three days. It took me three days to fully understand Whispering Pines' charm. It took about that long for Rosalyn too. I got the key for the apartment and gave it to my sister. While they wandered off to explore the property, I started on the paperwork, and Tripp brought the luggage upstairs.

"I set all the bags in The Nook." Tripp leaned against the door jamb and stared at me. "How are you doing?"

"Honestly, with you staring at me that way, I'm a little flustered."

"You know what I mean."

"She hasn't even been here an hour yet."

"That doesn't change the question." He crossed the room to stand behind me and squeezed my shoulders.

I set down my pen and melted beneath his strong hands. "We started out rocky because of the clutter all over the house. She's inspecting everything, and while she hasn't been directly critical yet, I can guess what's acceptable and what isn't. You, acceptable. River, questionable. Anything related to Wicca, unacceptable. Overall, I'd say I'm hovering at around a six out of ten, which is pretty good all things considered. Be warned, though, she's on her best behavior right now."

He kissed the top of my head. "So are you."

A valid point.

Having shown Mom the apartment, Rosalyn stopped in the office next. "She said, 'Far from five-star accommodations but it seems comfortable enough.'"

"Wow." I rubbed my sticky eyes. I should have slept longer this morning. Nervous energy had me up at five fifteen. "She's being really generous today."

"Don't be fooled. She's using her big-girl manners."

"That's what I told Tripp."

Rosalyn jerked a thumb over her shoulder. "I'm going to unpack. Tell me when it's time for dinner. Oh, Mom's waiting for you to escort her to her room."

I'd assumed Mom would want The Alcove, Dad's childhood room, and assigned the other rooms to our other guests. But what if The Alcove brought back memories of the last time she was here, which was when Gran told her about Dad's illegitimate son? It was probably best to let her choose for herself. I could reassign the rooms in thirty seconds if necessary. Dad wouldn't even look inside The Alcove when he came in December. He went right for it in January. As Mom did now before I could even offer her anything else. I was stressing over nothing. Which happened a lot.

"I forgot to mention," she began as I carried both of her bags upstairs, "your father was very pleased with the renovations you and Tripp made to the house. He felt you honored the original style nicely, and I have to agree. With what I've seen so far at least. It's sophisticated yet simple with quality furnishings."

Emotion tickled my throat. She claimed the words were Dad's, but my father would never describe a house that way. For that matter, I couldn't imagine him even noticing a house's style.

"Tell him I said thanks. Tripp and I spent many long nights poring over websites. Simple lakeside sophistication is exactly what we were going for."

"Perhaps that's a career possibility for you both. You could set up bed-and-breakfasts. They're quite popular, you know."

Like we were the ones graduating college and about to start the hunt for a job instead of Rosalyn. "We have careers, Mom. Pine Time has become Tripp's passion. And being the sheriff here—"

She let out a little gasp as she opened The Alcove's door, stood at the threshold, and stared into the room. The furniture was the same Dad had used as a boy, and we'd left it in all the same places. We touched up some scratches on the wood, updated the bedding and curtains, painted, and added fresh accessories. It was the same room otherwise, with the same gorgeous view of the lake and pine trees from the cozy window seat.

As I watched Mom's reaction, Briar's warning about hovering in doorways crossed my mind. She claimed doing so would lead to getting stuck and not being able to choose a path. Was Mom stuck? Were there pathways she needed to choose between? She was so focused on whatever she was seeing, she didn't even notice when, ever so gently, I pushed between her shoulder blades, encouraging her to step over the threshold.

"Your father loved this room," she murmured and peeked in the bathroom. "Oh, yes. He said the bathroom renovations were especially nice."

"He did?"

She turned a slow circle, taking in everything, and then went to the bay window and sat on the bench seat. "He said as a child his favorite thing to do on stormy or frigid days was to sit here and read or work on his models."

"His pyramids and ancient structures."

She nodded wordlessly.

"We left a few on display." I pointed to the tall bookshelf

across the room. "All the others are in a box in the loft over the garage."

"I'll take them home with me when I leave."

"All of them?" I didn't want her to take the ones in the bookshelf. I'd agonized over which ones to leave out and liked having them there. They added a personal touch to the room.

"Your father is renovating his study. I think seeing what you've done to this place, moving it forward rather than letting it remain stuck in the past, has motivated him to do the same."

Something about that statement made me happy. It was either that what we'd done to his childhood home motivated him or that renovating his study meant my parents were working on fixing the broken bits of their marriage. I wanted to ask how things were progressing with their reconciliation, but we'd have plenty of time to talk. For now, I should let her settle in and unpack before we went to dinner.

"Is there anything you'd like, Mom? Tea or coffee? A snack of some kind?"

"Thank you, Jayne, but I'm fine." She smiled and suddenly looked tired. A five-hour drive for someone used to staying within a one-hour radius of home, aside from an occasional three-hour jaunt down to Chicago, had to be tiring. Returning to the place where her marriage had first started to crumble had to be exhausting. "I think I'd like to check in with the spa and take a twenty-minute nap before we go get *grub*."

I gave her the wifi password and stood there awkwardly, as though we were saying goodbye already. She patted my shoulder and gave her signature tight smile. The signal that I could leave now.

"One of us will come get you when we're ready to go." I stepped into the hall, leaned against the wall, and felt all the energy drain from my body. My legs became heavy. My arms didn't want to lift. I knew I'd been anxious about her arrival, but I hadn't realized I'd been holding on to that much stress. Did I have any of Morgan's Chill Out tea downstairs? Did I have time to run over to Unity and get one of their hot stone massages before dinner? No to the second.

In the kitchen, I found a nice supply of Morgan's tea. I swear, the supply replenished itself because we drank a lot of it and never ran out. Caught up on his chores, Tripp joined me for a cup. Ten minutes later, Rosalyn emerged from her room next to the kitchen looking rested and happy.

"Are you two about ready to go get something to eat? You promised me Triple G."

Tripp took our empty mugs to the dishwasher. "I'm ready."

"Yay!" Roz headed for the stairs. "I'll get Mom."

Chapter 5

WHEN MY FATHER RETURNED TO Whispering Pines for the first time after almost two decades, I wasn't sure what to expect when I walked with him through the village where he'd grown up. We'd started at the sheriff's station so he could see where I worked. He'd gotten a little emotional when he'd seen the plaque on my office door with "Sheriff Jayne O'Shea" engraved on it. My mother had a distantly similar reaction. It had taken years for her to accept my career choice. I'm pretty sure the worldwide attention I got when handling the death of celebrity chef Ginger Wakefield finally convinced her it had merit. Regardless of how she felt about the job, she was not at all impressed with my "utilitarian" workplace. My predecessor, Sheriff Karl Brighton, hadn't been interested in frills, and after completing the B&B renovations, hanging curtains and putting down throw rugs wasn't at the top of my priority list.

Dad had become nostalgic when we walked along the Fairy Path and through the village commons. With eyes sparkling, he murmured again and again how so much had remained the same. Mom's "big girl manners" started to slip when we exited that same wood plank path and circled the massive pentacle-shaped garden at the heart of the village.

Her face pinched with distaste, and she repeated her question from earlier. "Does nothing in this village ever change?"

My nerves returned. Getting her to not hate the village would be a huge hurdle to clear. "Change is slower here than in other places, Mom, but new businesses give it a go fairly often. One opened right before Christmas."

"Hearth & Cauldron." Tripp pointed back down the path. "We just passed it. Reeva Long gives cooking lessons there to villagers and tourists. You do a practice meal first which gets served to brave customers, then you make it a second time and bring it home to have for dinner that night."

"Reeva Long," Mom mused. "That name is vaguely familiar."

"She wasn't here when you were." Because she left the village to raise the child who was the product of an affair between her husband and her sister. But I wouldn't go into those details. Especially not in Mom's first hours back in the village. "You may have heard of her, though. Her sister is Flavia Reed."

Mom brightened with understanding, not happiness. "Her, I do remember."

"Is Reeva doing classes this week?" Rosalyn asked.

"Hot cross buns, deviled eggs, and plum blossom cookies." Tripp had been talking about those cookies for a week. Something about baking with flowers appealed to his ever-evolving organic side.

"Fun." Rosalyn clapped. Her enthusiasm for Whispering Pines was almost over the top. I knew she liked it here, but she was probably pumping up the volume for Mom's sake. "We should do a class. Reeva is brilliant."

"Fun," Mom repeated with a tight smile.

I burst out with a laugh. "Sorry, but I can't see Mom in a cooking class."

"What are you saying?" There was a hint of amusement behind Mom's neutral expression.

"You taught me everything I know about cooking." I ticked off the list on my fingers. "Use only the best can openers. It's advisable to use a butter knife to open boxes so as not to get a nasty paper cut."

She looked sideways at me, and the hint of amusement became the tiniest possible smile. "Or break a nail." She flapped a hand at the little cottages that dotted the commons area. "There were exactly this many shops seventeen years ago. With all the tourist business you claim to get in the summer, I'd think new opportunities would arise."

I pointed west from where we stood next to Treat Me Sweetly. "There's a book shop tucked behind Ye Olde Bean Grinder. It's called Biblichor and has only been there for two years. It used to be in a back room of the library and was so popular the village council agreed to let India Paige, the owner, build a new cottage."

I'd stopped in there while on patrol plenty of times but hadn't spent much time in there as a patron. Since Gran had so many books, I felt like I had my own in-home bookstore.

"Biblichor?" Mom repeated. "Is that like petrichor?"

The scent released from the earth during the first rain after an extended dry period.

"Similar," Rosalyn responded. "It means 'the smell of old books.' Something to do with the organic bits of the paper, ink, and glue decomposing over time. Anyway, really cute place. There are four-foot-tall freestanding shelves scattered all around. Tall ones that reach the ceiling line the walls. She put in those old-fashioned ladders on rails so you can reach the top shelves. There are also three small fireplaces and tufted leather chairs and sofas scattered throughout so you can sit and read. I could spend all day in there."

"I didn't realize you knew the place so well." Feeling guilty, I made a silent vow to spend some time in there before my sheriff responsibilities kicked into high gear again.

"There's also the kids' clothing shop behind the resale store," Tripp added. "It's only a couple of years old."

"Two new shops in twenty years?" Mom shook her head.

"Two new cottages," Tripp corrected gently. "The council is very conscious of not overcrowding the village. They also don't want any new shops coming in that would take business away from someone who's already running something similar."

He sounded like a public relations guy singing the praises of our little village.

"Right," I agreed. "The hair salon next to The Inn, for example, opened shortly before I got here. The stylist and esthetician who own the salon originally had space inside the yoga studio. When the health center and yoga studio merged, they decided to open their own place. The people in their new location closed down their kitchenware store and moved to a fifty-five and older community somewhere south of here. Near Tomah, I think. Now, since there's no longer a dedicated housewares shop, Reeva Long has a collection in Hearth & Cauldron's retail room."

"You're splitting hairs," Mom insisted, uninterested in the details. "This village has stagnated."

I sighed, frustrated by her stubbornness. "Don't you think it's possible that Whispering Pines has simply found its rhythm?" She didn't respond. "From what I've seen and heard, the villagers don't want more. They've created a niche for themselves and make the majority of their income working twelve- to sixteen-hour days, seven days a week between Memorial Day and Halloween. After that, they enjoy home life, hobbies, and friends for the other seven months of the year. I'm still getting used to the lifestyle, but these folks are among the happiest I've seen."

Mom tipped her chin up and looked down her nose at me. "Even though there was already The Inn, rental cottages, and a campground, you and Tripp opening a bed-and-breakfast didn't cause problems with the villagers?"

I felt like I'd gotten blindsided by an investigative reporter. Tripp seemed as unprepared for the question as I was. We hadn't asked permission because my family owned the land. My parents had been okay with the plan, with strict guidelines and goals for us to meet, and that was all we worried about. Tripp and I had developed a friendly competition with Laurel over who could reach *no vacancy* faster, but I'd never asked her how she felt about Pine Time. No one had ever challenged us on it. The villagers were very protective of their home, and surely one of them would have said something if they hadn't liked the idea.

"Well, this week," I stammered, "The Inn ran out of space and the rental cottages and campground aren't open yet. Neither are the three hotels just outside the village limits on the east end." I'd almost forgotten about them. "Those hotels are almost always booked when they're open, which assures me there's plenty of need for lodging here."

I wouldn't let her convince me otherwise. Pine Time had been a good idea.

"I'm not sure it was *needed*," Mom objected, "but I imagine more up-to-date facilities are welcome with the tourists. The Inn and those rental cottages are, like most of the buildings here, in dire need of renovations."

Pine Time might not be as quaint as the cottages, but positioned next to the lake the way it was, it had plenty of atmosphere. That's what people came here for.

"We should eat." Rosalyn hooked an arm with mine and whispered, "She's hungry. Let's get her some food. Her mood should improve dramatically."

True. And I hadn't eaten anything since breakfast.

Mom eyed The Inn as we passed it. "I assume there are still only two places to eat here."

"Both The Inn's restaurant," Tripp began, once again using his tourist guide voice, "and Grapes, Grains, and Grub serve lunch and dinner. The Inn also serves breakfast. They take turns being open during the off-season since there are so few tourists."

"Since we've got around forty visitors here for Ostara," I added, "and plenty of villagers who want to celebrate the holiday together, they'll both be open this week. Hearth & Cauldron also serves lunch in quantities dependent upon how many people take classes each day. Treat Me Sweetly will have an abbreviated supply of ice cream, cookies, and pastries available." In two short months, they'd be back to full inventory and have a line of people out front waiting to get in. We could hardly wait. "And Ye Olde Bean Grinder serves coffee year-round."

Mom made a semi-interested *hmm* sound. "Rosalyn has been raving about the coffee shop. The current operator wasn't here seventeen years ago."

"She was," I corrected, "but she would've only been five or six years old."

Rosalyn sighed happily. "Violet is the world's best barista."

"I think she's some rare blend of green witch and kitchen witch."

And I'd said too much. Mom had warmed at the mention of excellent coffee, a passion all three of us shared, but froze right back up again when I said the word *witch*. Thankfully, I didn't attempt to babble my way out of it. Instead, I walked faster toward the village pub. Feed her. Everything would be better after something off Triple G's menu.

"We only expected the two of you," pub owner Maeve told Tripp.

"Sorry. I should've called. Rosalyn and Jayne's mom arrived earlier than we thought."

"Fortunately, we saved a four-top for you." Maeve gave a convoluted set of hand signals to one of her servers. "Hang on a minute. We'll grab two more chairs and place settings."

Maeve knew I preferred to sit where I could see as much of a room as possible. It was a cop thing. That meant reserving spots for us in the main dining room instead of one of the smaller dining rooms scattered throughout the building that used to be someone's home. Even when we sat on the deck out back, she put us in a corner where I could see all.

We had no sooner taken our seats when Rosalyn let out a squeal. She jumped to her feet, practically ran across the dining room, and threw herself into Reed's arms.

"I assume that's this Martin I've heard so much about." Mom ignored the menu in her hands and looked over her reading glasses at the man who had captured her younger daughter's heart. "If she wasn't going on about this village on the way up here, she was talking about him."

"He's a good guy," I promised.

"Maybe so, but her breakup with James isn't even six months old." She hummed, shook her head crisply, and returned to her menu. "It's too soon."

Tripp and I watched as Rosalyn pointed at us and then dragged Reed our way.

"Mom," Rosalyn held one of Reed's hands in both of hers, "this is Martin. He's going to join us for dinner."

I wasn't sure if I felt worse for Mom or Reed. Roz had thrown both of them into the fire. She grabbed a chair from a nearby table and flicked her fingers at Tripp and me. "Scooch over."

As Reed settled in and Rosalyn tracked down a place setting for him, I noticed Flavia in the corner diagonal from us. Her always sour expression pinched even more as she watched her son join my family. A few feet away, Reeva sat seemingly unaware her sister was behind her. Or, more likely, she was ignoring her. Reeva had also noticed Reed sit at our table. Was he supposed to meet his mother or aunt here, or had Rosalyn invited him to eat with us? Either way, the sister witches didn't appear pleased with our cozy gathering.

After our orders had been taken and drinks delivered, Mom proceeded to grill Reed on what it was like to be a sheriff's deputy.

"It's something different every day," he replied as though he'd answered that question a hundred times. "I think that's what I like best about it. I never know what the day will bring."

"Do you intend for this to be your permanent profession?" It sounded like she was interviewing him for the position of boyfriend to her youngest daughter.

"I recently graduated from the police academy." His chest puffed out proudly, but I heard the nerves in his voice. "At the top of my class. I've never been good at much, so it feels like the right fit for me."

"But you are," Rosalyn gushed. "You're good at—"

"How long," Mom interrupted with a pointed, silencing stare at her youngest, "have you lived in Whispering Pines?"

"I was born here."

"Flavia Reed is your mother?" Mom asked.

Reed's gaze darted to me. His message clear: *How do I respond?* "She is."

Mom made a *hmm* sound and drank from her glass of Chardonnay. I'd forgotten that she had either met some of the villagers years ago or had learned about them from Dad. Or me. I'd expressed either frustration or approval over many of the folks here during our phone conversations.

"How is everything going with your mom?" Rosalyn asked. "And Reeva?"

Really? She wanted to open *that* conversation here and now? Did she not see the witches in the corner casting hexes at us? Well, Reeva wouldn't do that, but Flavia would in a heartbeat. I expected the lot of us to break out in warts at any moment.

Fortunately, Morgan, Briar, and River walked in then. I jumped at the chance to postpone any horror stories about Reed's mother and aunt hurling spells at each other and introduced Mom to our friends, starting with River.

"River Carr." Mom gave him an appreciative once-over. Even she wasn't immune to his dark, sultry aura. "I've heard a great deal about you. Lovely to meet you."

"And you, Lady O'Shea." River took her hand and placed a kiss on the back.

I swear, she swooned for a moment before quickly collecting herself. "I understand you flew Jayne and Tripp to Maui and then kept an eye on the house while they were gone."

Uh-oh.

"As it was a rather subdued fortnight throughout the village," River explained, "I had no other task than to literally monitor the house."

Mom looked at me. "Perhaps if you had stayed instead of gallivanting to the tropics, you could have arranged some bookings for that . . . fortnight."

"Tripp and I needed a little R&R. The villagers had been talking about how quiet February is here for months. Even The Inn was empty that week. It was the perfect time to slip away."

"R&R?" Mom asked in a tone that made my mouth go dry. "You had several months off after you left the police station in Madison. And if I recall properly, Tripper, you wandered the countryside for five years. Seems to me you two would want to focus your energies on your proposed business instead of getting 'a little R&R.'"

Horrified. My pants could have fallen to my ankles right here in the middle of Triple G, and I wouldn't have been more embarrassed than I was at that moment. My instinct, to deflect attention off myself by bringing in reinforcements, took over and before I realized I was doing it, I grabbed Morgan's arm.

"Mom, do you remember Morgan? Rosalyn and I used to play with her in the commons when we were little."

Morgan inclined her head in greeting. "Blessed be, Mrs. O'Shea."

I watched as Mom's gaze started at Morgan's wavy raven-black mane that hung to the middle of her back. Proceeding downward, she paused a half-second later, probably to analyze the Triple Moon Goddess pendant at her throat. She paused again at her seven-month-swollen baby belly before completing the journey to her black leather mid-calf lace-up booties.

While Mom was checking her out, Morgan leveled a glare on me that was the equivalent to her hissing, "A pox on you for dragging me into this."

"Morgan Barlow," Mom confirmed. "I do remember you. I understand you have quite an interest in plants."

Morgan rested her hands, with matte-black nail polish and silver rings on every finger, on her belly. "Yes, from the tiniest sprout to the mightiest tree, plants are my passion." Her eyes darted to me as she gave a throaty laugh. "Of course, I am a green witch."

A naughty green witch. She knew how Mom felt about Wicca and magic and all that. I suppose I had that coming.

Mother gave her signature tight smile. "That is what your costume would imply."

And then, in a move that could only have been meant to take the attention off her daughter, Briar stepped between them, hand extended, which Mom automatically took.

"Georgia, merry meet. Dillon has told me so much about you during our many chats."

Confused by the interruption, Mom asked, "And you are?"

"How rude of me. I'm Morgan's mother, Briar Barlow." She paused, a glint in her eye. "Dillon and I grew up together. I lived in his house for a tick."

The moment Briar said her name, Mom snatched her hand away. "The house was Lucy and Keven's then. It's ours now." And then pointedly a half-beat later, "As is this land."

The unvarnished message: they could sell and evict me, Tripp, and every villager at a moment's notice. My rather urgent assignment over the next five days was to convince Mom that Whispering Pines was worth saving. If I failed to get her on board, she'd tell Dad to contact their realtor. My ultimate dream was to buy the land and house from them. But I couldn't imagine how many millions of dollars that would mean. Or how I could ever get my hands on that kind of money. I was freaking out over a new car loan. Speaking of which, I did own my ten-year-old falling apart Jeep Cherokee outright. What were the chances of the bank accepting that as collateral on a multi-million-dollar loan to a small-town sheriff?

"None of it is really yours, though," Briar replied. "Lucy left everything to Dillon."

A sour lump formed in my stomach. Why, in the name of whichever Goddess was watching this nightmare play out, was Briar poking the bear?

"Dillon is my husband," Mom countered, an unmistakable note of acid in her voice. "What's his is mine. What's mine is his."

Briar clucked her tongue, but before she could say another word, River cleared his throat and took her by the elbow. "Perhaps we should order our dinners."

He held out a chair for her at the table next to us. Maeve meant well. She knew how Tripp and I often came here to eat with River and the Barlows. Tonight, however, a little separation would have been better. Like them eating at The Inn instead.

"What was that?" I hissed at Mom after they'd stepped away.

"What was what?" She drained her wine glass and signaled for another.

"All you had to do was say 'nice to meet you.' Would that have been so hard?"

"She started it." She folded her hands in her lap and cleared her throat. "You bring me into a building filled with people who call themselves witches and you think I'll smile and accept that without question? You are well aware that my opinion since the first time I came here is that this village is full of kooks."

I'd hoped that after so many years away, she would be willing to see the village with fresh eyes. We should have had dinner at home. This was too much too soon. My fault.

The five of us managed to chat politely about safer topics after that. Mom let her guard down for a brief window and declared her minestrone soup with spring vegetables and rustic roll a flavorful start to her meal. Then she said the maple glazed salmon on her dinner salad was perfectly prepared, the lettuce crisp and nicely dressed.

"Thank God," Rosalyn whispered in my ear.

"Maeve isn't Wiccan," I whispered back, "but she must have a kitchen witch on staff and instructed them to mix a little something extra into Mom's dinner."

Whatever it was, Mom's mood lightened significantly once her belly was full of food and Chardonnay. Her attention turned to the other laughing, chatting diners dressed in all manner of outfits from jeans and sweatshirts to *costumes* like

Morgan's. She seemed curious if not a little confused by them. So, in an attempt to help her better understand, I invited Morgan back to the table.

Chapter 6

HAVE YOU LOST YOUR MIND? Jayne in my head demanded. By the looks on Tripp's and Rosalyn's faces, they were wondering the same thing.

At this point, I couldn't flap a hand and tell Morgan, "Never mind." Well, I could, but I remembered feeling like a complete outsider when I first came to Whispering Pines. All these strange Wiccan phrases and celebrations. The villagers' obsession with the moon and keeping lights dim at night so they could see more stars. I watched as Mom stared at the other diners with varying looks of confusion and thought, knowledge is power. If she understood a little more about Wicca, the villagers, and the village in general, maybe she wouldn't feel so uncomfortable and negative about the place I'd come to love. Tomorrow's gathering at The Inn would have been a better time for this, but I'd already set things in motion.

"I was hoping," I told Morgan, "that you could explain what Ostara is exactly." I could have asked Reed. He grew up in a Wiccan house, and even though he'd stopped practicing years ago, he still understood everything. Morgan was more passionate about the topic, though.

She hesitated, staring at me like she was once again

wondering why I kept dragging her into my issues. Then she pulled a chair over from her table and sat between Rosalyn and me, straight across from Mom.

"Jayne tells me you're agnostic. Is this true?"

Mom cleared her throat and clutched her still half-full wine glass like a protective shield. "That's correct. I've studied many religions, searching for a proper fit, I suppose you could say. None of them sufficiently swayed me or felt right, so I put my religious life on the back burner. As you're aware, the girls' father was raised Wiccan, but Dillon stopped practicing when he left for college and never chose another path."

Did he tell her he'd attended a coven gathering when he was here at Christmas? Or that he'd conducted private rituals in Gran's worship area in the loft over our garage?

Not your business, Jayne. Stay out of it.

Having established a level playing field, Morgan continued. "Wicca, as you're likely aware, is a Pagan nature-based religion. We closely follow the ever-changing seasons and acknowledge every full moon with celebrations we call esbats. Wiccans also take part in eight other major celebrations throughout the year known as sabbats. We worship various goddesses and gods — "

"Goddesses."

All eyes lifted to someone behind me. I turned to find Maewyn Barnes there.

"Don't include all of us in your explanation." Maewyn gestured between herself and two other younger members of the Chicago coven. "*We* worship and honor only goddesses."

The two with her nodded vigorously. Others in the coven grumbled, disagreeing with her. A few even booed or hissed softly.

"Yours," Morgan replied, "is the definition of a specific type of Wicca." I knew Morgan's tone of voice and mannerisms well enough to determine that whatever that type was, she wasn't fond of it. "The Whispering Pines coven welcomes women, men, and others. We often honor gods as well as goddesses."

Maewyn snorted. "I shouldn't be surprised that someplace as remote as this would follow old-school beliefs."

Ariel Birdsong placed a hand on Maewyn's shoulder. "No need to be that way, Mae. We're ultimately all part of the same sisterhood. This is a time for celebration."

"Exactly." Maewyn jerked away from her. "It's a *sister*hood."

"Why are you here then?" Wanda rose from a table in the center of the room and took two steps forward like she was about to charge at the younger member. Rosemary and another woman at her table with long wavy silver-gray hair and a band of Celtic knots tattooed around her upper arm jumped up and held Wanda back before she could take a third step. "From the day you joined our coven, you've been trying to change things. If you can't accept it—"

"Then you change it," Maewyn insisted as though this was obvious.

"Or you keep searching," Rosemary suggested calmly. "I've been a member of this coven since before you were born, and the high priestess since you were a child. We're happy with it and each other just the way we are."

Wanda pulled free from their grip and put her hands in the air, indicating she wouldn't attack the girl. "Why should we change because you, a new member, aren't happy? Why don't you form your own coven? This one is getting a little large. It might be time to divide."

Rosemary frowned, not liking that idea. Or maybe it was that Wanda suggested it so publicly. Or that Wanda had gone over her head.

"I'm here," Maewyn continued, unfazed, "to celebrate my beliefs. Those beliefs being that Wicca is for women." She took in Tripp, Reed, and other nearby men. "Men get everything else in the world. This is ours."

"You're embarrassing yourself," Amaya hissed, stepping forward now. "And us. Stop before you do or say something you'll regret."

Someone from the crowd echoed, "Yes, stop, please."

Rosalyn nudged me with her elbow and whispered, "Don't you think you should mediate?"

I turned to Reed. He was the acting sheriff this week. His eyes grew impossibly large, and he shook his head. The thing was, we didn't get to choose our assignments. If he wanted more responsibility, he had to perform the duties that made him uncomfortable too. But his panicked, deer-in-the-headlights expression combined with Maewyn's firm opinions regarding men meant this might not be the best moment for him to take charge.

"Everyone, calm down," I called out as I stood by the petite girl. Seriously, how did that much attitude fit inside such a tiny body? "First of all, Ms. Barnes, we were having a private conversation. Eavesdropping is rude. Second, this is a community gathering." I spoke louder so everyone could hear. "We're all here to eat, drink, and converse with our families and friends. As sheriff, I encourage your coven to set aside time tomorrow or the next day for public discussions about the different Wiccan sects. Some of us, myself included, would find that very interesting. This, however, isn't the time for that."

She glared at me with those black-brown eyes. They looked like dark pits of anger, righteousness, and defiance. Maewyn was a little scary.

Hold tight, Sheriff Jayne ordered. *Do not back down or you'll have a world of trouble on your hands with this one.*

That reminded me of a time ten years ago when Rosalyn and I had a staredown over who would get the front seat of the car on the way to Chicago. Mom wanted to attend some kind of salon convention during a week when we had two days off school. She pulled us out for the entire week and splurged on a swanky hotel as a way of keeping us from complaining about having to go with her. Even now, I had no idea why the front seat was so important to Rosalyn that day, but I was the older sister. There was no doubt in my mind, I was going to sit in the front. I'd never felt more victorious than when she broke eye contact first and slumped into the back.

Like Rosalyn that day, Maewyn was trying with every attitude-stuffed cell in her body to intimidate me. I was the sheriff, though. She wouldn't bully me or anyone else in my village. After another few seconds, she stepped back but never dropped her gaze.

"Morgan," I stated, "go ahead and say what you were going to say about Ostara. Some folks here may not be aware of how we do things in Whispering Pines."

Morgan rose to her feet in that graceful way she had and glided to the center of the room. "Ostara is two days from now, on Thursday. On that day, we will celebrate the arrival of spring or the Vernal Equinox. As is true during the Autumnal Equinox in September, day and night will be in perfect balance with twelve hours of daylight and twelve of darkness."

She spoke with such reverence for the natural world, even Maewyn finally looked away from me and turned her attention to Morgan.

"With each passing day," she spun slowly, addressing the room as a whole, "daylight hours will increase, allowing nature to honor and sustain us with its bounty. Ostara, coincidentally, is the name of a goddess."

Maewyn seemed almost triumphant as she turned to her coven members. "See? Like I said, Wicca is about goddesses."

The grumbling from the tables grew louder and more

agitated. They didn't seem to be agreeing or disagreeing with Maewyn but simply wanted her to stop causing a scene.

"Ostara," Morgan continued as though delivering a keynote speech, "is a maiden goddess and represents potential, growth, and the resurgence of life after a long, dark winter. She was also known as Eostre, which is obviously very similar to the Christian Easter. Ostara's origins are thought to be Germanic, and it is said that she has much in common with the Norse goddess of fertility."

"That's right," Maewyn called out, inserting a supplement to Morgan's speech. "Ostara is a celebration for a *goddess*. Estrogen comes from the root word Eostre – "

"Which is imperative for women's fertility," Morgan interrupted and placed her hands on her belly. "As I've already stated, the Vernal Equinox signifies a lengthening in the amount of time the sun spends overhead warming and nurturing us. For that reason, we also celebrate the Sun God at this time. During the equinox, the Sun God joins with the Maiden Goddess Eostre who conceives his child and enters the Mother phase of the triad." With compassion, she approached Maewyn. "I know you know how vital the Maiden, Mother, and Crone are to Wicca. Their symbol is a full moon flanked by two crescent moons." She paused for a moment. "I understand your coven is called Circle of 3 Moons. We cannot have the Mother Goddess without the Sun God."

"Donors," Maewyn replied instantly. "That's all men are good for. Preservation of the species."

"Oh, here we go," a man in the group moaned. It might have been Reed, but I couldn't swear to it. He'd probably heard arguments about the value of men from his mother since he was a boy.

"That's right," Maewyn snapped. "We've formed our own space within the society you thought you would always dominate."

"Mae." Amaya was in front of her in a flash. "Enough already."

Maewyn stepped around Amaya and, in the general direction of where the voice had come from, taunted, "Can't handle it, can you? Can't handle when women claim their power."

"Stop!" a female voice in the crowd called out to soft cheers of encouragement from those around her. "No one wants to hear this."

"Wanda's right," another voice added. "Go form your own coven."

Maewyn, looking equal amounts hurt and angry, flung a hand toward Wanda. "I can't believe you all agree with her."

"That's not it." Amaya let out a tired sigh. "Wicca is our religion, not a platform. All I want, and the others here, too, is to learn more about our religion. That's why I joined this coven. You joined us, what, three or four months ago? All you've done since day one is debate every little thing."

The crowd of Wiccans, villagers, and a few random tourists was growing uncomfortable with this confrontation. So uncomfortable that Maeve sent over Jagger, Triple G's bouncer and the largest man I'd ever been face to face with, to break it up.

Maewyn was the approximate size of one of Jagger's legs, but that didn't stop her. She looked up at him and laughed. "What are you going to do? Throw me out? Try it, freak. You lay a finger on me and I'll have the sheriff here charge you with assault."

Amaya grabbed her by the upper arm. "Honest to God, what's the matter with you? Are you drunk? High on something?"

Jerking her arm free, Maewyn spun to face her.

The escalating anger combined with Jagger's appearance made me think of an evening this past November. Most of the village had gathered right here in the pub for Thanksgiving dinner. A "disturbance" broke out that night, and a young woman ended up getting stabbed. I wasn't about to let anything like that happen again.

Moving slowly closer, which made Maewyn back away from me, I corralled her toward the back of the main room. "That's enough now. Morgan was explaining the meaning of Ostara for me and my family. I have no idea why you've tried to turn that into a debate, but you're the only one arguing, and you're making everyone very uncomfortable."

"I'm not allowed to speak my mind?" She glared like an angry toddler. "Because people don't like it when someone speaks the truth?"

"That's not what I'm saying. Something you might not understand about Whispering Pines is that we're a community where no one person is above anyone else."

"Except for you," she challenged. "Right, Sheriff?"

I knew she meant my authority as an officer of the law. But what Maewyn and most of the villagers didn't know was that the O'Shea family had rights here the others didn't have. For example, if Dad was present, we could take a vote right here and now to kick everyone off our property. Gran wrote it into the bylaws. Majority vote won. In the case of a tie, Dad got two votes. On more minor issues, like overruling the village council on day-to-day village matters, one of us could do that on our own. To me, using that authority was the very last option. Whether Maewyn liked it or not, I did have rights others didn't. Knowing that emboldened me to do what I was brought here to do.

"Ms. Barnes, I don't know what's got you so worked up, but my job is to keep the peace. I'm asking you for the last time to stop making a scene. Maeve owns this establishment. I know her and can tell she's very close to making a formal complaint against you. If she does, I will take you to the station and you'll spend the night in a holding cell."

She pouted but didn't challenge me on this, so I let her go back to her table.

Near the middle of the dining room, Laurel was trying to get everyone's attention. When her too-quiet, too-polite pleas of "excuse me" didn't work, Maeve let loose with the ear-piercing whistle she used at closing time.

"I've got a short announcement," Laurel began, giving a nod of thanks to Maeve. "Tomorrow is the day before the Ostara festivities. As in previous years, The Inn will host a gathering. There will be activities for everyone, kids to adults. And a Whispering Pines gathering wouldn't be complete without food."

A soft cheer rose from the more relaxed crowd.

"Briar and Morgan Barlow are inviting you all, villager and visitor alike, to join them for a seed planting gathering at their cottage on Ostara at ten o'clock."

This brought murmurs of excitement. Any green-thumbed witch would be honored to plant in the presence of the Barlows.

From across the room, Reeva waved, signaling Laurel about something.

Laurel pointed at her in acknowledgment. "Right. Almost forgot. Reeva asked me to announce that she'll be holding special classes at Hearth & Cauldron tomorrow on making various Ostara-themed recipes. Hot cross buns, deviled eggs, and—"

"Plum blossom cookies," Tripp blurted excitedly. "I'll be there."

"How encouraging," Maewyn crooned. "The men here do the women's work. Just when I was sure this saccharine-sweet village was backwards. No, you've flipped roles. I applaud that." And she literally did.

Her tone this time was more condescending than

confrontational. Still, if she pushed it much further, she and I would take a walk to the station.

"We have not flipped roles," Maeve insisted. "More than half of the businesses here are owned by women. Our founder was a woman; Lucy O'Shea, our sheriff's grandmother." She gave a respectful nod to me, Mom, and Rosalyn. "That's partly why many of us came here. To get away from the patriarchy and sexist attitudes prevalent in much of society."

Maewyn's applause turned into a raised fist. "Preach it, sister."

"However," Maeve raised her voice and ignored the fist, "don't for one minute think that means we disrespect or discount our male villagers. Or that any of us feel either inferior or superior to another."

Ribbing Maewyn a little more, Wanda loudly asked, "If cooking is women's work, what would men's work be? And if there is *men's work*, does that mean women aren't allowed to perform those tasks?"

The woman with the armband tattoo and long silver-gray hair stood, placed a hand on Wanda's shoulder, and went to Maewyn, who had turned a fierce red with either embarrassment or anger. In a calm make-love-not-war tone, this woman suggested, "You must see that life is easier if we don't categorize or apply labels. The continuation of our species requires an egg and a sperm. At this moment in evolution, no human carries both. In that sense, everyone is equal."

"Don't ever," Maewyn growled, "tell me a man is equal to me."

There was such venom in her voice it stopped me cold. Maewyn wasn't just angry, she looked ready to kill. What exactly set her off, and what had made her this way? Was she bullied? Abused? Should I be worried she would hurt someone?

"You're limiting yourself, child," the woman continued. "Surely you're aware that there are many countries, and a handful of states, that recognize more than two genders?"

"Skye Blue." Rosemary pulled the tattooed woman away from Maewyn. "Let's not add that discussion to the mix right now. The energy in this room is getting toxic."

"You're right, it is." Maewyn grabbed her sweater from the back of her chair, knocking the chair over as she did. I started toward her, and she held out a hand. "Don't worry about it, Sheriff. I can't take any more of this. I'm leaving." And she stormed out.

All of that rage threatening to boil over in her. And more anger spreading through the coven members. This was a group of supposedly like-minded people with similar beliefs. Why were they so angry? What was going on that the rest of us couldn't see? Of course, the only group of Wiccans I'd had exposure to was the Whispering Pines group. And if I thought about it, there was some anger swirling among them too.

I sat back in my chair, feeling a little shell-shocked. Then, as though putting an exclamation mark on my thoughts, I spotted Flavia still standing in the shadows of that far corner. She wasn't paying any attention to us this time. She was too busy shooting visual daggers into the back of her sister's head. Reeva, sitting with Ruby, Violet, and Ivy, seemed oblivious. Or she was ignoring her. Sisters were good at that. Especially when doing so ticked off the other one.

"Sure didn't see all that coming," I told my tablemates.

My mother made a disapproving *tsk* and finished her wine. "Your father told me he hoped I'd see you in action. It wasn't as impressive as I expected. Of course, he didn't explain that 'action' meant you breaking up the equivalent of a schoolyard squabble."

Rosalyn came to my defense. "Preventing trouble is a big part of her job, Mom. If that had turned into a physical altercation, someone could have gotten hurt. Bar brawls are nothing to joke about."

As much as I appreciated knowing Rosalyn got it, I put a hand on her arm and shook my head. "Let it go, Rozzie."

I glanced across the dining room, checking that peace had been restored now that Maewyn the Instigator had left. The Circle of 3 Moons coven had returned to their dinners and/or tablemates, but closer inspection showed that all the tension hadn't left with Maewyn. There was a lot of leaning close and talking, followed by nasty glances being cast about. Most aimed those glances toward the table that held the coven's top tier—Rosemary, Wanda, Marie, Calliope, and Skye Blue. The looks seemed to say, *it's your job to fix this, so do something.*

Whispering Pines was more or less a peaceful place. Villager squabbles, like the Benji Wallace/Abner Kramer near-death dispute over a fishing shanty in January, were really quite rare. Most of our trouble came from elsewhere, which had to be expected when a place welcomed as many outsiders as we did. But sometimes it felt like the village had lured those people here with the sole purpose of causing trouble. Like now. A sabbat should be a time of relatively quiet celebration.

During his visits, Dad had gotten a firsthand look at a few of those outside troublemakers. He saw me capture a fugitive, track down a murderer, and identify a hit-and-run driver who'd committed manslaughter. Unfortunately, in order for Mom to see what he saw and be *impressed* with my job, something equally big would have to happen.

My gaze shifted from tables full of disgruntled coven members to my mother. "Don't lose hope, Mom. Around here, things tend to go from schoolyard to impressive really quickly."

Chapter 7

REED LEFT OUR TABLE TO find out why his mother was glowering in the corner. Since all of our B&B guests were still here, I suggested we stay a little longer at Grapes, Grains, and Grub. I wanted to try and leave on a more positive note so angry witches wouldn't be Mom's lasting memory of the pub. Business-savvy Maeve seemed to be thinking the same thing. As though wanting to salvage her business's reputation with the reigning matriarch of the O'Shea clan, she arrived tableside with a tray loaded with complimentary servings of Triple G's signature desserts.

"Rustic strawberry-rhubarb tarts," she identified while setting a plate before each of us, "with vanilla bean ice cream straight from Honey at Treat Me Sweetly."

"Is that cake?" Rosalyn's eyes went wide at the plates still on the tray.

"It is. We call it the Boozy Irish." Maeve smiled, knowing how good it was. "The drink is the inspiration behind it, and we only have it on the menu during March in honor of St. Patrick's Day. Guinness beer is mixed into the chocolate cake. There's a shot of Jameson whiskey in the chocolate ganache between the layers, and Bailey's Irish Cream liqueur is blended into the frosting." She winked as she set slices in front of us. "Don't eat and drive."

My tension level dropped again as I watched Mom take a bite of each and then practically lick both plates clean. That was saying a lot because she rarely ate dessert.

Right before we left, I pulled Reed to the side.

"You don't have to say it," he insisted before I'd even opened my mouth. "I know I choked earlier. I think I have a mental block when it comes to women, especially Wiccan women, arguing." He gave me a sheepish smile. "The first step is admitting the problem, right?"

His mother and aunt. Yeah, those two could scar anyone for life.

"Can I count on you?" I asked, thinking of the tension still present among the coven members. "Will you deal with the goings-on for the next few days, or do I need to?"

A big part of me wanted him to assure me that, as my deputy, he could step in for me whenever necessary. The other part wouldn't mind having an excuse to slip away to check on things now and then. Which would be easier to deal with? Warring witches or my judgmental mother?

Witches, no question.

"You can count on me, boss. I got blindsided."

"Because you were distracted by my sister?" I still couldn't fully wrap my head around that relationship. "Things like that can't stop you from doing your job, Deputy. Nothing can."

"It's not that," he insisted, but the flush across his cheeks said it might be a little bit that. "The Ostara celebration has always been an exciting event. Most events around here are. But this one in particular with more hours of sunlight and warmer weather. What's not to love?" He frowned, a truly sad look. "The anger and the tension around here, you feel it, right? That's not normal. Not for Whispering Pines."

Overall, yes, the folks here were happy, but there had been tension in the village since the day I got here. I couldn't speak to what was historically normal and what wasn't, though. Or for how long things had been abnormal.

"Not seeing something coming can never again be an excuse," I reiterated. "If you're doing this, it means no picking and choosing which crimes to investigate and which to hand off."

"But that's what you always do. Any tasks you don't like, you give to me. So if I'm acting sheriff, you're acting deputy, and I should be able to do the same thing. Right?" The sparkle in his eyes assured me he was joking. "Honestly, boss, I'm on it."

"All right, I'm handing over the reins. You're officially driving this wagon."

He winced. "Please tell me that's the end of that analogy."

He knew me so well. "I was going to say something about the visiting coven being like an out of control herd of stampeding horses, but I won't."

"Glad you know when to stop."

"I'm going home. There's a gaggle of witches at my B&B." I tilted my head. "Gathering of witches? A cluster? What's a group of witches called?"

He stared, waiting for me to fill it in, before saying, "A coven. Go home, boss. And let Tripp drive. You've had too much Boozy Irish."

It was a beautiful clear night with a nearly full moon and a billion stars on display. The hint of warmth in the air was especially welcome. My mother smiled as she looked around at the towering trees and cute cottages as we walked to the west side parking lot. Until she saw me looking at her and then she rearranged her face into a more neutral expression. Too late. I'd already seen it. The Whispering Pines magic was starting to affect her.

Once we were home, Mom watched as I handed out keycards to the waiting witches and explained that their luggage was in The Nook at the top of the stairs. The younger group grabbed their bags and wandered across the yard to the boathouse. The others went off in search of their assigned rooms.

I explained to Mom how the check-in process normally worked, and she gave an approving nod.

"Can I get you anything?" Tripp asked her. "Coffee? Tea?"

"A cup of tea would be lovely. Peppermint to soothe my too-full stomach if you have it. I must admit, Rosalyn was right about the grub at your pub." She chuckled, presumably amused with her rhyme.

Except for the Maewyn situation, I considered the night a success. "I'm glad you enjoyed dinner, Mom."

She reached out and inspected the ends of my hair. "So dry. You are in desperate need of a trim. When was the last time you had a haircut?"

Behind her, Rosalyn pointed at me, mimed a belly laugh, and mouthed, *I told you.*

I cringed. "When did I leave Madison?"

"Oh, Jayne." Mom sighed, disappointed. "When I encourage my customers to create hair and skincare routines, it's not only for vanity reasons. Beauty is the bonus that comes from the effort." She dropped my crispy ends and touched her fingers to my face. "It's important that you take time for yourself. We all have busy lives, but even a few minutes a day has value. You can't give one hundred percent if you're not at one hundred percent."

Tripp brought her a small tray with a teacup, a cozy-covered teapot that held two cups of hot water, and two honey straws from Bennett our local beekeeper.

"Thank you, Tripp." She yawned as she took the tray.

"This has been a very interesting first few hours in your village. I'm going up to my room to enjoy this tea while I perform my own nightly rituals. Goodnight."

"Goodnight, Mom." I touched my cheek. I swear, I could still feel the warmth from her hand there.

Rosalyn took Mom's place next to me and gave me a shoulder bump. "Knocks the knees out from under you now and then, doesn't she?"

While Tripp went to make three more mugs of peppermint tea—we'd all overeaten tonight—Rosalyn and I sat on opposite ends of one of the sofas and intertwined our legs. I was about to make a smart comment about Mom being under the influence of booze-laced cake when Amaya appeared outside the patio door and swiped in using her keycard.

"Oh, hey." She held up an unlit cigar. "I know, no smoking inside the house or apartment. The girls don't want me smoking on the deck either. Is it okay if I do out here?"

The first woman I'd ever seen smoke a cigar was Cybil the fortune teller. It immediately explained the rasp in her voice. To me, it required a bit of attitude for a woman to pull off a stogie, and Cybil had oodles of attitude. Amaya, with her black headwrap, thick dark eyebrows, and confident stride did too.

"Sure." I pointed to the right side of the patio. "There's a standing ash and butt holder tucked into the corner."

"Oh, I won't smoke the whole thing. A few puffs will do me." She pulled the door halfway shut, then opened it again, came inside, and dropped onto the couch across from us. She sat with her long legs spread in a V, elbows resting on knees, hands and stogie hanging between them. "I wanted to apologize for Maewyn."

"Someone else's actions are never your responsibility." I almost looked behind me to see if Morgan had said that. Deep thoughts. Must be aftereffects of the cake.

"I know." She eased back and propped her right foot on her left knee. "I guess what I mean is, I'd like to explain her."

Tripp arrived with a tray loaded with mugs, tea bags, honey straws, and a carafe of hot water. He offered Amaya a mug, but she declined. Then he sat next to me and settled in to have a mug and listen to our discussion.

"I've known Maewyn for three years," Amaya explained. "She lives near my occult shop and came in one day looking for a job. I hired her and since the first day have been trying to help her control this need to constantly impose her opinions on everyone." She stared at her own hands as if hoping the answers for understanding her friend would appear on them. "Sometimes it's like she can't stop herself. Almost like she's got some kind of Tourette's syndrome, but she doesn't blurt out curse words. Well, she does, but not involuntarily."

Why would she accept that behavior and keep her on staff? Maewyn must offend the customers.

Amaya placed a hand, with multiple silver and gold rings stacked on the middle finger, to her upper chest. "I fully support women and their struggles, but I like men." She grinned and shrugged. "Women, too, if you know what I mean. I've been trying to help Mae find more of a balance for her passion."

This explained why Amaya jumped up and tried to quiet her down at Grapes, Grains, and Grub. She was used to dealing with Maewyn's outbursts.

"Doesn't she scare people off?" Rosalyn asked, voicing my exact thoughts.

"Sometimes," Amaya agreed. "On Friday nights, we host women-only gatherings. On Tuesdays, men are also welcome. Mae gets the Friday night crowd so pumped up. I'm telling you, the shop practically vibrates with energy. I do three times the sales on those nights than the other nights combined. Even factoring in if those she offended hadn't walked out during the week. When she's really in the groove, talking about how women can do it all and have it all" — she made explosion hands by her head — "five times the sales."

"You're not concerned about those upset customers?" Tripp asked.

"Or your karma?" Once again, I was tempted to look over my shoulder for Morgan.

"I did worry about that the first few times. My customers, not my karma. Then I found that a lot of those people came back when Maewyn wasn't working. A lot of them say she poked at something inside them and gave them thoughts to meditate on. They actually agreed with what she was saying but left because they didn't want to deal with those feelings at the moment. Mae will push you to talk if she finds the tiniest way in. And it isn't only about women's rights. She talks about everyone's right to have a safe space in our world. She discusses the environment, healthcare, the planet, and sometimes politics, but I nix that right away. I do *not* want that kind of energy in my shop."

"Is this what she was trying to do tonight?" I asked. "Get people worked up and thinking about Wicca? Or women? Or Wiccan women?"

Amaya released a tired sigh. "I think so. Like I said, her passion gets the better of her sometimes. That's all I wanted you to understand."

Rosemary wandered into the great room then. "Control over her passion will come with age." She pointed toward the front of the house. "I came down to read in the sitting room and couldn't help but overhear your discussion."

"Why should she stifle her passion?" Amaya challenged.

"Controlling and stifling are not the same thing." Rosemary sat at the opposite end of the couch from Amaya and adjusted her ivory shawl around her shoulders. "Someone can be the planet's most passionate person on a topic and never once need to yell to get their message across."

"She doesn't always yell," Amaya insisted. When Rosalyn and I stared, she relented. "A lot but not always."

"Have you ever noticed," Rosemary continued, lowering her voice with each word, "that if you whisper, people will get quiet and lean in to hear what you are saying?"

I looked. All four of us had.

"They will tune you out and walk away if you yell for too long." She tapped an earlobe and then the middle of her chest. "Hurts the ears and the soul."

Amaya rolled her eyes. "Or perhaps with age comes complacency. Maybe it becomes less about control over one's method of delivery and more about giving up and letting passion die."

Rosemary looked to me and Roz. "This is what we always hear from the younger members of our coven. That we've given up on the rest of the world and only care about what's important to ourselves. What they don't realize is that we've spent a lifetime whittling away that which doesn't fit in our lives. Regardless of passion, a person can't be effective at everything. The older members and I are at the stage where we're paying attention to those topics that are most important to us. To some, that means simply living our lives. At our age, we've earned that."

"I don't mean to be rude" — Amaya stood — "but that's my cue to go about my business. If you listen to her long enough, you'll notice that she always says 'younger' not 'newer.' The older members only care about themselves. This whittling away statement is just their hippie-dippy way of saying they aren't going to bother putting forth the effort to make the coven a better fit for everyone."

Amaya crossed the room and was out the back door before any of us could comment.

"So impatient." Rosemary frowned. "Religion isn't a club that should be molded to suit the masses. There are many fine options available. If one group doesn't suit your needs, keep searching."

"Sounds like there's a lot of friction in your coven," I suggested gently.

She sighed. "You have no idea. I've been the high priestess for fifteen years. The Circle of 3 Moons coven is my life's passion. It's like my baby." She put her hands to her heart. "I care deeply about every member and have done my very best to guide them in Gerald Gardner's teachings."

"Who's he?" Rosalyn asked.

"Founder of Wicca." At her surprised expression, I clarified, "Read about him in a book at Shoppe Mystique."

Rosemary gave me a mentor-esque smile, impressed with my knowledge. "I'm simply trying to protect my coven from becoming diluted, not to change Maewyn's or Amaya's beliefs. All I ask is that they not try to change us."

She grew quiet then and started chuckling.

"What's funny?" Tripp motioned at the tea mugs.

Rosemary bowed her head in thanks and took one. "I was thinking of what Wanda always says about our younger members. 'They read three books on Wicca, buy a pentacle, or Goddess forbid, take an online course and think they know everything about the religion.'"

I thought back to when I first came here. A young woman named Keko Shen had come to the village specifically to meet Morgan. She wanted to learn from her. Morgan explained to her, and me, that Wicca wasn't something that could be taught in a week or even a month or two. Like any religion, it was a lifetime practice that you had to devote yourself to. That's probably what Wanda was trying to say.

"I don't want you to think we're here to cause trouble, Sheriff," Rosemary assured. "All of us, old and young, came here to celebrate Ostara. The sabbat, not the Goddess. One thing all of us in the coven agree on is that the Wiccan vibes are very strong in this village. Those members who haven't been here before have heard the rest of us sing its praises." She placed her palms together. "We are honored that you have welcomed us here. I vow to do my best to maintain the peace over the next two days. Just like you." She slid to the edge of her cushion and pushed herself up to stand. "Thank you for the tea. I'll bring the mug back in the morning if that's all right."

"Absolutely fine," Tripp responded. "Breakfast is at seven thirty."

"We'll be here. Goodnight, everyone."

We waited until we were sure she was all the way upstairs. Then Rosalyn slumped against the couch. "Wow."

"That coven," Tripp began, "is almost like a smaller version of the village. Half welcoming change and the other half fighting it."

"I think I've had enough witchy drama for the day." Rosalyn yawned and stretched. "My room is calling. I must answer that call."

Before turning in for the night, I helped Tripp get organized for breakfast. That meant putting non-refrigerated ingredients in a basket on a shelf in the pantry and refrigerated ingredients in a specific spot in the refrigerator. That way he could grab it all in the morning and get right to work. Then we performed the rest of our nightly closing routine, which included Meeka doing a last patrol after we'd shut off all the lights except a lamp in the great room and the light over the stove. Then we trudged up two flights to our apartment.

I remember my head hitting the pillow and giving Tripp a goodnight kiss. After that, I was out cold until his alarm went off at five. I fell back to sleep and woke again when the house phone rang. Tripp answered it and used the phone's intercom function to let me know the call was for me.

I groaned as I rolled over and slapped for the extension on my nightstand. "This is Jayne."

"Hey, it's Laurel. Maewyn Barnes's roommate is at the front desk. She says Maewyn is missing."

Chapter 8

I HATED DAYS THAT STARTED this way. "What do you mean Maewyn is missing?"

"Well," Laurel began, "Iris Mohan, Maewyn's roommate, came down around five thirty. She told Emery she was looking for her roomie. Maewyn wasn't in her bed, hadn't slept in it, or even been in the room at all last night. Emery checked with Gardenia, who worked the night shift until three this morning. Based on Iris's description, Gardenia thinks she saw Maewyn go up to the room at about four-twenty yesterday afternoon but didn't notice her leave. Emery came on at the end of Gardenia's shift and says he didn't see her either."

I yawned. "That sounds like missing. My mom is here until Sunday. Sorry I forgot to introduce you."

"I figured that's who the woman at your table was."

"Yep. I want to spend as much time with her as I can, so Reed is acting sheriff for the rest of the week. Call him with this, okay?"

There was a pause before she replied, "You couldn't have told me that before I went into all that explanation?"

"Could have. I should at least know what's going on,

though. We'll probably stop in at the festivities later, so I'll check in with Ms. Mohan then."

After brewing and drinking a cup of coffee, I took a shower and debated about what to do with my mother today. We'd for sure go to the Ostara celebration. We could go to the Barlows' cottage tomorrow and plant seeds. But then what? Honestly, unless you were into cross-country skiing or snowshoeing, there wasn't much to do around here in the winter other than eat. The hiking trails were too muddy or we could go for a stroll through the woods. Although, Mom probably didn't have appropriate hiking shoes. And Morgan thought *I* was a city girl the time she led me through the forest to Blind Willie's cabin. I was rustic as they came compared to my mother.

"What am I going to do with her?" I sighed, thinking how she was like a little kid that needed entertaining, and pulled the curtain aside to see Meeka sitting on the rug, staring up at me, her head tilted in question. I yelped. "You startled me. I thought you were downstairs."

She'd let all the heat out of what should have been a cozy, toasty bathroom. That's what I got for pushing the door shut but not closing it.

I dressed, towel-dried my hair, and went down for breakfast. It took mere seconds to understand why Meeka had come up by me rather than staying with Tripp like she usually did. The witches were gathered around the dining room table discussing options for the next sabbat, which would be Beltane on May first, and they were loud. On the positive side, it sounded like no one agreed with anyone this time, not just old ones versus young ones.

I debated asking if any of them had heard about Maewyn being missing, but since they weren't talking about it, I assumed they didn't know. Bringing it up could cause unnecessary panic. Maybe she'd gone to another witch's room for the night or hung out beneath the almost full moon. Wouldn't be the first time a city slicker had become enchanted by the beauty of nature here.

"Good morning, Proprietress," River greeted from his standard spot at the dinette table across from the kitchen.

"Morning, River." I took the seat next to him. "I was hoping I'd find a quiet moment with you. Let's chat."

He paused with his buttered toast halfway to his mouth. "Did I do something?"

"It's what you haven't done yet." When he didn't catch on right away, I nudged, "The ring?"

While Tripp and I were at River's condo on Maui, he'd asked us to find a black box in the master bedroom closet and bring it back with us. We found two boxes. The first was full of promotional materials for his company, Blackbird Industries. A *Facts About Blackbirds* section on the back of a pamphlet talked about how the birds are connected with the otherworld, that they can have a hypnotic effect on people, and will guide you to where you want to go while keeping away those who may want to do you harm. It made me shiver even now to think of what I'd read because it was a lot like River's personality. Tripp decided our renter/friend was a shapeshifter.

The second box held an even bigger surprise. It was a ring that was far too extravagant to be a token of friendship. It had to be an engagement ring. The band was made of black gold. The centerpiece was a large oval-shaped black opal swirled with bursts of blue, purple, green, red, orange, and yellow. Encircling the opal were three rings of tiny black diamonds. It was truly stunning and perfect for a certain green witch I knew. And, as of last night at the pub, it still wasn't on Morgan's finger.

"When are you going to give it to her?" I demanded. "How long do we have to pretend like we don't know about it?"

"Until the time is right." River took a bite of his toast and chewed while I stared at him. "I did not tell you to look at it. Your impatience is your own doing."

"You did tell me to," I practically yelled, then lowered my voice. "You literally sent me a text that said, 'Go ahead. Open it.' I can get my phone and prove it to you."

"Granting permission is not the same as forcing you to follow through with a deed."

I stared at him. "If I let it slip, it's not my fault."

He squinted and held my gaze. "Never fear, Proprietress. You will not let it slip."

"You just did that mind-meld thing on me, didn't you? I can't talk about it now, can I? You're horrible."

He chuckled, amused with himself, but said no more.

I stood to grab a mug of coffee as Mom entered the room. She paused to press her cheek to mine and then took the seat next to River I'd just vacated. Since when did we do the cheek thing? If we grunted at each other in the morning, it was rare. Usually the fact that we got out of each other's way near the coffee pot was greeting enough.

"What did Laurel want?" Tripp gave me a quick kiss and continued assembling breakfast platters for us.

"We have a missing witch." Halfway through the explanation, the front doorbell rang.

"I'll get it." I unlocked the deadbolt and had barely opened the door when a teenage girl with red-blonde hair and a face full of freckles burst in.

"You've got to help me," she pleaded. "My mother is in labor."

I now had a new least favorite way to start the day.

When I started to give her directions to Unity, she stopped me. "I'm not sure I have time to get her there."

"It's only five minutes away."

The girl shook her head. "Her water broke, and she says

she feels like pushing."

I knew enough about active labor to know the urge to push meant things were close. "All right. Take me to her."

In the driveway, a mostly rusty teal-green Volvo sat diagonally in front of the garage. The girl led me to the passenger's side where I found a woman with long dark-copper hair panting in preparation for an oncoming contraction.

"I'm Jayne. I own this B&B. What's your name?"

"Freya . . . Nygaard," she managed between breaths.

"How often are your contractions coming?"

Before she could answer, the pain hit hard, so I looked to the girl.

"I'm not sure," she responded. "Like I said, her water broke about two miles outside of town and they started coming faster. I stopped at that grocery store. They sent me to the clinic, but the door was locked."

Locked? Unity should be open around the clock with so many tourists here.

"The closest hospital is an hour away," I murmured mostly to myself.

"That's why I stopped here. I saw your sign on the side of the road and didn't know what else to do."

A feeling of panic spread through my chest. Cops didn't do roadside deliveries. We could but called for the fire/paramedic crew immediately and kept calling with each contraction to get an update on their ETA.

As the contraction eased, Freya slumped back and took deep, slow breaths.

Get it together, Jayne in my head ordered. *Make a plan.*

A plan. Plans were good. Whispering Pines didn't have paramedics, and I wasn't comfortable transporting a woman in the late stages of labor.

"What's your name?" I asked the girl.

"I'm Runa." She pointed to the backseat where a toddler with strawberry-red hair and huge blue eyes stared at us. "That's my baby sister, Elin." She considered her statement for a second. "That might be the last time I can call her that. If this one's another girl, Elin will be my middle sister."

"Let's get your mom inside. Looks like you're right. It's not a good idea to bring her to Unity. We might be delivering in your car if we do."

Runa didn't seem crazy about bringing her inside either. "Can you deliver a baby?"

I barked out a single, slightly hysterical-sounding laugh. "No. But I'll get someone here who can. They can talk me through things over the walkie talkie until they get here."

"Walkie talkie?" Freya demanded. "What kind of backwards spot on the map did you bring us to?"

"If you would've agreed to get in the car an hour ago like I asked," Runa shot back, "we'd be at the hospital by now."

"We're not backwards," I promised. Our only cell phone reception is via wifi, and the trees interfere with that."

"So what are we going to do?" Runa guided us back to the baby, unconcerned with our technology issues.

I looked over my shoulder to see Tripp and River standing on the front porch. I waved to them, and they rushed right over.

"This is Freya Nygaard," I told them. "She's in labor. We need to bring her inside."

Tripp helped Freya out of the car. The second she was standing we could tell by her soaked shin-length skirt that her water had broken very recently.

"Here." Runa handed me a blanket from the back seat. "So she doesn't drip everywhere."

I draped the blanket around Freya's back while Tripp and River locked their arms to form a makeshift chair for her to sit on. Once she was secure, they headed toward the house. I ran ahead, startling all the women in the dining room into silence when I burst through the front door.

"Where are we taking her?" Tripp asked.

"What's the problem?" Marie jumped to her feet. "Is she injured or in labor?"

"Labor," I responded, wondering how she came to those two options so fast. "I need to call for someone at our healing center. Looks like the baby will be here very soon. We need a room." I glanced at Calliope who was staying in The Side room. "She's got two other kids with her. Your room has those bunk beds."

Calliope started nodding before I could finish my thought. "Take it. I'll move in with one of the others."

"I'm a certified midwife," Marie answered my unstated earlier question. "Have been for twenty years. I can help."

"Freya will like that," Runa approved from the doorway. "Half the reason she took so long to agree to going to the hospital is that she wanted a midwife to deliver her at home. Hers was with another mom. Sounded like there were complications because she was still laboring when I dragged Freya out to the car."

"I'll call for one of our medical folks to come over too," I told Runa. "They'll bring the proper equipment."

While securing her dozens of braids into a single bundle by wrapping and knotting two braids around them, Marie followed Tripp and River upstairs.

I took two steps toward the office when Runa said in a gentle tone, "I swear, I'm not being a brat. With the dripping everywhere comment and what I told her about her not leaving our house, I mean. Freya was being so unreasonable. We talked about this months ago. She understood that if she had to go to the hospital, we'd need plenty of time to get there. She agreed then, but today she kept wanting to wait 'five more minutes' for the midwife so she could have a home birth. She never listens." She closed her eyes and exhaled a centering breath. "Crap. I forgot Elin in the car."

Runa seemed more like an exhausted caregiver or co-parent than a teenage daughter. And it bothered me the way she called her mother by her first name. Regardless of how old the child was, it was a matter of respect to the people who brought them into the world. Guess I was old-fashioned that way.

"How old are you?" I asked Runa.

"Fifteen." She held up a hand, stopping the statement she knew was coming next. "Yes, I'm an old soul, blah, blah, blah."

I smiled. As Gran would say, Runa was a pip. "Go get Elin and your bags. I'll call for backup."

I paused at the dining room door when Amaya asked, "You took pictures?"

Kegan stood between the table and the doorway, cell phone in hand.

"Not this time," Amaya demanded. "You've got to stop posting pictures of random people without their permission."

Kegan slid her phone into her back pocket. "I know. I wasn't going to." But her tone made it obvious she was.

Since Amaya seemed to have that under control, I continued to the office, closed the door, dropped into my chair . . . and jumped when Meeka's face appeared between my knees. "Too many people?"

She gave a little *ruff* and leaned against my leg.

I patted my lap and let her jump up as I reached for the phone.

"Unity," a voice answered, "this is Drake."

"Hey, Drake. This is Jayne at Pine Time. We've got a situation over here."

"Dead body?"

Why was that always everyone's first guess?

"Guest in labor. The daughter says they stopped by the clinic, but no one was there."

Drake groaned. "She must've missed me by literal seconds. Sanjay had an emergency at home, of the burst pipe variety. He said the place was empty, and since I was about to walk out the door for my shift, I told him to go."

"The daughter saw our sign on the side of the road and brought Mom here. I'd bring her to you, but I'm not sure we have that much time. One of our other guests claims to be a midwife and is with her now, but I'd feel a whole lot better if one of you were here too."

"No problem. Jola is on call today. I'll send her right over. Hang tight."

"Easy for you to say." I hung up and gave Meeka a squeeze. "You stay in here, girl. Things will calm down soon."

For the most part, the house was already quieter in that the ladies in the dining room had returned to their breakfasts. Tripp, however, came racing down the stairs looking panicked.

"What's wrong?" I asked.

"We need a plastic sheet or about a hundred towels to protect that mattress. She's going to mess it up big time, and I don't want to replace it again."

I placed my hands on his chest to slow him down. "Hang on, where are they? I thought we agreed on The Side." The new mattress was in the Jack room. A bullet had shredded part of the old one. But we didn't talk about that.

"In between contractions," Tripp explained through a sigh, "Freya insisted she wanted separate rooms. One for her and the baby and another for Runa and Elin. She agreed that the Jack and Jill set up would do."

That was understandable. Little Elin didn't need to be around her laboring mother. Runa didn't either. Now I'd have to tell scary Wanda that she'd have to share a room, though.

"Are you okay?" I asked Tripp, biting back a grin. Mr. Calm and Cool was freaking out. And looking a bit pale. I turned him toward the great room. "Sit before you fall down. Head between your knees. I'll find something for the mattress."

He nodded and swayed as he walked. "There's a fresh roll of plastic sheeting in the basement by the painting supplies."

That would work.

By the time I'd brought the sheeting up to the room and then went back to the basement for old towels, Jola had arrived. She followed me upstairs but froze in the hallway outside the Jack room instead of going inside.

"Come on in," I beckoned. It took a second before I understood her hesitation. The last time she'd been to the house, she'd been curled up on the floor in the bathroom shared by the Jack and Jill rooms, cowering from the gunman in the Jack room. The one who'd shot the mattress. I stepped in front of her. "Can you do this? Should I call Drake?"

She blinked and seemed to come out of a daze. "No. I can do it. Just, you know, memories."

"I understand. There's nothing to fear this time except the language of a woman suffering labor pains."

As if on cue, Freya let loose with a stream of profanity, the likes of which I'd only heard from drunken frat boys.

Funny enough, that put Jola at ease, and she laughed. "We'll never fully understand until we're there. And then moments after the baby arrives, the worst of the pain is forgotten."

That's what people claimed. I wasn't buying it.

I stood by as Jola introduced herself to Marie, who filled her in on the details. When Jola gave me a thumbs up indicating everything was under control, I went to the Jill side in search of Runa and Elin. I wanted to understand how a laboring woman and her children ended up on my doorstep.

Chapter 9

I FOUND RUNA SITTING IN an overstuffed lounge chair in the corner of the Jill room with her feet propped on the matching ottoman and Elin in her lap. The toddler had her thumb plugged into her mouth and appeared to be sound asleep.

"Are you two okay in here?" I asked.

"No need to whisper," Runa assured. "Elin can sleep through a fire alarm. Literally. Ours went off one night when I burned popcorn in the microwave. She didn't budge."

There was something about Runa that seemed very familiar. I was positive I'd never met her before but could swear I knew her.

"Where do you live?" I asked. "Must be close to here if you were heading north to the hospital."

She waved a hand vaguely westward. "We're about a half hour from here. I was taking her to the hospital in Superior."

A mental map of Wisconsin popped to the front of my brain. "Superior? If you live a half hour from Whispering Pines, the clinics in Hayward or Ashland are closer."

"Yes, but the doctor who delivered Elin works in Superior." She wrapped an arm tighter around her little sister and paused before continuing. "Elin almost didn't make it. She was breech, and the cord was around her neck. And Freya had problems too. The midwife told her considering all that, it might be better to deliver in a hospital. Freya insisted on a home delivery. When her midwife couldn't make it this morning, I figured going to the guy who was familiar with her history made the most sense."

"Your mother is in expert hands right now. I don't know Marie, but I do know Jola and would trust her with my life."

Runa released a little of the grip she had on Elin and nodded at the room in general. "I like this room. The whole house is nice. Thanks for taking us in. I've got Freya's credit card, by the way. I promise we can pay for both rooms. Even if we're here for a few days."

We'd find out for sure when I ran the card.

"I know what you're thinking." Runa plucked at a hole in her UWM Badgers sweatshirt and wiggled her foot with a taped together shoe. "We wear raggy clothes and drive a crappy car. Clothes aren't a big deal to us, and the Volvo is only crappy on the outside. The engine and interior are almost brand new. Well, newly replaced. Freya's last guy was into cars. He fixed up the guts and was going to do the bodywork next. Then Freya told him she was pregnant, and he took off. Don't feel sorry for us, though. We're fine. My grandparents are loaded."

And yet, the three, almost four of them lived in the middle of Nowhere, Wisconsin. To be fair, some people loved the solitude and space this part of the state provided. Others stayed or came because it was all they could afford. A few found it was easy to disappear up here.

"We don't normally provide lunch or dinner," I told Runa, "but considering the circumstances, we'll make an exception today. Let me or Tripp know when you or Elin want something to eat."

"We can go into the village. You have restaurants, don't you?"

"Yes, but you said you're fifteen. You've only got a driving permit, right?"

She shot me a look so withering it took me by surprise.

"Sorry, Runa, but I'm also the sheriff here. I can't knowingly let you break the law."

She sighed. A sound as unamused as the look she'd just given me. "Fine. I'll let you know when we'd like a snack."

I stepped into the hall as Freya screamed again. Was there anything even close to childbirth that men had to suffer through?

At the bottom of the stairs, I planned to go straight to the kitchen since I hadn't had breakfast yet. Then I remembered the Nygaards kicked Rosemary and Marie out of the Jack and Jill rooms. We needed to do a little rearranging.

"How are things going up there?" Rosemary asked.

"Based on my extensive knowledge of childbirth" —I held my thumb and index finger about a quarter-inch apart— "everything is great. There's something I need to discuss with you."

I explained Freya's desire to have a private room for her and the baby and how it was best that Runa and Elin be nearby.

"The most logical way to make that happen," I paused before breaking the news, "is to put them in the Jack and Jill rooms. Freya is still in labor. That could go on for a while."

"Marie and I need to go somewhere else then," Rosemary concluded as though this was a given.

"She already gathered your things and moved them down the hall."

"That's fine." Rosemary shook her head, unconcerned with that. "Wanda and I are okay with sharing—"

"Hold on." Wanda pushed her shoulders back and her eyes hardened. "You're telling me we have to share a bed?"

Somehow I knew she wouldn't take the news well. "We only have those two rooms available. The Side room has a queen bed and a bunk bed with a full-size mattress on the bottom. The Treehouse has one king bed. You can pair up however works best for you."

"What kind of discount will you give us?" Wanda asked.

"*Dios mio*," Calliope hissed. "Wanda, a woman is having a baby. That's an event to celebrate, not profit off of."

"Obviously," I began, "you only need to pay for the two rooms. I could take an extra ten percent—"

"We'll accept no discounts," Rosemary insisted, "and we're happy to pair up."

Wanda crossed her arms, scowled at Rosemary, and then at me.

Rosemary sighed. "Stop it. We've been friends for two decades. We could all use some good karma points." She shot a stern look at Wanda. "Some of us more than others."

Wanda swatted a hand with crooked fingers at Rosemary. They reminded me of Briar's hands. I'd put money on Wanda being a green witch. Or at least a dabbler. Gardening wasn't for sissies.

I placed my palms together and bowed to the three. "Thank you so much for understanding. I know this visit hasn't turned out like you hoped, but I'm sure once you're at The Inn and enjoying the events the village has planned, everything will work out fine." I turned to leave and spun back. "If there's anything at all Tripp and I can do for you, say the word."

"Discount?" Wanda asked and actually smiled when Calliope gently swatted the back of her head. Glad to see the tough woman had a bit of softness in there.

I found Tripp, River, Rosalyn, and Mom gathered around the dinette.

"What on earth is going on up there?" Mom asked with a horrified expression.

"A woman is giving birth."

"You say that like it's a normal occurrence." She held both hands in front of her, silencing my response. "Never mind, I forgot. I'm in Whispering Pines."

From anyone else, that statement might be funny. From my mother, it held far more disdain for the village than humor.

I grabbed a plate and filled it with French toast, scrambled eggs, and fruit. Then I added a muffin. "They were on the way to the hospital when the pains came on fast. Her daughter saw our sign on the side of the road and pulled in here."

Marie entered the kitchen then. "Looks like we'll be a while. I didn't get to finish my breakfast. Is it all right for me to take more?"

"Of course." I indicated the spread on the kitchen island. "Help yourself. I thought Freya's water broke, though."

"It did." Marie loaded a small plate with fruit and a muffin. "That means the baby is on the way, but not necessarily quickly. The contractions have slowed. Don't worry, this is normal. Jola and I have everything under control."

She took her plate and a mug of coffee upstairs with her, and I turned to Mom and Rosalyn. "Should we go into the village and check out the festivities at The Inn?"

"You and Tripp can't both leave," Mom objected, assuming I'd meant everyone. "You have customers in the house. Am I to assume it's common practice to let perfect strangers have the run of the place and for you to not be present for your guests?"

"No, Mom, that's not our practice." In fact, that was a big downside to running a B&B. We couldn't leave the guests alone, which meant one of us had to be here at all times.

During the tourist season, I was at the station all day which left house-sitting duties to Tripp. "The only time Tripp and I are away from the house at the same time is when either Arden or Holly are here cleaning."

"I'll stay," Tripp told us. "I've got to clean up, make crackers for the wine and cheese social tonight, and prep for tomorrow's breakfast." To Mom, he explained, "Part of Jayne's job is being with the public. She needs to be in the village, circulating through the crowd. We've found that even at otherwise mellow events, the sheriff's presence is a good thing."

My heart warmed. I loved how we had become such a great team. How we knew each other so well and understood, both technically and emotionally, the details of each other's jobs.

River pushed away from the table and stood. "You may both leave. I will be in residence until the dinner hour. The Ladies Barlow are engaged with the celebrations and preparations for tomorrow's seed planting. This allows me to perform my own duties. Go participate in the events, Master Tripp. I'll attend to any concerns the guests may have."

Despite Mom's sour expression, Tripp agreed. "Thanks. I'll clean up first and won't be gone long. I do have to make crackers."

And even though Reed was at the top of the call list today, Tripp was right about me needing to mingle among the tourists. Public safety was ultimately my responsibility. I should also check in on Maewyn's status. Funny that no one from the coven seemed to know she was missing. Or was it that they knew but didn't care?

Chapter 10

SINCE TRIPP WOULD NEED TO leave sooner than the rest of us, we took two vehicles. I drove Mom's new metallic beige Lexus and couldn't get over how nice it was to drive a quality car.

"Can't believe you got a hybrid," I commented. "I didn't realize you were so environmentally conscious."

She picked a dust speck from the chocolate-brown leather seat and sent it out the window. "I was tired of stopping for gas all the time."

That made a lot more sense.

We parked both cars behind the station and walked along the Fairy Path to the commons. It was another beautiful early spring day in the village. I took Tripp's hand and breathed in the semi-warm breeze. I'd lived in Wisconsin my entire life and knew to appreciate these days but to not put away my winter wardrobe yet. The temperature could easily drop again, and spring snowstorms could blow up with little warning. That was the excuse the fishermen used for leaving their shanties out on the lake. They were willing to push it as far as possible for one more day on the ice. If it was me, I'd bring them in.

"Look at the eggs." Rosalyn pointed out clusters of brightly colored eggs scattered around the trees. "But Easter isn't until next month."

"It must be something Wiccan," Mom said with the same tone she'd use to say, "It's probably something contagious."

The Inn's front lobby looked like spring had exploded all over it. Vases filled with daffodils, hyacinths, and tulips were everywhere. Considering only tiny flowers called snowdrops were growing in the Pentacle Garden and throughout the woods, the green witches must have grown these indoors.

Banners in spring colors hung on stands in the corners. Candles in spring green, light yellow, and pale purple sat beneath hurricanes and flickered on any surface not occupied by a vase of flowers. The promise of things new and fresh stood out dramatically against the dark-paneled, slightly crooked walls of the building.

"Happy Ostara," Emery called out from behind the desk. "Well, technically it's not until tomorrow. I should really say, welcome to our Ostara celebration."

The second I let Meeka off her leash, she made a beeline for the dining room. She knew the chances were good that someone had dropped something edible in there. If she didn't find crumbs, she'd sit in front of people and give them her hungry eyes until they gave in and offered her a nibble.

"Follow Meeka," Emery told us. "There's plenty of food and other activities. There's a cookie decorating table, a coloring station for kids and adults, and multiple egg decorating tables."

As soon as we entered the dining room, I switched from Regular Jayne to Sheriff Jayne, but a more mellow version of Sheriff Jayne since Reed was in charge. I scanned the room for my deputy but didn't see him anywhere. Hopefully he was searching for Maewyn. No sign of Laurel, either, so I couldn't ask if she'd contacted him. I'd ask Emery. He'd know.

"What would you like to do, Mom?" I swept a hand across the entire dining room. She'd remained neutral about the promised festivities until we entered the lobby and she saw the decorations. Then I noticed a bit of sparkle in her eye.

She cleared her throat. "We just ate breakfast, so more food can wait. I'm not interested in decorating cookies or coloring." Her gaze landed on the egg tables at the far side of the large room. "I am curious about egg decorating, however."

At tables set up along the side walls, children were dipping eggs into cups filled with colored liquid. That was the way Rosalyn and I used to do it when we were little. More tables were set up in front of the floor-to-ceiling stone fireplace. There, people were involved with a more complex version of egg decorating. Villagers and visitors alike had taken seats along the two long tables as Ruby from The Twisty Skein gave instructions. Beckett, the beekeeper, appeared to be her helper. I hadn't seen him since the Mabon/Autumnal Equinox celebration in September.

"Remember," Ruby was telling two of the coven members, "the wax goes where you don't want color. And you start with your lightest shade and work toward the darkest."

"What are they doing?" Mom asked her.

"We're making *pysanky* eggs." Ruby, as usual when instructing people on a craft, was all smiles. She invited Mom to sit at an open station. "The eggs' yolks and whites have been blown out, and the shells thoroughly washed. This is a shell I made."

She held up an egg that had white flowers, leaves, and vines on a ruby-red background, her signature color. "The patterns can take a while to draw, but the dying process is quite simple."

The crafters at the various stations had not only hollowed-out eggs before them and cups with colored liquid, like at the kids' tables, but also candles and pencil-sized sticks with what looked like tiny funnels on the tips.

"These are *kistkas*," Beckett explained of the pens. "The tips hold small amounts of beeswax." He dropped a few pellets in the funnel of one and held it over the candle's flame. "Once the wax has melted, you draw it on the egg."

No wonder Beckett was here. He probably brought the wax.

"When your design is complete," Ruby continued, "and the wax has hardened, you put your egg into the dye color of your choice. It's best to draw your design on with a pencil first and then add the wax rather than to try free handing a design with the kistka."

"The trick," Beckett said, "is to think wax equals white, or whatever color your egg is. Or if you're adding many colors, wax equals no color change."

"The history behind coloring eggs," Ruby informed, "is that they were believed to protect against evil while bringing happiness and prosperity into the creator's home. And, as we learned at Grapes, Grains, and Grub last night, Ostara is about fertility. Eggs are symbols of fertility. Chickens, of course, lay eggs and frisky little rabbits are quite fertile, which is why those two creatures play a role in our celebration."

"The Easter bunny, chocolate eggs, and marshmallow Peeps," Rosalyn noted with childlike whimsy.

"That's why we saw eggs scattered in the woods." I knew someone would explain it to us.

"Jayne?"

Someone laid a hand on my shoulder. I turned to find Laurel there.

"Sorry to interrupt," she said, "but could we talk for a moment?"

"Sure." I bent to tell Mom, "I've got to step away. Are you okay making eggs?"

"I am." Her attention was firmly on the crafters around

her. There were clearly some who'd done this before and others who were as new to it as she was. "This intrigues me. Go do what you need to do."

Rosalyn joined the adult coloring table, and Tripp was getting a lesson on decorating cookies from Sugar, so I followed Laurel into the lobby where it was quieter and we could talk without being overheard. Meeka tagged along. There was a table with hot cross buns, deviled eggs, ham, and other hors d'oeuvres, but nowhere near as much food as there had been for Yule. The Westie preferred her eggs scrambled and ham wasn't her favorite. Besides, she probably sensed there was something K-9-related going on. Meeka was as eager for tourist season to start and be busy again as I was.

"Did you get in touch with Deputy Reed?" I asked Laurel.

"I did." She signaled to a young woman standing near the registration desk to join us near the fireplace. "This is Iris Mohan. Maewyn Barnes's roommate. She'd like to talk with you."

Early twenties, five foot six, medium-brown skin, tattoos covering both arms, gold septum ring, black hair in gleaming dreadlocks to her waist.

"I'll check in with you later," Laurel announced and left us to talk.

"Hi, Iris. I'm Sheriff O'Shea. What's going on?"

Before she said a word, I got a street-smart Chicago vibe off her. She arched an eyebrow and took a half-step back as though surprised. "You're the sheriff?"

"I am indeed." It was my age. Older people accepted my position right away. The closer a person was to my twenty-seven years the harder it was for them to believe I was the sheriff. "What's up?"

She gave me a sideways glance before saying, "I talked to your deputy earlier. I'm really worried about Mae, though, so wanted to go straight to the top."

"Did you have a problem with Deputy Reed?" He was fresh out of the academy but experienced with the job. I'd be shocked if he messed something up.

"Not a problem exactly. He seemed" — she pursed her lips and wiggled them left then right — "unconcerned is probably the best word. He asked a bunch of questions and wrote down what I said. I think he thinks she just took off. Like maybe she went for a hike or headed home." Her dreads swayed as she shook her head. "She wouldn't leave. Not without telling someone. Besides, all her stuff is still here."

"I understand you're rooming with Maewyn. Will you take me up there so I can have a look around?"

The request put her at ease, and her shoulders sagged with relief. My guess was that Reed hadn't bothered to go up there. I had no idea what I might find that would be of help, but it couldn't hurt to take a look.

As we climbed the creaking stairs, I asked Iris, "Why are you so sure Maewyn didn't leave?"

"I was up until a little after one last night," she began. "I'm sort of a night owl. Then I woke up this morning at like six, which was weird. I usually sleep until nine or nine thirty. Mae wasn't in the room, and her bed hadn't been slept in, so it was like the lack of her presence that woke me up, if that makes sense."

"I understand. What did you do after you realized she hadn't been there?"

"I walked over to the parking lot to see if her car was still there. It would be a problem if she had left because a couple members rode with her, and we filled every available space in all the cars. Well, except for Wanda. She kept saying she needed time alone and drove herself. She's kind of a loner."

"What kind of vehicle does Maewyn drive?" I didn't have my notepad with me so grabbed a sheet of letterhead paper and pencil from a basket on a small table in the third-floor hallway.

"Camry. Pine green. It's like fifteen years old."

I wrote that down and followed her to a room at the center of the hall. The first thing I noticed was that one bed was neatly made, and the other had a tangle of bedclothes at the foot. Meeka instantly started investigating the room by sniffing in the corners, beneath the bed, and at anything lying on the floor.

"I know Mae came up here at some point after she left the pub last night." Iris pointed out a pair of black ballerina flats on the floor next to the desk in the corner, and a charcoal-gray sweater draped over the desk chair. "She was wearing those shoes and that sweater."

"I was there. I remember the sweater." She'd snatched it from the back of her chair so quickly she knocked the chair over. I pulled out my cell phone and took a picture. "She was fuming when she left."

"She was," Iris agreed. "She probably went for a walk. That's what she does at home when she gets worked up over something. It depends on how angry she is, but the average is a ten-block square."

"It sounds like you know her well. Are you roommates in Chicago?"

"No, we're friends, though. She came into my parlor about two years ago."

"Parlor?"

"I do tattoos, piercings, and massage. Just chair massage and only by request. It helps people relax if they're nervous about the needles. I don't own the place. Been working there for five years."

"Is that what the red marks on your hands are from? Ink?" I pointed out red stains on her hands at the base of both pinkies.

She looked. "Oh, no. We wear gloves to protect us from ink and such. I use a rowing machine and get a little aggressive with my strokes, I guess. Anyway, Mae came in the first time about a year and a half ago. She was pissed off about something and wanted to get a tattoo."

"What kind?"

"The female symbol. You know, the circle with the cross beneath it. She wanted one with a raised fist in the center of the circle."

"Did she get it?" A tattoo would be an easy identifier if this turned out to be a recovery instead of a rescue.

Iris laughed. "I've been doing this long enough to know when to suggest people wait a while and when to move forward with ink. I didn't have to say anything to Mae. After ten minutes of ranting, she walked out. She came in once a month for the next six months. Same thing. Pissed off and needing to vent. The eighth time she came in, she'd decided to get the symbol, without the fist, right here." She rubbed a finger over the fleshy part on the top of her right hand between her thumb and index finger. "It's like the size of a dime. She was afraid of needles."

"I assume you got to know her pretty well over those six months."

"Like I said, we're friends. The fourth time she came in, it was almost closing time, so we went out and got a beer. She attracted quite a crowd at the bar. Some cheered her on. Others told her to get lost. Only they used a more colorful phrase than 'get lost,' if you know what I mean. By then, I'd been a member of Circle of 3 Moons for about a year. When we got to the point where I felt like my religion was a safe topic for us to discuss, about nine months in, I told her about Wicca. She thought it sounded cool and asked to come to a coven gathering. A few months later, she asked to come to another one."

"So she's been a member of the coven for how long?"

"Three or four months."

"Her beliefs don't line up with the others', though, do they?"

"No. I'm not sure if she read about Dianic Wicca or if someone told her."

"Dianic?"

"A type of Wicca that worships the Goddesses but won't give the time of day to Gods. You heard her last night. What you see with Mae Barnes is what you get. She is who she is. If you don't like it, you can get fu —" She instantly turned a deep berry red. "Lost. You can get lost. Sorry."

"No worries." I'd heard far worse from the laboring Freya Nygaard this morning. "All right, so you know she was here at some point last night. You think she might have gone for a walk to calm down. If that's the case, she probably wouldn't have gone on the hiking trails. They're a mess right now with all the snowmelt, and even with the near full moon, the woods are dark at night."

"And she's a city girl," Iris noted. "She's not much for nature walks."

"That leaves walking along the highway."

Flashes of searching the snow-filled ditches during a blizzard in January for a missing car filled my mind. That hunt had ended horribly. I prayed this one wouldn't, but this was Whispering Pines.

"The other reason I don't think she left," Iris supplied, "is her devotion to Wicca. She liked those first few coven gatherings enough to join. There was a lot about it that seemed to click with her, but when she found the Dianic version, Wicca that also supported her feminist beliefs, it became like an obsession to change 3 Moons."

"Why? Why not find a new coven?"

She shook her head. "No clue. Me and a few other

members told her the same thing. That she needed to quit pushing or join a different coven. Rosemary is so patient, but she came close to kicking her out a couple times."

"What does this have to do with your certainty that she didn't leave?"

Iris looked at me like I was slow. "Three full days of everyone together instead of only a couple of hours at a time? No one has to go to work or get home to their kids or cats or partner. She's basically got a captive audience. I'm not sure if she's trying to convince others to form a new coven with her or if she's still determined to convert 3 Moons to Dianic. It honestly could be either. Whatever she's up to, she came here with a purpose. Leave the first night? No way."

Her argument made sense. From the minor and limited interactions I'd had with Maewyn, she seemed confident and determined, if not overly aggressive.

"I believe you," I told Iris, who slumped onto her unmade bed with relief. "Do you mind if I look around the room?"

"Mae will have a tantrum if you touch her stuff."

I couldn't help but laugh at her word choice. A "tantrum" sounded exactly like what Maewyn's reaction would be.

"This is kind of important, though," Iris reasoned. "Yeah, take a look. She's got stuff in the bathroom too. The pink bag is hers."

Iris scooted to the head of her bed, leaned against the headboard, and pulled her legs into crisscross. She took out her phone and started scrolling while flipping the fringe of her geometric print scarf back and forth.

"Don't post anything about this," I cautioned. "Nothing more than 'I'm looking for Maewyn. Anyone know where she is?' We don't want to create a panic." Or scare off a potential suspect if this went the way things tended to go in this village.

"No worries," Iris assured. "You may have noticed that the coven is calmer today. It's amazing the chaos one person can create. If anyone notices she's not around, they'll breathe a sigh of relief before going searching for her."

And this was coming from her supposed friend. With more sorrow than judgment, I stated, "I'm glad she's got one person on her side."

"She's got more than me. They're in Chicago, though."

Since I was closest to the bathroom, I started there. The "pink bag" was an eight-inch-long by three-inch-wide by three-inch-deep zippered bag with a glittery unicorn horn coming out of the top. A smiling horsey face decal filled the front. Inside were standard generic products available at any Walmart. Toothbrush, toothpaste, and floss. Face wash, moisturizer, and a small collection of cosmetics including blush, mascara, and eyeliner. Nothing here of interest. Other than the unicorn. Like Wanda smiling when Calliope smacked her in the head, it seemed Maewyn had a soft side too.

Her suitcase didn't offer much more in the way of clues. Only clothes tossed haphazardly inside. Everything was black, dark gray, or deep purple. Meeka gave it all a good sniff, and nothing inside caught her attention either.

"Does she have a purse?" I asked Iris.

"No. She only carries her cell phone in one of those cases that doubles as a wallet. She clips her car keys to the zipper, but those are right there on the desk."

Two charms, a pentacle and the earlier discussed female symbol with the raised fist, joined three keys on the ring.

"Any idea what the keys are for?"

"One's for her car, one's for her apartment, and the other is for Amaya's occult shop."

"What about her phone? Is it here?"

Iris shrugged. "No clue."

"Call the number. Maybe it's in the room somewhere."

She did so and kept her eyes locked on mine as she listened to it ring. After a few seconds, she frowned. "It went to voicemail." She listened and then said, "Hey, Mae, it's Iris. I'm looking all over for you, girl. Call me so I can quit freaking."

"I'll pass all of this on to Deputy Reed. He's solid, so don't worry about that. If you felt like he wasn't concerned earlier, it was probably that he was trying to determine what he could eliminate from his search and what he should focus on. Don't worry. If she's still in the village, we'll find her."

I hurried down the stairs to look for Reed and ran into Morgan in the lobby.

"Thank the Goddess. I was hoping I'd find you." She put her hands to her lower back and winced.

Chapter 11

WAS MORGAN IN LABOR? IT was too early. She wasn't due for two more months. What should I do? Call Jola? No, she was with Freya. Marie was a midwife. She could stay with Freya, and Jola could come help Morgan. No, I should find Briar.

"Why are you looking at me like that?" Morgan asked.

My eyes darted to her hands still at her back. "Are you in labor?"

She traced my gaze and laughed gently. "Good Goddess, no. Some day when a small human is laying on your tailbone and bladder, you'll understand." She half-waddled to the lobby's sitting area next to the fireplace, lowered less gracefully than usual onto a couch, and propped her feet on the coffee table. "I'm taking a short break and went for a walk around the garden. The sun is glorious today, isn't it? I have to get back to the shop shortly, but I stopped in here to see the setup."

Morgan was gushing. Her emotions were amplified lately. Had to be that baby.

"What did you want to talk about?" I sat on a leather chair next to her.

"Our mothers. I'm concerned they're going to end up in a catfight."

"Are they in the dining room? Do I need to call in reinforcements?"

"No, Mama is at home preparing for tomorrow." She winced and then smiled as her right hand went to the side of her belly. "She's kicking. Whenever I stop moving, she starts. I envision many hours in the beautiful rocking chair River made for her nursery, keeping her asleep."

Sliding over onto the couch, I reached my hand out and paused. Morgan gave me the okay, and I placed my hand next to hers. She was right, that baby was squirmy today. When I pulled my hand away again, Meeka stood with her paws on the sofa cushion, sniffed at the baby bump, and jumped back a blink later when a spot near her nose popped out. Was that a foot? A knee? Maybe an elbow. I smiled. The two were playing already.

I circled back to the topic of our mothers. "You're talking about the incident at the pub last night."

Morgan drank from her ever-present water bottle. "I am. And I hate to say it, but most of this animosity seems to be coming from your mother."

"Only in that she came to town. Briar started it with her 'I lived in the house' comment." I expected an objection but didn't get one. "What do you think is going on?

"What's the commonality?"

"Me. But I haven't said much to Mom about Briar."

"It's not you." Morgan exhaled, both she and Baby Girl seeming calmer now. "What are the universal things women fight about?"

"Status. Territory. Friendships. Men." Oh. "Dad."

"I believe that's it."

"Do you think they ever had anything going on?" That was the question many wanted the answer to.

"As in a romance?" She shook her head. "Mama insists their relationship is one of best friends or close siblings."

"And that's hard for everyone to believe, isn't it?"

I thought of that movie from the late '80s *When Harry Met Sally*. One of Rosalyn's favorites. Harry tells Sally that men and women can't be only friends because sex gets in the way. I didn't believe that. River and I, for example, were friends. I recognized that he was a very handsome man, but I didn't want to sleep with him.

Morgan glanced at the clock on the mantel. "I need to get back to the shop. Would you care to walk with me?"

"Sure. I'll spend all the time in the sunshine I can."

I attached Meeka's leash, and once the three of us were out on the red brick pathway, Morgan linked her arm with mine.

"You're wondering if they're lying, aren't you?" she asked.

"We all know Dad can hide the truth." Meaning Donovan. I pushed thoughts of my rotten half-brother out of my mind the moment they entered. "Which is basically the same thing. But there's no reason Briar would lie to you."

"No, she wouldn't. Mama can't keep secrets from me."

I glanced sideways at her. "As in she wouldn't, or she literally can't because of something witchy?"

Morgan cast a sly smile but didn't reply. "While she may not have romantic feelings for Dillon, she does love him deeply. You know how territorial she can be. I think that's what last night was. He's been hurting for years because their marriage has been shaky. Mama blames Georgia."

"And Mom blames Gran and Dad." Love was so complex. "I agree, we need to keep an eye on our mothers. Or lock them in a room together and let them duke it out."

"Mama has magic on her side."

"Mom has territorial rights and a scorned heart."

Morgan considered that. "Should be a close fight."

Our paths diverged at Shoppe Mystique. She went inside, and I cut through the Pentacle Garden to one of the five benches placed between the points of the star. I chose one that was facing the lake and currently flooded with sunlight. Meeka joined me on the bench and turned her furry face to the sun too. Morgan was right, it was glorious. After taking a few seconds to appreciate the warmth, I pulled my walkie talkie from my belt.

"Sheriff O'Shea for Deputy Reed."

A few seconds later, "Right behind you."

I looked left to see him coming from The Inn.

"Emery said you were out here with Morgan. I figured we should touch base on our missing person."

While I relayed everything Iris had told me, he added to the notes in his notebook.

"She told me most of that," Reed acknowledged, "but not the part about Barnes going out walking."

I wanted to say that if he'd taken the time to investigate their room, that information would have come out. He was leading this investigation, though. I'd let him run it his way. Besides, I needed to get back to my mother. Thanks to Morgan, thoughts of her and Briar rolling around on the floor in a hair-pulling, face-scratching catfight were now distracting me.

"You want to tell me what to do next, don't you?" he guessed.

Of course I did. "Do I need to? I mean, you're on it, right?"

"I spoke with Iris Mohan and the others at Barnes's table last night." He checked his notes. "None of them knew what might have happened to Ms. Barnes, but they had a lot to say about their fellow witches."

"Eight of them are staying at Pine Time. I got a good look

into their dynamics when we got back from Triple G last night."

He flipped a page in his little book and read a quote, "'They don't understand that we are serious about this. They don't see that our ways aren't wrong just because they're different.'"

"Let me guess, Amaya? The one with the headwrap."

"No, Ariel Birdsong." He grinned. "Side note: She told me she chose her name because she feels a connection to birds. Says she's jealous of their ability to fly and be free."

He tried and failed to hold back a laugh, but I agreed a little with her jealousy. How amazing would it be to soar along the treetops?

"It's the same thing we hear with the villagers here," he continued. "The older witches say the 'youngsters' don't respect the religion. With the Originals, it's that anyone new in the village is trying to change things. 'Things are fine the way they are.'"

Something I'd heard more than once. That statement could have come from Flavia, Cybil, Effie, Sugar . . .

"What's your plan going forward?" Before he could protest, I added, "I'm only curious, not looking to try and alter it."

"There are a few more coven members I want to talk to who spent a lot of time with Maewyn. I'll track down Ms. Mohan and talk with her again. I didn't realize I'd left without getting the whole story from her." He paused and thought a moment. "I'll go for a drive along the highway and look for her. It's a long shot, but if she did go for a walk last night, I agree that's the most likely route."

"Sounds good to me." Other than it seemed he was going to do everything himself. "Remember, I'm a call away if you need me to help with anything."

Inside The Inn, Reed took off to find the folks on his list, and Meeka and I returned to my mom, Rosalyn, and Tripp. Rozzie was still coloring, but at the kids' table now. I paused to see what the kids gathered around her were so fascinated by. She was shading only the lines of her picture and leaving the rest white. Coloring on the lines, not inside or outside. Rozzie always had to be different. Mom and Tripp were making eggs. Tripp, the simple dip method. Mom, the intricate beeswax style.

"I had no idea you were so crafty," I told her, inspecting her creation. She stuck to the white shell with a single-color approach, but the designs were surprisingly complex for her first attempt. A completed egg sat across from her on a tiny stand. The white parts formed simple flowers, daisies I think, and two sets of parallel lines circled the shells, one set at the top and one at the bottom of the egg. She chose deep pink for the color.

"That one is for your father. Ruby told me that the ribbons, or lines, represent eternity and flowers are for love and happiness." She flushed slightly, and my heart fluttered at the implication. "This one is for me. The suns and circles with dots in the center both stand for prosperity or good fortune. Green is for balance and rejuvenation." The flush intensified. "The dye is dry, so now I can remove the wax."

I watched, impressed, as she held the egg over the candle's flame. As the wax melted, she wiped it away, revealing the simple but clean design.

"Wow, Mom," Rosalyn appeared on my left. "That's really cool. I want to try one."

All the spots at the table were full, so Ruby told her she should come back later. "We'll be here until sunset tonight and back at dawn tomorrow. Well, sunrise tomorrow. Dawn is when we'll light the bonfire."

Finished with his eggs, Tripp stood at my side and wrapped an arm around me. "I should get back to Pine Time soon, but I want to go over to Hearth & Cauldron and learn about hot cross buns and deviled eggs."

"And plum blossom cookies?" I teased.

"And the cookies. Would you ladies care to join me?"

"I would," Rosalyn chirped immediately.

"I would too," Mom agreed, rubbing any remaining wax around the egg as a coating. "Ruby, may I leave these here to finish drying?"

"Of course." Ruby took the pink and green eggs and set them on a table behind her. It was covered with plain brown craft paper and dozens of decorated eggs. Next to each creation, she wrote the artist's name. While Mom and Rosalyn went to use the restroom, I looked at the creations. One, in particular, stood out to me. Not only did it not have a name beneath it, it was dyed black with the brown eggshell showing through. Pretty, but kind of intense in comparison to the other mostly pastel ones.

"That one is interesting, isn't it?" Ruby asked.

"By your tone, I'd say the color is significant."

"Everything about it is significant. Ask ten witches what a color means, and you're likely to get ten different responses. I find it meaningful that the person combined black dye with a brown egg when we've got nearly every color of egg available."

I looked to the basket of emptied and cleaned shells waiting for decorations. Beige to tan to copper to brown. Blue from pale to robin's egg. Even a few green ones. The standard white looked sort of dull in comparison.

"The brown of this shell," Ruby continued, "could suggest caution, indecision, searching, or protection. It could also be associated with the earth or grounding. Black, of course, can signify negativity, binding, or banishment."

"Black can also have positive connotations, can't it?" Morgan told me once that black was the purest shade as it contained all colors. That's why she wore so much of it. Also because her customers expected witches to dress in black.

"Black and brown could mean purity and grounding, but the design tells me they created it with negative intent." She pointed out the simple pair of zig-zag lines crossing the egg north to south and east to west. "A wave or saw pattern traditionally stands for death. The placement of the lines are significant as well."

The conversation I had with LaVonne LeBeau about hot cross buns came to me. "It symbolizes the equinox, the time when day and night are equal. Do you have any idea who made it?"

"No clue. There have been so many people at the table today. I asked Beckett if he saw who left it because I wanted to label it with their name. He didn't know either."

I reached for the egg, then stopped and asked, "May I?"

Ruby nodded.

Taking a sheet of paper towel from the roll on the table, I lifted the egg with two fingers and turned it over. On the side we hadn't seen was a circle and more zig-zag lines.

"What does a circle mean?" I showed her.

"A sun would have lines coming out of it for the rays. That could mean a full moon."

The zig-zag lines next to the moon needed no interpretation. They clearly formed the initials *MB*. Maewyn Barnes?

"The moon is full tonight," I murmured, mostly confirming what I already knew.

"Technically," Ruby corrected, "it was full a little before nine this morning. It looked full to the naked eye last night and should through tomorrow. True 'full' only lasts for a few moments."

"Would you let me know if anyone comes looking for this egg? A name would be best, but even a physical description could be helpful."

"Of course." She gave me the look I'd seen many times on many faces. It said she knew I was on the trail of someone.

I wrapped the towel around the egg. "Can I take this?"

"Feel free. I don't want that death egg on the table with all the other cheery Ostara eggs."

Death egg. "One last question, did anyone touch it?"

"I didn't. Becket didn't. I didn't notice anyone handling any of the eggs so my guess is no, but I can't be positive."

Then we might be able to get fingerprints off it. I needed to find my deputy again. If this egg was meant as a harbinger of death and Maewyn wasn't dead already, she would be soon.

Chapter 12

WHILE TRIPP AND I WAITED in the lobby for Mom and Rosalyn, I pulled out my walkie talkie again and called for Reed. Thirty seconds passed without a reply, so I called again.

"Talking with someone right now, Sheriff. I'll get back to you."

"Meet me over at Hearth & Cauldron when you're done."

"Will do."

"Something you need to take care of?" Mom was standing about a foot away from me when I turned around.

"No, everything is fine." It wasn't, but Reed was in charge, and I needed to spend more time with Mom today. I'd already spent more than half an hour talking to Iris and at least another thirty minutes with Morgan and Reed. "My deputy is going to meet me over at Hearth & Cauldron for a quick chat when he's done with what he's doing." I stepped toward the front door. "In the meantime, are we ready? Let's go make hot cross buns."

Mom arched a judgmental eyebrow and looked down her nose at me. "Jayne, if there's something else you need to—"

"No, nothing. Everything's under control." I held the door open. "Let's go."

When we got to Hearth & Cauldron, Tripp was disappointed to the point of pouting to learn that Reeva wouldn't be giving instructions on plum blossom cookies. "I was looking forward to learning how to bake with flowers."

"Don't worry." Reeva patted his arm. "We've still got nine weeks before tourist season starts. We'll make something with flowers before then." She let her eyes wander across the group of eight students before her. "Due to the larger than expected number of students today, we'll only have time for you to make the recipe once instead of twice."

To save time, we'd learn how to make the dough for the buns but because it took so long to rise, we'd use the batches from the previous class that were already rising in the warming drawers to do the assembly.

"But how do we know they did it right?" the orange-haired witch asked. "What if our buns don't turn out because the dough is bad?"

Reeva stacked her hands, right laying on top of left. "This will be more of a skills class, but by the end, you will have a full understanding of how to make the dough and assemble the buns. I'll give you each a copy of the recipe, and if you have questions when you get home, you may email me."

This satisfied most of the class.

We started by softening currants and dried fruit by simmering them in either apple juice or rum, our choice. While the mixture cooled, we prepared the dough. After kneading until our arms were ready to fall off, we put our dough in the warmer and grabbed a bowl from the previous class.

I kept thinking about that "death egg" and looking for Reed so wasn't paying attention to Reeva. We were supposed to add the cooled, softened fruit to the dough before shaping it into balls, but I started forming first.

"Jayne, you're not baking with intent." Reeva's tone held

great patience, but her expression held obvious disapproval. Loud enough for everyone to learn from my mistakes, she said, "Whenever you enter the kitchen, leave everything else outside. Food comforts as well as sustains. If you bring troubles to your altar, those troubles will show up in your meal."

Finally, the bell over the door jingled as Reed walked in.

I took off my apron, handed it to Reeva, and leaned close. "There's something going on if you get my meaning."

Her lips pursed. "I do *get your meaning,* and if you knew Martin was coming, you should have simply observed the lesson and let someone else have your spot."

"Sorry. You're right." I stepped closer and whispered, "I wanted to bake with my mom."

Her arched eyebrow let me know I wasn't really baking with her, though, because I was distracted. Reeva could say a lot with that eyebrow.

I motioned for Reed to follow me into the dining room, but it was almost full of would-be diners. Effie and Cybil, two of our elder fortune tellers and Original villagers, cast knowing glances at us, seemingly able to tell by looking at us that something potentially upsetting was going on. Reeva hadn't set tables out back yet, so the patio was clear of patrons. Reed and I went out there to talk.

Before I could say a thing, he gave me an update. "I was talking with Gardenia when you called. She confirmed seeing Barnes at The Inn yesterday afternoon around four-twenty. She didn't see her leave but thinks that must've been when she stepped into the bathroom. The lobby was quiet until the end of her shift." He paused to study me. "What's going on?"

I took the wrapped egg out of my jacket pocket and pulled the paper towel away from it. When Reed reached for it, I blocked his hand. "No, it might have fingerprints."

"Okay. Whose prints?" He took a wide stance and hooked

his thumbs in his belt loops. As I explained the probable significance of the egg's design, he became more interested. "You think Barnes is still alive?"

"I have no idea. Equinox isn't until tomorrow. But the full moon is today."

"What do we know?" Reed asked while pacing in front of me.

I held up a finger for each option. "We know we've got a missing person. Barnes either took off on her own, was kidnapped, or killed."

He chewed his lip as he weighed the options. "You said the saw pattern indicates death. So this egg is most likely a warning note."

"That's what I'm thinking. The message being that Barnes either died at the technical full moon at eight-something this morning or will die tonight when folks normally celebrate a full moon."

"Or, assuming the killer is following technical times, at the moment of the spring equinox." He pointed out the crossed jagged lines representing the balance of light and dark. "That will be a few minutes before four this afternoon."

"Jayne?" Rosalyn stuck her head out the back door, her eyes on Reed, not me. "Hi, Martin."

Reed lifted a hand in a wave as I asked, "What's up, Roz?"

"Mom wanted me to check on you. Is everything okay?"

Mom did? Her focus hadn't strayed from her crush. "Everything's fine. Shouldn't you be baking something?"

"The eggs are boiling." She smiled and pointed over her shoulder in the general direction of the kitchen. "I'll tell her you're okay."

Once she left, I asked, "How do you want to handle this?"

He blushed, probably thinking I meant Rosalyn, then realized I meant the egg. He took it from me. "I'll take this back to the station, dust it for prints, and see if I can get a hit."

"All right, I'll start—"

"Nothing," he insisted. "I'm good. You've got family here."

"Reed—"

"Boss, I've got this under control. I'll put out a call to the guys who helped us search for Jacob Jackson that time. They know how to hunt for a missing person. I'll set up home base at the station and check in with you as we learn things." When I didn't respond, he added, emphasizing each word, "I've got this. Go be with your family. Rosalyn will put things together otherwise and either freak out or want to help."

He knew my sister well. "You may be running things, but this will ultimately come down on me. I want regular updates."

"I already said that."

"Hourly."

"Even with the moonlight, we don't want the guys roaming around in the dark. I'll cut off the search at sunset and check in with you then. Unless we find something sooner."

I hesitated before agreeing. "Fine, sunset. But if I don't hear from you—"

He released an impatient sigh. "I'll stay put at the station and manage everyone from there. I spoke with Iris Mohan again. She basically confirmed what you said earlier. There are a few more coven members I want to talk to, and I'll have them come to the station so I can stay put."

After scanning for possible flaws, I relented. "All right. Your plan seems solid. Good luck. Stay in touch."

Reed took off for the station, and I returned to my mom and sister. At least that had been my intention. Effie and Cybil were still at the table to the right of the door next to the potbelly cast-iron stove. Their granddaughter, Lily Grace, and

Sugar from Treat Me Sweetly had joined them.

The four glanced up when I paused by their table. Effie looked like a kid caught with her hand in the cookie jar and blurted, "Nothing. We aren't talking about anything."

No, nothing at all suspicious there.

Being Ostara week, the Whispering Pines kids had today, tomorrow, and Friday off of school, so it wasn't strange to see Lily Grace with them. Sugar, however, was a different case. "What are you doing here? I figured you'd be selling sweets from open to close today."

"What are *you* doing here?" Sugar shot back. "I figured with all these witches around, you'd be patrolling our village and keeping it safe."

"The village is perfectly safe," I assured and immediately felt a twinge in the back of my neck, like someone with a voodoo doll caught me fibbing and jabbed me with a pin.

"I want to learn how Reeva makes hot cross buns," Sugar explained. "Her recipe has something mine doesn't."

"You're saying Reeva's are better than yours?" Cybil taunted. "That she's the superior kitchen witch?"

"I'm a baker. I want to put out the best product I can." A shadow crossed Sugar's face for an instant. "I learned my lesson with Gin Wakefield. Until Reeva returned to the village, I held the title of Most Skilled Kitchen Witch. My ego isn't so big that I can't learn from someone with even better skills."

If anyone had an ego that could get in the way, it was Sugar. She'd been devastated by the Wakefield tragedy, though, and grew from it. I was proud of her.

I started to walk away, but my curiosity got the better of me. Grabbing an unused chair from a nearby table, I squeezed in between Sugar and Lily Grace. When looking for answers from a crowd, focus on the weak link. I set my elbows on the table, propped my chin in my hands, and stared at Effie until she looked up.

Her penciled-on eyebrows arched impossibly higher. The color faded from her light-olive complexion, and she flashed a too-innocent, too-big grin. "What?"

"What were you four talking about?"

"What makes you think—"

Cybil swatted her upper arm. "Why do you try? You can't keep a secret to save your soul."

I looked pointedly at Cybil this time. "We all know that's not true." Meaning they'd both held on to the Donovan secret for more than forty years. I'd never seen overconfident Cybil blush before. It was a little unsettling. "Look, the less you all say, the more I think it's something I should know about. Spill it."

Sugar waited for her tablemates to give the okay and explained, "We were talking about the events at the pub last night. That girl with the attitude and the woman with the big hair were arguing about changing things they don't like."

"We chatted with some of the women sitting near us," Effie took over. "It seems the girl isn't satisfied with much of anything regarding the coven she just joined. They said her first night there, she started demanding changes. She doesn't even know the religion well enough to understand what she's asking for."

"There's nothing wrong," Cybil insisted in her raspy voice, "with leaving well enough alone. Things don't always need to *improve*." She made air quotes around the word improve, her long multi-colored nails clacking together as she did.

They were talking about Maewyn and the Circle of 3 Moons coven, but they could have been talking about me and Whispering Pines. It was no secret that Cybil, Effie, and many of the others who'd been here most of their lives didn't like that things were different from how they had originally been. Unfortunately, their matriarch died. No one could lead the village the same way Gran had. Change was inevitable.

"I don't know why you all have to be so dramatic about everything." Lily Grace reached for a deviled egg from the plate at the center of the table. "The argument at the pub struck a nerve. The Originals don't want things to change." She popped the half-egg into her mouth and wedged it in her cheek. "Like that's some huge secret." She pointed at her bulging cheek. "These are really good."

"Technically," Effie pointed out in her gentle way, "Cybil and I are the only remaining Originals."

"And Blind Willie," Cybil added.

"And Willie," Effie agreed. "Sugar and Honey, Dillon, Briar, Laurel, Flavia and Reeva." Her voice broke, and she looked to Cybil and her granddaughter. "Rae and Gabe, wherever they are . . ."

"The Pack," I supplied.

"Right." Effie cleared her throat. "The Pack members all are part of the Original family lines but only the adults were considered Originals. You, Morgan, Lily Grace, and the others of that generation are even further removed."

"Removed from what?" Lily Grace asked. "Because we're not old we don't have a voice around here? We should take what we're given and be grateful?"

Not even a little surprised that the teen expressed my thoughts so bluntly. "You know that each generation puts their own twist on things."

Cybil pointed at me. "That's exactly what we're talking about. You kids don't have to keep twisting things. Look at Morgan. She's almost a clone of her mother."

"But she's welcomed River into her life," I argued. "And their daughter's. That's a complete break with the Barlow family line. And you can't tell me a father being involved with his child is a bad thing."

"Yeah." Lily Grace raised a fist in the air while the other

three replied with muted mumbles.

"Jola moved back here," Cybil blurted as though just thinking of her, "and suddenly the healing center and the yoga studio are merged."

"What," I began, dumbfounded, "could possibly be wrong with that?"

Cybil slapped a hand on the table. "What's wrong with the way it was?"

"I think it's great," Lily Grace said. "Do you remember leaving a yoga session, all loose and warm, and having to walk fifty yards through snow or rain to get a massage or acupuncture treatment?"

"We don't do yoga." Sugar raised her chin like this was a badge of honor.

"If anyone in this village could use some mellowing . . ." I teased softly.

"Well trust me, it sucked." Lily Grace popped another egg in her mouth. "I'm totally making these at home."

"The setup worked fine for decades," Cybil insisted. "And those of us who had to suffer walking those torturous fifty yards are perfectly mellow."

I laughed. "Yes, Cybil, you and Sugar are the poster children for Zen."

"What about this place?" Sugar swept a hand across Hearth & Cauldron. "Was this necessary? Was there anything wrong with getting together on a Sunday and learning to cook from each other?"

I realized months ago that if Sugar could have one wish, it would be to be twenty years older and a true Original like Effie and Cybil.

"And yet," I pointed out, "here you are, waiting with Lily Grace to learn how to make hot cross buns and deviled eggs. Look, ladies, I understand what you're saying, but you've got to admit that you have to look hard to find anything legitimately new in Whispering Pines. Both of my parents commented on how little has changed here."

"Not all changes are visible," Effie intoned like she was having a vision. "Attitudes can do more damage than objects."

"Sounds like a prophecy." Sugar folded her hands on the table and sat at attention, waiting for more.

And more came when Lily Grace placed a hand on my arm. "It's up to you. Complete your last task because the time is coming. A reminder is on the way."

"Your last task?" Sugar repeated slowly like she was trying to solve a puzzle.

Effie and Cybil could sit here all day and spit *prophecies* at me. The only one who could stop me in my tracks and make me listen was the teenager on my right. I knew what my last task was. Like Rosalyn and I had in October, Mom and I needed to resolve our problems. But what reminder? What did I need to remember?

Lily Grace blinked. "Crap. I had a vision, didn't I?" She glanced at her hand still on my arm and snatched it away. "And, of course, it was about you."

"Sorry to interrupt." Reeva stood between Cybil and Effie. "Sugar, Lily Grace, the next class is going to start in about ten minutes. Please be ready."

Lily Grace grabbed all the uneaten eggs and buns from the plates around the table.

"Hey," Cybil objected when she took her bun, "I was going to eat that."

"Something new," the teen explained through a mouthful. "Visions make me hungry."

Tripp appeared in the doorway between the kitchen and dining room. When he spotted me in the corner, he came over. "Here you are. We were wondering where you went."

I was right here, spending time with people other than my mother. Again.

"Our class is done," he continued. "I'm going to head home. Actually, I need to make a quick stop at Sundry first. We need yeast and currants. I want to make these buns for breakfast tomorrow." He paused, his head tilted to the side. "You okay, babe?"

I stood. "I'm fine. Got a little distracted here. Where are Mom and Rosalyn?"

He gestured toward the kitchen. "Talking about yeast doughs with Reeva."

Lily Grace was right. This was up to me. And I couldn't fix something if I wasn't in front of it. Or with it, in this case. If Mom and I were going to resolve our issues, we needed to spend more time together.

Chapter 13

SINCE OPENING HEARTH & CAULDRON a few days
before Christmas to teach classes, Reeva had also been slowly
filling the shelves of the retail third of the shop with unique
kitchen and household items. There were pieces handmade by
villagers or treasures obtained from antique stores she visited
on acquisition trips. Baskets in every shape and size. Mason
jars pre-filled with ingredients for muffins, breads, or cookies,
the recipe attached with a length of twine. My favorite were
the hand-tooled, ancient-looking leather recipe binders.
"Because," Reeva insisted, "every kitchen witch needs a
grimoire."

My mother was currently captivated by the kitchen
utensils.

"These are adorable," she gushed over a salad serving set.
The spoon was spoon shaped, but the fork resembled a pine
tree. "All pine and all made from trees from the property?"

By which she meant the O'Shea Family property. Her
business mind was spinning.

"That's what it says." Rosalyn pointed out a small framed
sign on a shelf between a pine bread box and a utensil holder
with pinecones carved into them.

"I had no idea the people here were so talented," Mom mused as she studied a child's plate that looked like a bunny. The face would hold the main dish, the divided ears the side dishes. "Rozzie, you would have loved this. You hated when your food touched."

"She still does," I teased and gave my sister a hip bump.

An eight-foot-long shelf of vintage items, both kitchenware and household pieces, caught my attention the second I saw it. I was about to start searching through the collection when Reed burst in and literally pulled me to a quiet corner near the front door.

"Problem with the search?" I glanced pointedly at his hand on my upper arm.

He released me like he'd received an electric shock. "Sorry. No problem, in that we don't need to search for her."

My first *hopeful* thought was, she returned on her own? But my deputy wouldn't be freaking out if that was the case.

"What's going on? Why didn't you call me on the talkie?"

"I didn't want to risk anyone overhearing us. Even on the 'secure' channel."

"Did you find Barnes?"

He nodded slowly. "On the lake."

This also took me a moment to work through. During tourist season, that would mean in a boat. But it wasn't tourist season, and the lake was frozen.

I whispered, "Don't tell me she's dead."

"That's part of the problem. She's lying out there, near one of the fishing shanties, and isn't moving."

"And? Is she dead? Did you check for a pulse?"

"Verne Witkowski's shed went through this morning. Granted, it was over a shallow spot where the water is warmer which means the ice is thinner. You know that spot a little past your place where the weeds grow?"

I knew where he meant. I rescued a man from drowning

in that location back in July. Wait until Tripp heard about this. I told him the ice was looking thin and that the fisherfolk should bring in their shanties.

"Why do I care about Verne Witkowski's shed?" I asked. "Where is Barnes? Anywhere near that same spot?"

"No, she's closer to the marina docks. I didn't go out to her, but I'm ninety percent sure it's her. I used a pair of binoculars."

Inhaling, I counted to ten instead of screaming at him to get to the punchline already. "Who found her?"

"Brady Higgins. She's lying near his shed."

"Did he check to see if she was alive or dead?"

"No."

Inhale. Exhale. "Why not?"

"The ice is making thawing sounds, so we're a little concerned about how stable it is around Brady's shed."

"Thawing sounds?"

"Best if you witness it for yourself."

The necessity to see things for oneself was fairly common around here. "All right. Give me a minute. I need to tell my mom and Rosalyn that I'm leaving."

The two had moved on from the wooden pieces to a rack of cookbooks.

"Hey," I began and didn't need to say more.

"What happened?" Rosalyn asked.

"There's a problem on the lake. I'm sorry, but I need to go take a look."

Mom frowned. "What kind of problem could happen on a frozen lake that you need to investigate? Is that your jurisdiction?"

"All of Whispering Pines is my jurisdiction, including the lake. The fire department deals with water rescues."

"Water rescue?" Rosalyn repeated. "The lake is frozen. Did someone fall through?"

"I'm not exactly sure what's going on. Reed told me there's an issue, so I'm going to check it out."

"Do what you need to do." Mom's encouraging tone told me she understood, which eased my mind a lot. "Will you be long? Should we wait somewhere for you?"

I dug Mom's car keys out of my jacket pocket and handed them to her. "You two do what you like. Shop, go to The Inn and decorate more eggs, go back to Pine Time. I'll either call Tripp or get a ride from someone here."

"Is there danger involved with this?" Mom asked. "You don't have to go out on the ice, do you?"

"I won't know until I get there. Don't worry. I'm no hero. I'll let those who know how to do rescues take care of this."

Normally, we asked people to stay on the wooden pathway and not trample the plants. This wasn't a normal situation, though, so Reed led me through the woods behind Hearth & Cauldron and straight south to the marina.

Mr. Powell, Schmitty, Rourke O'Connor, and a bereft-looking Verne Witkowski were standing on one of the four boat docks there. All of them were staring out at a woman, presumably Maewyn Barnes, who lay about thirty yards away near Brady Higgin's obviously tilting fishing shanty. The woman was small. From this distance, to those who didn't know it was a body, it looked like a rolled-up tarp set next to the structure.

I was about to ask what the plan was when a noise, like someone playing an electronic synthesizer, came from . . . the lake?

"What the hell is that?" I whispered.

It did it again, and this time I thought of laser guns being fired in a space battle. Next came a sort of whooshing sound, like something big was swimming beneath the ice and pushing the water around.

"What is that?" I demanded, and the locals laughed at me.

"Wouldn't have believed me if I told you," Reed said, "would you?"

"That's the sound of ice thawing? I live on the lake. Why haven't I heard it?"

"Not sure on the science of it," Mr. Powell offered, "but it probably hasn't been warm enough until now."

I noticed his right pant leg was soaked to mid-thigh. "Did you fall through?"

He nodded and pointed to an open spot along the shoreline near the edge of the dock. "That's why none of us have gone out to get her."

The guys tended to let Mr. Powell be the sacrificial lamb, so to speak. They wouldn't let him get hurt, but if anything could happen, it would happen to klutzy Mr. Powell.

The lake made cracking, popping, clinking sounds that I'd normally associate with thawing ice. Then it made the laser blaster noise again.

"How should we do this?" I asked. "Is she in danger of going through?"

"Possible but doubtful," Schmitty replied. "The ice is thick enough to hold what's there for now, but we're not sure how much more weight it can bear."

Verne shook his head. "That shack is leaning. It could easily break through at any minute." His voice had a hopeful edge to it. Probably didn't want to be the only one to lose a shanty.

"Yeah. I think it was built leaning, though," Schmitty told him.

Rourke added, "Everything Brady builds looks like that."

"Where is Brady?" I looked around.

"He was real shook up after finding the body," Reed replied. "I got a statement from him, and he left. He'd heard about Verne's hut going through and came to pull his out of here. That's when he found the victim."

"His is the only shanty in the bay," I noted. The next closest one was a few hundred yards to the southeast.

Rourke shot a pointed look at Verne. "Everyone puts their houses out across from the hotels. That's where the boat launch is."

"Then why is Brady's here?" I asked.

"Because," Schmitty began, "he claims he'll have all the fish to himself if he sets up away from everyone else. So he uses the launch and drags the thing clear over here. Problem is the water is shallower in the bay. The fish are out where it's deeper. And Brady wonders why he never catches anything."

"I catch in the shallows," Verne insisted. "Fish like the weeds."

"And weeds like the shallows." Schmitty bit back a laugh. "Which is why your hut—"

"Yeah, never mind." Verne swatted at him.

Schmitty turned to me. "We've been standing here debating how to get to her."

I waited but had to push for more. "And?"

"We decided to try an inflatable raft," Reed told me, his acting sheriff confidence returning. "The marina has a tough one that won't get shredded by the ice."

I waited for one of them to make a move toward the marina. No one did. "What are we waiting for?"

"Keys," Reed said as though that should be obvious. "The raft is inside the marina shack. Either Gil or Oren is on the way."

"What do we do in the meantime?" I wondered aloud.

Reed shrugged. "Listen to the ice."

The woman wasn't moving, so she was either unconscious or deceased. There was a rescue rope on the side of the shack. We could try throwing it out to her, if we could even get it that far. That wouldn't be much help if she couldn't grab it and hold on. Reed was right. We weren't going to risk anyone breaking through by sending them out there.

So we stood there, waiting for Gil or Oren to show up, and listened to the whale-call of the lake. It sounded like it was trying to communicate. Gran always told me the lake had a personality. She must've heard this sound every spring but never mentioned it. Maybe because it was normal, so she never gave it a second thought.

I could almost hear her saying, "Oh, that sound? That's just my lake waking up."

Gil arrived within ten minutes. While he got the raft from the marina shed, Reed ran over to the station van that he'd parked on the beach and got the camera bag. We were debating which of us should ride out to the woman and document the scene when Mr. Powell pointed at Reed and me. "You're both staying here."

"He's right," Schmitty agreed. "We might be volunteers, but we're trained in rescue operations. We meet every weekend through the off-season to keep our skills up so we're ready for the tourists."

"I didn't know that." I looked at Reed. "Why didn't I know that?"

"You never asked?" he suggested. To the others, he asked, "Who's going out, and who's pulling the raft back?"

"Verne is the biggest, so he'll pull," Schmitty decided. "Me and Rourke will go out and get her."

"Gil and I will help pull." Reed handed me the camera. "You document from here."

"What would you like me to do?" Mr. Powell asked. When everyone exchanged glances but didn't respond, he nodded. "I'll supervise. I'm good at that."

I gave the camera to Schmitty. We needed pictures of the scene. "Once you get out to her, take a bunch of pictures before you touch her."

Schmitty inspected the camera, looked through the

viewfinder, and gave a satisfied nod before hooking the strap around his neck and tucking it safely inside his jacket. "How many is a bunch?"

"At least a dozen from multiple angles. Don't worry too much about closeups. We can zoom in."

With a rope tied to the nose of the raft, Schmitty and Rourke used strong paddles to push the raft along the ice out to the victim. She still hadn't moved, and I'd lost hope that this was a rescue operation. We were recovering her body. I took a few pictures with my cell phone as they made their way out. Once they'd reached the woman, Schmitty pulled out the camera. We could hear the sound of the shutter clicking from the docks.

When Schmitty gave him the okay, Rourke reached over the front of the raft and pressed his fingers to her neck. "She doesn't seem to be breathing. She's cold and stiff to the touch, so I can't get a pulse."

Reed paused respectfully before ordering, "Get her in the raft and come on back."

"Hang on," I called, shooting an apologetic look to my deputy. "Before you move her, look around. Does anything seem out of place?"

"Like what?" Schmitty asked.

I reminded myself that they were rescuers, not investigators. What would look like evidence to me might not to them. "Anything that isn't snow, ice, or water."

"What are you thinking?" Reed asked.

"Blood. Bullet casings. A dropped glove. A cliché cigarette butt. Anything that might indicate foul play."

Reed nodded, realizing he should have thought of that.

"Plenty of footprints," Rourke called, "but they're all trampled together. Don't see anything else."

"Bring her in, then," Reed responded.

They positioned the raft next to the victim. Schmitty, at

the bow, took her by the shoulders. Rourke, near the stern, hooked his arms beneath her hips.

"Look at the position of the body." Reed pointed. From this distance, it looked like they were moving a mannequin. "Rourke said she was cold and stiff. Looks like full rigor to me."

I nodded my agreement.

"Then she's been dead two to twelve hours," Reed murmured, mostly to himself, and wrote in his notebook. "Possibly longer because the ice and cooler air temperature will slow the progression of rigor."

With the victim in the raft, Schmitty waved his arm in the air. The signal for the others to pull them back.

I continued taking pictures with my cell phone until the raft was on shore, and the men were out. I got the camera from Schmitty and took more. We emptied the memory card every time we used it and always kept extra batteries in the bag. I'd rather have way too many shots than to miss something important so kept clicking. The victim was belly down in the raft, so I didn't have a clear view of her face. I could, however, see her right hand. On top, in the fleshy bit near her thumb, was a tattoo of the symbol for woman. No doubt, this was Maewyn Barnes. I should've made her spend the night in a jail cell. She'd probably still be alive.

She had on the same fashionably torn black jeans I'd seen her wearing at the pub, a heavy sweater, and combat-style Dr. Martens with scuffed toes and worn soles. I pictured her walking the streets of Chicago, working off her bouts of anger. Barnes had gotten a lot of use out of those boots. The black stocking cap on her head and silky blood-orange scarf around her neck indicated that while she may not have been dressed to be outside all night, she was well-prepared for the equivalent of a ten-block cool-off walk.

"Leave her right there," Reed instructed. "We need to call

the medical examiner. This one will definitely require an autopsy."

"You can use the phone in the shack if you'd like," Gil offered.

"I'll take that offer," Reed said. "Sheriff, you'll stay with her while I make the call?"

I nodded while staring at Barnes. Something was off. Not only the fact that she was dead, but something about the body felt wrong.

From where we were on the beach, we could easily see The Inn about two hundred yards away. If I squinted, I could make out the south wall of Grapes, Grains, and Grub. My gaze traced an invisible trail from the pub to the third floor of The Inn. Maewyn and Iris's room was on the front side. They had a great view of the commons area. I looked through the back wall of the building, across the hall, and into their room. There, I saw Maewyn changing shoes and switching sweaters.

No one listens to me. They all think I'm a raging man-hater. Close. I don't hate all men. If only the coven queens would try to see things my way, 3 Moons would be perfect. Why is it such a big stinking deal for me to ask them to consider shifting their focus? I thought we were supposed to be a unified group. They listen to the others. What do I need to do to get them to listen to me for two damn seconds?

Maybe Iris and Amaya are right. Maybe I'd be happier at another coven. Even though I wouldn't have my friends with me.

I need to walk. I need to calm my racing brain. How many walks, how many miles have these boots taken me on? It's chilly. I'll need my heavier sweater and my —

"Boss?"

I blinked. The moaning lake was in front of me. The raft to my left. Reed on my right.

"What did you see?" he asked.

He'd tried numerous times, but Reed couldn't "see" a

scene through the victim's eyes the way I could. I could say it was only me telling stories to myself, but I was close a good portion of the time. Maybe it was a gift. Maybe Reed simply needed more time on the job.

"She was walking. Like Iris said." I pointed to her feet. "Look at those boots. They've been worn a lot."

"She walked out onto the lake?" Reed looked from Barnes out to the spot where she'd died. "She might have slipped and fell, hit her head hard, and was knocked unconscious."

"Could be. I hadn't considered that she'd gone for a walk on the lake."

"You think someone dumped her out there?"

I stared at Barnes's body. What was this thing gnawing at my brain that I couldn't resolve?

"What are you thinking?" Like Tripp leaning close to me in the car yesterday, Reed stepped behind me to follow my line of sight.

"It's right on the tip of my brain and won't reveal itself. She went for a walk" — I tapped a knuckle to my temple, trying to knock it loose — "but I'm not sure what happened after she left The Inn."

"That's frustrating, but you're not a mind reader, Sheriff. That's why we investigate."

"Sheriff Jayne?" The happy but confused voice of Violet sang out in stereo from my walkie talkie and Reed's.

I unclipped the unit from my belt. "This is Sheriff O'Shea."

"Tripp called the Grinder. He said something about a baby being here. Well, there. At the B&B. Does that make sense?"

I smiled. In the midst of a tragedy, life continued. "It does. Thanks, Violet."

We needed to get another walkie talkie unit for Tripp at the house. Relaying messages through Violet worked, but it was inconvenient.

"Something you need to take care of?" Reed asked, echoing my mom's words from earlier.

"It's not urgent." I gave him a two-minute explanation of how the Nygaards ended up at Pine Time.

"Dr. Bundy won't be here for a while." He fished in his pocket and pulled out the van keys. "Go check on your guests and come back in an hour." He nodded across the semi-frozen singing lake. "It's not like we have a crime scene to investigate. I'll stay here with the victim."

"All right, that works. Call me if something comes up."

I got into the van, Meeka laying on the floor in the back, and let out a big sigh. My job, my B&B guests, and Mom and Rosalyn. Then there was Tripp and my personal life. It wasn't even tourist season yet, and I already felt pulled in too many directions.

Chapter 14

I HADN'T TAKEN THREE STEPS inside Pine Time's foyer when I heard the unmistakable sound of women's squeals coming from the second floor. After another three steps, a baby's cry rang out loud, strong, and angry. I would've had the same reaction to all that noise. Poor kid.

Tripp rounded the corner from the kitchen, laughing and pretending to plug his ears. "They've been doing that for at least ten minutes."

Maybe he wasn't pretending.

I tilted my head back for a kiss. "How many of them are up there? I saw Mom's car, River's Bentley, the Prius, and the Explorer outside. Who's missing?"

"The Explorer is Amaya's. Her three roommates are with her in the boathouse last I knew. The Prius is Rosemary's. I think she's upstairs with Calliope. Not sure about Wanda."

"That's right. Wanda's Audi isn't in the driveway. How's the wine and cheese preparation coming along?"

"Crackers are cooling on a rack. When our guests are ready, I am too. Would you like a glass?"

"I'd love one, but I've got to go back to the docks in an hour." I frowned. "Dr. Bundy is on his way."

Tripp's arms dropped to his sides. "Uh-oh. What happened?" He looked more and more shocked with each part I told him. "Maewyn? Why? Because she was brave enough to speak her mind?"

His reaction surprised me. "Don't tell me you agreed with her."

"She discounted my entire gender. No, I didn't agree with her, but I did admire her passion."

"How many conversations have we had on the sundeck or snuggled on the couch at night? All light-hearted and intelligent on various topics. Some we agreed on, others not so much."

"And we never walked away angry."

"That's how I know there are ways to be passionate about topics without resorting to yelling, screaming, and name-calling." Is that what happened to Maewyn? Had someone disagreed with her to the point that they took it too far? "I'm going to meet our new houseguest. Then I've got to get back to the lake, but it shouldn't take long. Our acting sheriff needs a little backup on this one."

In the second-floor hallway, Marie was standing outside the Jack room looking pleased. She smiled when she saw me. "Such a joy to help bring a new one into the world. The contractions slowed, as you know, but once they picked up again, everything went smoothly."

Her accent was delightful. That lilting tone had to be soothing to laboring moms.

"That's great. Freya's daughter, Runa, told me she had a hard time delivering Elin."

Marie nodded. "You learn a lot about a woman during labor. Many times, especially as we got toward the end, she said, 'Please don't let this one be breech.' She wasn't."

"She?" I smiled. "Another girl?"

"She's got a good start on her own little coven," Marie

teased. "Although the Nygaards aren't Wiccan. She did ask us a lot of questions about why we were here and what exactly Ostara was."

"Sounds like they stopped at the right place. Thank you so much for your help."

She placed a hand to her heart and bowed her head. "My sincere pleasure."

"Is there anything I can get you? Something to eat or drink? Tripp is setting up for the afternoon social. Wine and cheese. Crackers and fruit."

"River brought up a tray earlier, but a glass of wine sounds lovely. I could do with a little washing up first."

I pointed to the end of the hallway. "You and Calliope are in The Side room now, to the left of the corner room. We appreciate you all being so accommodating. You two will have to thumb wrestle over who takes the bed and who gets the bunk bed. I hope that will be all right."

"Calliope told me earlier. She and I have been friends for many years. We'll be fine. Speaking of Calliope." She laughed. "It's always fun to see the effect an infant has on a person. Wait till you see. She's in there now, baby talking in Spanish. As for Rosemary, she loves babies but . . ." Marie swatted a hand in the air. "Long story. Do you know if Wanda is back?"

I shook my head. "Her car isn't in the driveway."

"Probably found a quiet place to relax. She said that bookstore had nooks and crannies that make her feel invisible. Which is just what she wants." Her smile turned sad. "Excursions like this one make her anxious. She has a hard time being around so many people. Anyway, I'm off to celebrate a birth with a soak in the tub and then some wine before dinner."

Marie started down the hall, and I poked my head into the Jack room. Rosemary and Calliope were making their way to the door. Jola stood next to the bed on Freya's right. Runa and Elin had piled onto the bed with their mother, who held Pine Time's newest guest.

"May I come in?" I asked.

"The more the merrier," Freya answered. "Come meet my new daughter. Runa, take Elin out of the way so she can get a good look."

I gazed at the fair-skinned, deep-copper haired little bundle currently latched on to her mother's breast. Her blue eyes were huge like Elin's, and she stared at her mama as though to say, "So you're the one who's been giving me the ride all this time."

"She's beautiful," I said and meant it. To my surprise, or maybe my horror, a small spot in the center of my chest warmed.

You want one? Jayne in my head teased.

Not now, I thought back at her and was again surprised at my response. When had I shifted from a solid, definite no to not now? It had to be watching Morgan all these months and how excited she, River, and Briar were to welcome their little one.

Freya pressed a fingertip between the baby's mouth and her nipple to release the suction. Then she covered up, lifted the baby to her shoulder, and softly patted her back.

"Have you chosen a name yet?" I couldn't look away.

When a tiny burp sounded from the little one, Freya cradled her in her arm and turned her toward me. "Meet Tyra Nygaard."

"And what does Tyra mean?" Runa asked in a leading way that indicated all of their names had been purposely chosen.

"Tyra," Freya began, "means thunder goddess. This little one has been unexpected from the day we found out she was coming. Like a sudden thunderclap that disrupts your moment. Then today, she came on fast and strong. Once she was ready, that is."

Little Elin placed a tiny finger to her own chest. "Light."

"That's right." Freya gestured for Runa to bring her back. The teen rolled her eyes, as if to say, "make up your mind," and plopped Elin on the foot of the bed. Elin scrambled up to her mother, who reached out and placed a hand to her middle daughter's cheek.

"Elin means torch of light, and that's exactly what she is every day. A beam of light brightening our world."

"And what does Runa mean?" I asked, loving this way of choosing a name that has a meaning for the person.

Freya returned her attention to the baby. "Runa means secret lore."

Runa's mouth pinched in a pucker, and her eyes seemed to turn from blue to cold, stormy gray. What did that mean? She didn't like her name?

Jola pulled me to the far side of the room by the bathroom. "Everything went perfectly other than that she tore a little."

It took me a half-second to understand what that meant. When I got it, my whole body grimaced in empathy with Freya's plight.

"She'll be fine. I recommend that she stays right where she is for a couple days."

"Not at a hospital?"

"Giving birth is a natural thing, Jayne. In plenty of civilizations, women pop out a baby and continue with their day. I don't recommend that, but Freya will be fine."

I must have made a face because she laughed at me.

"Marie is a highly skilled midwife. I learned a few things from her. She agrees that a hospital stay isn't necessary. We're going to take turns checking on Freya and Tyra, but all they both really need right now is rest. There are vaccinations Tyra should get that Freya has approved. I'll get the doses from

Unity and bring them over. Freya will need to get checked out by her OB when she gets home, and Tyra will need to see a pediatrician. We'll maintain a detailed chart for her to take when they leave."

"What about food? What about Runa and Elin?"

Jola shook her head. "Relax. You don't have to do anything. They have a good stash of baby supplies, including a new car seat and diapers. Runa assured us she will watch Elin and go to Sundry to get whatever else they might need."

And just that fast, a war raged in my mind. I'd already told Runa she couldn't drive by herself with only a permit. With everything going on around the village, though, I couldn't promise my assistance, and neither could Tripp. I'd have to have another talk with the girl.

Across the room, Freya held the baby out to her oldest daughter and snapped, "Take her. I need a rest. And Elin needs something to eat. She's obviously getting hungry."

Interesting. Freya must mean one whose emotions change rapidly. No, that wasn't fair. She just gave birth. And she tore. I shuddered.

"I'll stay until after dinner," Jola explained. "Marie will check on them through the night, and I'll come back tomorrow. That way Marie won't miss out on any more of the festivities."

When Jola returned to the bedside, I beckoned Runa over to me.

"Three girls will be all sorts of drama," she mused. "But I sure wouldn't want to be the only boy in this household."

"So you're happy that you have another sister."

She shrugged in the way only a teenager could. "I guess. I'll be out of there before the real hormones kick in."

"Jola told me you'll be taking care of Elin and whatever your mother and the baby need."

She sighed as though exhausted. "That's why I'm here."

"I want you to listen to me closely, then." She faced me and looked straight into my eyes. "Considering the circumstances, I'm willing to make an exception to what I said earlier about you driving on your own. As long as your record is clean, you have my permission to drive by yourself within the village. That means from here to the east side parking lot near Sundry, the general store. Do not, for any reason, leave the village limits."

Her expression remained neutral. No sign of relief or of having won a victory. There was something in her eyes, though. Like regardless of whether I gave permission, she would take that car if necessary. After another second or two, she softened, and a small smile turned her mouth.

"Thanks for understanding, Sheriff. Freya won't allow anyone but me to watch Elin, and I don't want to walk that far with her."

"No one but you? Even when you're in school?" I joked.

"I do online high school. As long as I get my assignments done on time, I have the flexibility to study whenever I want. That usually means when Elin is sleeping." She sighed. "Toddlers are really demanding. It was easier when she was a baby."

That sounded like personal experience, not just simply observing or parroting something her mother might have said.

"Are you saying childcare is your responsibility? Always, not only when your mother is giving birth?"

"Most of it is. Freya works two jobs, all the hours she can get. We've got enough to live on, but she's always worried some big bill will pop up and wipe out our savings. She works, and I'm the help."

Not I help, but I am the help.

"Earlier, you told me you had plenty and that your grandparents were loaded."

"Yeah, that's the last resort." She repeated it with

emphasis, "The *last* resort. Don't worry, the charge for the rooms will go through. I also pay our bills."

This girl was definitely an old soul. If she hadn't told me, I never would have guessed she was only fifteen. She looked and acted much older. Again, she reminded me a lot of someone I knew.

"Anyway," she continued, "the cops in our town agreed to the same thing, driving within city limits, so I'm used to it. I'll need your permission to have Elin in the car too. I won't be able to leave her here."

I bristled at that one. Driving herself around was one thing. But Elin . . .

"Our cops said it was okay for me to drive her around two months after I got my permit. Before that, I pushed her a mile in her stroller and brought food home in a backpack. We had to go to the grocery store every other day because that's all I could carry. It was great when the weather was nice. The fresh air was good for us."

She spoke like she was Elin's mother.

"I have a new, properly installed car seat in the backseat of the Volvo. Check it out if you want." When I obviously still wasn't completely on board, she sighed dramatically and pulled her permit from her back pocket. "It's not like I'm going to run with her. Go ahead, check my record. I've never even gotten a parking ticket, let alone been in an accident. Never had any non-traffic related issues either."

Was there a danger of her running? Now would be the perfect chance with her mother laid up and focusing on baby Tyra. No one keeping an eye on her. Although, if she was telling me the truth, it didn't sound like she ever had much supervision.

"If my plan was to run, I'd already be gone." She thrust the card at me.

It verified her name was Runa Nygaard. "Address is current?"

"Yep."

"No middle name."

"None of us have a middle. It takes Freya long enough to come up with one name. She'd still be debating and my permit would say 'Baby Girl Nygaard' if she had to choose a second one. Not only would it have to be Scandinavian, Norse in particular, because she thinks we're descended from Vikings, it would have to mean something."

"Speaking of which, I'm curious about your name. What does 'secret lore' mean?"

Runa's expression went blank. No, not blank. It went dark. A blend of anger, annoyance, and embarrassment.

She glanced back at her family—Freya holding the baby, Elin sitting next to her on the bed—and then back at me. "Freya is far from the beatific mother figure she's presenting right now. In her mind, she's perfectly maternal, caring for her daughters better than anyone else could. Even though I do most of the parenting." She grew quiet for a minute. I waited. "I told you before, Tyra's father took off when he found out she was on the way. Elin's father was a drunken fling in the bathroom at a New Year's party."

Understanding for the storm of emotions swirling in this girl grew.

"As for me." She sighed and shook her head. "My grandmother says Freya was the result of a . . . let's say a date who wouldn't accept the word no. Turns out, I was too. Great *lore* to pass down the bloodline, hey? Nice to give me a name that constantly reminds me of how easy to manipulate the women in my family are."

In other words, that she was the result of a rape.

"You know a physical assault isn't the woman's fault, right? It's not a matter of them being manipulated or easy or any of the other accusations people like to throw at them."

She turned away. Too angry to discuss the truth.

I changed the topic. Sort of. "What about your mother's name? Does it have any significance?"

She laughed but not happily. "If you ask Freya, she'll tell you it means lady. As in, the high society type. If you do even a little research into Norse mythology, you'll learn that *Freya* is the Goddess of lust, sex, fertility, war, and death."

Without another word, Runa returned to her mother and sisters. I was okay with that because I honestly wasn't sure how to react to that last revelation. I slipped out of the room and went in search of Tripp. I found him in the kitchen, his focus on the notebook in front of him. He was jotting down in detail the breakfast spreads, cookies, and wine-and-cheese pairings for the next few days. The group in the boathouse was only staying three days, checking out Friday morning. Marie's group was checking out Sunday morning. My mom's day spa was closed on Mondays, but Rosalyn had an afternoon class. They hadn't decided if they were leaving Sunday or super-early on Monday.

"Got your plan together?" I asked as I sat on the barstool across from him.

"Just about. I'll need to make a Sundry run probably on Saturday." He looked up from the notebook. "What's wrong?"

He knew me well enough to pick up on my mood with only a glance. I told him what Runa had said.

"She claims her mother is a warrior sex goddess of fertility and death?" He paused and considered this for a moment. "Pretty much covers all aspects of life."

I couldn't help but laugh at that. "I'm not sure if I'm more concerned about her home life or her obvious lack of respect for her mother."

"It's hard sometimes," he mused, "to tell a difficult life from a different one when you've had things easy the way we have."

When he was thirteen, Tripp's mom ran off in search of a

better life for him, ended up addicted to drugs, and died from an overdose in a dirty bathroom stall. And he still thought he had things easy. That's what happened when you grew up knowing you were loved. He lived with his aunt and uncle who still adore him like he's their son. As for me, my dad spent most of my teens and early twenties overseas digging for pieces of lost civilizations. My mother buried her loneliness and pain with work. Even though neither of them was around much, I had everything I needed. I guess that meant I had things easy.

"My point is," he continued, "Runa doesn't appear neglected. Both girls seem well-nourished and healthy. You're also getting the story filtered through a teenager's perspective."

"That's true." Whispering Pines was relaxing all the street-smart cop instincts out of me. "You think she's telling me a story?"

He put his hands in the air. "Not saying that. We don't know them so can't really make that call."

"Also true. Help me keep an eye on the girls? I'm not taking responsibility for them, and I know you'll be busy with food prep and B&B tasks. Just try to note if they come and go?"

He reached across the counter and pushed a lock of hair behind my shoulder. "Can't help yourself, can you?"

"Goes with the territory. Public safety and all that."

"I'll do my best."

"Can't ask for more." I glanced at the clock on the microwave and jumped off the stool. "I've got to go. Dr. Bundy will be at the marina any minute now."

Chapter 15

REED CALLED OVER THE TALKIE when I was in sight of the marina. "Dr. Bundy is here. Where are you?"

He sounded impatient. Discovering that being sheriff wasn't as easy as it looked? Or maybe, like me, he was frustrated over another death in the village.

"I'm seconds away. I can see Dr. Bundy getting out of his car."

I pulled up next to him, let Meeka out, and slammed the station's van door shut.

"Are you aware," Dr. B began, "that nothing happened here when you were on vacation?"

"You're saying I should go back to Maui?"

He chuckled. "That would be a tough assignment, wouldn't it?"

"Things happened. Reed had to deal with villager complaints. Someone threw snow over their neighbor's fence. Someone else blocked a neighbor's driveway with their trash cans. I chalk it up to spring fever." Dr. B blinked at me. "I'm joking. I get your point, no one died."

If I took the time to analyze this more deeply . . . No, not going there.

The paramedics followed us with a stretcher and body bag. We trudged through the parking lot and then along a well-worn but slightly mucky path to Reed at the docks. Meeka got mud on her paws but didn't roll around in the puddles this time. Good girl.

"By the way," I told Dr. Bundy, "Deputy Reed is handling this investigation so address any questions to him."

"Part of his training?" the medical examiner wondered. "Or are you stepping down already?"

"Never fear, Doc. I'm not going anywhere. I can handle anything this village dishes out."

At the raft, Dr. Bundy made a sad humming sound when he saw Barnes. "She could be my granddaughter."

"The victim was found about thirty yards offshore." Reed pointed out the location as the ice sang out again, surprising Dr. Bundy as much as it had me. "She was face down. Her airway wasn't blocked by snow, but it might have been and it melted. There was only a small amount of water near her face."

Dr. B confirmed that there was no pulse, declared her deceased, and motioned for the paramedics to turn her over. "I'll check for drowning during the autopsy. It's possible to drown in as little as two inches of water. If she'd been drinking or passed out for some other reason and her face was in a puddle, that could be the reason for death."

While they talked, I turned my attention to our victim. I slowly circled the raft, Meeka on my heels like a shadow, and scanned Barnes from head to toe. Her scarf kept jumping out at me. Something about it caught my K-9's attention too. She sniffed the scarf and then Barnes's sweater. Then the scarf again and back to sweater. Why? What was it about that scarf—

"It's orange," I blurted.

Both men turned toward me, and Reed asked, "What's orange?"

"The scarf around her neck. When I was in the room, I looked through Barnes's possessions. I didn't pull every piece out of her suitcase, but the items I saw were black, dark gray, or deep purple."

They both stared like they were waiting for me to connect the dots for them.

"Barnes didn't wear bright colors." I pointed. "Whose scarf is that?"

"You just said you didn't pull everything out of her suitcase," Reed stated. "Maybe it was down at the bottom or inside a pocket you didn't look in. It was chilly last night. Maybe she borrowed it from someone."

I shook my head. "I don't think so. Meeka keeps going back and forth between sniffing the scarf and her sweater. I don't speak K-9 but I'm guessing they don't smell the same. It's possible that she borrowed it, but this scarf is made of lightweight fabric. Chiffon or silk. It's a fashion accessory, not a piece meant for warmth. What's hiding beneath it?"

Dr. Bundy knelt and used the end of a pen to lower the scarf about an inch. Reed and I leaned close and saw marks on Barnes's neck. There were two oval-shaped bruises near her trachea and scratches across the front of her throat.

"Damn," I whispered and took more pictures.

"She was strangled?" Reed asked.

"That would be my initial assumption." Dr. Bundy looked over his shoulder at us. "Have you come up with a timeline yet?"

Reed shook his head. "We found her a little more than two hours ago. Until then, we were treating her as a missing person."

I thought back to my interview with Iris last night. "Her roommate believes she stopped in their room sometime after dinner."

Reed cleared his throat. An indicator for me to step back

again. "That would have been late afternoon. The front desk clerk saw her arrive at four-twenty, but no one saw her leave."

Had she been killed in her room? Highly unlikely. There was no sign of struggle, and I couldn't imagine the killer hauling her out of The Inn without someone seeing. Unless they waited for Gardenia to step into the bathroom again.

The doctor groaned as he pushed himself up, bent at the waist with his butt sticking out before standing straight. "Ever notice that babies and old fogies stand up the same way? Once she comes out of rigor, I assume I'll find petechiae around her eyes. Of course, as you know, lack of petechiae doesn't mean she wasn't strangled."

Reed nodded along with the ME's words. "We're probably safe to assume murder, in this case, right?"

"Unfortunately," Dr. Bundy agreed.

"What are the marks on her neck?" Reed asked, pen poised over his notebook.

Dr. B held a hand to his own throat, thumb near trachea, fingers beneath ears. "The bruises on her trachea are likely from the killer's thumbs. It's a very strong digit. Other marks may also be visible or become visible with time." He wiggled the fingers beneath his ear. "I wouldn't expect to see a line of four, though. The ring and pinkie fingers are especially weak."

"And those other marks?" I traced a finger down the center of my neck indicating the scratches on Barnes. Reed cleared his throat again. Fine. I'd be quiet. As long as he asked the pertinent questions.

This time, Dr. Bundy raised both hands to his neck, fingers curled into claws as though trying to grab hold of something. "They're likely scratch marks from her own fingernails. She would have tried to pull the killer's hands or the scarf away. I'll check for skin beneath her nails. She may have got the killer, too, so check your suspects' hands for scratches."

"Good tip. Thank you." Reed wrote that down and

glanced down at Barnes. "What would she have experienced?"

Dr. Bundy frowned. "Severe pain. If you've ever had a blow to the throat, even a gentle one, you'll know. Multiply it in this situation. Unconsciousness would have come fairly quickly, although to her it probably seemed like forever. If the killer was compressing the carotid, which is my guess, the victim would have passed out in ten seconds."

"How long—"

"Death takes four to five minutes," Dr. Bundy replied before Reed could finish the question. "Strangulation deaths, especially manual ones, bother me greatly." He held his hands in front of him as though strangling someone. "What kind of rage or derangement is required to hold your hands around someone's neck for four minutes? I timed it once on a dummy. Four minutes is a long time. Not only to maintain a physical grip, but also the determination to finish the job."

I frowned, understanding his horror.

We watched in respectful silence as the paramedics gently placed Barnes in the body bag and then took her to the ambulance. She hadn't been a pleasant person, but in her own way, she was making a difference. She was getting people to talk about issues they didn't normally even want to think about. And, hardest of all, she was likely a sad, lonely, angry person in need of help she'd now never get.

"Unless either of you has any other questions," a mellow Dr. Bundy stated, "I'm going back to the office."

Neither of us did.

He gave us a nod. "You know how to reach me if you come up with any. I'll call with the results as soon as we have them."

"Thanks, Doc," we answered in unison and watched him walk away.

Reed inhaled and blew out a long breath. "All right. Looks like I've got more people to talk to."

I waited for him to ask my opinion or for my help. When he said nothing more, I asked, "Did you want to go whiteboard?"

"I can do that in the morning."

"You know, the biggest reason I'm happy you're back is that I can bounce ideas off you and get your input when making a plan for an investigation. Turns out, that's far more valuable than I realized."

Reluctantly, he suggested, "How about we meet first thing in the morning to whiteboard then?"

I stared at him. "I'm here now, and everything is fresh in our minds. It's been a long day, but I'd rather not have two long days."

He sighed. "Let's head over to the station."

~~~

Meeka curled up on her cushion in the corner of my office at the station while I took a seat in a guest chair. Reed stood before the whiteboard and twiddled an erasable marker through his fingers like he was trying to decide how to proceed. He pulled off the cap and wrote *Victim: Maewyn Barnes* and *Manner of Death: Strangulation* at the top of the board.

"Manner is still open to revision," he qualified, "based on the autopsy."

"Strangulation appears to be a safe starting place," I agreed. "So what do we know? Sorry, that's your line."

He drew a timeline from one end of the board to the other beneath Barnes's name and added a vertical hash mark on the far left end. By the mark, he wrote *1600*. "We know she left Grapes, Grains, and Grub shortly after four o'clock." He added another mark a few inches to the right and wrote *1620 – The Inn*. "Gardenia saw her enter The Inn at four-twenty."

"You came and got me at Hearth & Cauldron around thirteen-twenty hours."

He added that to the board on the right side. "I got the call from Brady Higgins that he found Barnes on the lake at approximately twelve thirty. Mr. Powell and his crew were there setting up for the bonfire and attempted to go out to her. That's when Mr. Powell broke through the ice." He drew another vertical mark at the right end of the timeline and wrote twelve thirty. "There's our window. I'll alter it as I learn more."

He took a few steps away from the board, crossed his arms, and stared at it like he was hoping it would start filling itself in. After a long few seconds, he stepped back up and wrote *Suspects* below the timeline.

"Who do we like?" He considered the question and added:

Wanda Bishop
Rosemary Chauderon
Skye Blue
Amaya
Iris Mohan

"Last person to see the victim alive," he murmured as he added Iris's name, "is worth considering. Anyone you'd like to add?"

I didn't remind him that Iris stated she never actually saw Barnes before she went missing. "I don't know that I'd consider them suspects, but I'd interview Ariel Birdsong and Kegan Cleareye."

"Cleareye?"

"That's what she calls herself. Probably has something to do with the fact that she's always taking pictures." I shook my head. "I don't think she's serious about Wicca. It's more an opportunity to get fodder for her Instagram page. Anyway, they sat at Barnes's table last night. They may have some insider information. Oh, Selina Flores too. She's mastered the art of fading into the background and rarely speaks. She might have observed something."

"Or done something." He added their names to the board. "Can't trust the quiet ones."

"Marie Nurse was busy helping bring a baby into the world so don't add her. Calliope Jones is worth talking to."

"And there are plenty of other coven members who may have seen or heard something."

I waited until he was done adding names to the board and scribbling notes onto his legal pad and asked, "What would you like me to do? Who should I talk with?"

He shook his head. "I've got it, boss. You spend time with your mom and sister. Tell Rosalyn I'm sorry we didn't get to see much of each other this visit."

I sat there, silent, until I had his attention. "Since you became my deputy, when have I conducted an investigation without your help?"

He stood straight, shoulders back. "In January when you and Tripp had to track down and rescue Benji Wallace from the fishing shanty with Schmitty's help."

"Fair enough, but you were at school."

"I should've been here to help."

"Did you forget about the blizzard? There's no way you could have made it here safely."

"Speaking of which, they had to help you search for the hit-and-run victim in the middle of that storm." He grew quiet for a moment. "And there was an active shooter in the B&B with you and eight other people. Rosalyn told me she was scared to death."

Reed wouldn't look at me.

I softened my voice. "You were at school. In no way

should that be considered a negative. In fact, I can't tell you how glad I am that you got that education. I can only teach you what I know. Now you can share with me what you learned from the instructors there."

"I should have—"

"Deputy Reed," I raised my voice again and stood in front of him like a drill instructor. "That's enough. All those times you drove back here for the weekend to be here in case I needed help? The phone support you gave me when you should have been in class? You have gone above and beyond."

He blinked twice and swallowed hard. "Yes, ma'am."

"I asked you to be acting sheriff this week because I know you can handle it. Not because I'm trying to test you or set you up for failure."

He nodded.

"Had I known there would be a murder—"

"I've got this, Sheriff." He turned to me like an eager-to-please puppy. "Don't take it away. I'll find the killer."

It was almost dark outside, and we were both running on fumes after such an involved day.

"I think we should call it a night," I told him. "You are still the acting sheriff, however, so that's your call to make."

His mouth curved in a tiny smile. "I concur. Go home, boss. Spend time with your mother. We'll meet back here in the morning and divide up the suspect list."

"I like that plan." I whistled for Meeka, who jolted awake. "Let's go home, girl."

The three of us stepped out the back door. The only vehicle in the lot was the station van, and Reed drove that. I looked up at my deputy, "I'm going to need a ride."

Chapter 16

REED STARED AT MY HOUSE like he was trying to use x-ray vision.

"Put it in park and come inside," I told him. "Rosalyn wants to see you as badly as you want to see her."

I didn't have to tell him twice. He beat me to the entrance, covering up his eagerness to see my sister by holding the door open for me. Meanwhile, the moment I'd slid open the van's door, Meeka had spotted Blue the cat sitting in the far corner of the front yard like a neon-blue-eyed gargoyle. The Westie raced straight through the mushy mounds of snow dotting the yellow grass, getting muddier with every step. Great. She'd done so well earlier. Now she'd need another bath before bed instead of a simple paw washing. I really needed to keep her on a leash until the yard dried up. Like that would work.

In the great room, all of our guests — less Wanda, Freya, and her girls — were gathered for wine and cheese. Rosalyn had just taken a full glass from Tripp when she saw Reed and I enter the room. She let out a squeal and rushed over to us.

"Hey there," she gushed. "Are you off the clock for the night?"

"I am. The sheriff helped me with a plan for tomorrow.

We're going to get a little rest and clear our heads before starting again in the morning."

"What's got you so busy?"

Reed tilted his head in the general direction of the village. "Would you like to go grab dinner? I'll tell you what I can."

Rosalyn shoved her glass at me, the only sign that she even knew I was standing there. It was full of something pale pink. White Zinfandel, I guessed. Not my favorite, but at least it was more sweet than dry.

"Ah, young love." Tripp sighed dramatically when I got to the wine and cheese table. "Are they leaving?"

"Yep. Going to get dinner."

"There's a pound of shrimp for scampi thawing in the fridge for the four of us," he objected. "I could add more pasta and make a bigger salad to stretch it so Martin could join us. *And* I opened that Zin specifically for her."

"I doubt the wine will go to waste." Mom studied the bottles he'd chosen for tonight. "And I adore shrimp scampi, so let's not skimp on those servings. Oh, Airén." She tapped the label. "I've heard of this, but never tried it."

He took the bottle of white wine from her, poured a sample, and explained, "The Airén grapes are grown almost exclusively in Spain and are most often used for brandy or blending with other grapes for wine. In this one, the Airén is on its own." He handed her the glass. "It's not fancy, but it should go well with the shrimp. I thought we'd give it a try."

Mom swirled the glass, inspected . . . whatever one inspected when one swirled wine in a glass, and took a loud sip. And then another. She nodded. "You're right, not fancy. It will be fine with dinner, however. I'll take a glass of Sauvignon Blanc for now, please."

While he poured, she filled an appetizer plate with crackers and goat cheese. The plate had a slot cut into it for holding a stemmed glass so guests wouldn't have to set down their drink in order to eat. Tripp bought the plates purposely for these gatherings and had been ridiculously excited when he found them.

"How did your investigation on the lake turn out?" Mom asked.

I waited until she had her drink and motioned for her to follow me to the side so we could speak without the coven members hearing. "Not well. A girl died."

Mom gasped. "How tragic. Why are you here and not searching for the killer?"

"Reed is first contact for issues like this right now. I helped him make a plan, and we'll attack it in the morning."

She eyed me as I sipped the Zin. "And why is your assistant in charge of a death investigation?"

Unprepared for the question, I tipped the glass a little further and drank a little more. "Because I'd hoped to spend more time with you and Rosalyn. You haven't been here in almost twenty years, Mom. It's kind of a big deal. And we haven't seen each other since May."

"What is that saying? With great power comes . . . Oh, you know the one."

"Comes great responsibility," I finished for her. "It's from a movie."

"You've got the modern version of the quote right. The original comes from the Bible. Not that exact phrase, obviously, but a verse from Luke. 'For unto whomsoever much is given, of him shall be much required: and to whom men have committed much, of him they will ask the more.'"

I stared, literally openmouthed. "How do you know that?"

"That the phrase originated from the Bible or the verse itself?" She hooked her glass into the slot on the plate and popped a piece of goat cheese in her mouth.

"Yes. Both."

"It's hanging in my office. Your father had a small print of the verse created, framed, and delivered to me when I opened Melt Your Cares." Her voice quavered a tiny bit. She paused and cleared her throat with a sip from her glass. "He told me that I was taking on a great task. Great as in large. Not only had I invested a huge amount of money before we'd even opened for business, I had promised my small but mighty staff of three at the time that I would provide them with a weekly paycheck." She looked down at her crackers.

I couldn't remember ever seeing her look so vulnerable. "Were you scared?"

"Very much so. I was risking the decent, steady income from the salon where I worked. Between my assistant manager paycheck and the money your father sent us, we were comfortable enough but—"

"But you can't get rich off other people's money." Her expression was both shocked and pleasantly surprised. "That was the reason you gave Dad when he asked why you wanted to open your own place. I wasn't eavesdropping, I swear. I came to your room to ask you something and heard you say it."

She held my gaze for a moment and then blinked twice. Then a third time.

"I didn't understand it at the time, Mom, but that took a lot of courage." My chest tightened with emotion. "A *lot* of courage."

"I'm so sorry to interrupt." Marie touched my shoulder, breaking the moment. "I was about to leave for dinner with the others, and Freya asked me to find Runa and Elin. Have you seen them? They seem to be missing."

"Missing?" The thought that immediately slammed into my brain was, there's a serial killer in Whispering Pines. First Maewyn Barnes, now the Nygaard girls. Then Runa's comment when I gave her permission to drive within village limits shoved that thought out of the way. *It's not like I'm going to run with her.* Maybe that's exactly what she did. "When did you last see her?"

"It was a while ago," Marie admitted. "My focus is on Freya and little Tyra. Freya sent Runa to the store for food and Pull-Ups for Elin. That was, gosh, three hours ago."

"Three hours?" I choked on a piece of cheese. "And Freya is only now wondering where they are?"

"She was sleeping." Marie's calming tone suggested she understood my meaning: did the woman ever parent her children? "I was here to keep an eye on the baby."

"That's not your job, Marie. I appreciate your help more than I can say, but you're here with your coven for Ostara."

"It may not be my job," she agreed, "but it is my calling. And that means I do what's necessary when it's necessary."

I sure couldn't argue with that. "You think they went to the general store?"

"Yes. It's also possible they're at the clinic."

"Unity?" I glanced at Mom. "Whispering Pines' day spa."

Marie nodded. "Yes, Unity. Jola told me she was concerned Freya was placing too much responsibility on Runa. The poor thing is only fifteen. Jola told the girl if she wanted to go to Unity, she'd arrange some pampering for her. 'On the house,' she said."

"You'd better go." Mom nudged me with her elbow and took the glass from my hand. "Find the girl."

"Girls," I mumbled, a memory playing at the back of my mind. I blinked, and whatever the memory was, it turned to dust as fast as it had formed. "Elin is with her. All right, since it's been three hours, I'll start with Unity. It's unlikely they've been wandering around Sundry all this time. I shouldn't be long." To Marie, I added, "Go to dinner. Mom can pop up and check on Freya until I get back."

Mom's glare made it clear I was in trouble for

volunteering her that way, but she didn't object.

"They're both sleeping so should be fine," Marie assured her and joined the others.

In the front yard, Meeka was still chasing Blue but trotted over to the Cherokee when I whistled for her. I set her on the tailgate, and Blue leaped up next to her an instant later. The cat settled into the back corner of the crate, and Meeka followed. Immediately, the pals started batting at each other.

"I'm not sure which will cause less distraction. You two being contained together or one of you wandering free."

Blue licked a paw, doing her best impression of pure innocence. Meeka sat with her back to the cat but kept glancing over her shoulder as though preparing for an ambush.

"All right, but if there's any fighting"—I shook my finger at them—"I'll pull this vehicle to the side of the road and separate you two."

When I got to the tiny lot behind Unity, Blue stood from her curled position, stretched, and gave a little *mrow* to Meeka before taking off into the woods. Just hitching a ride across the village, apparently. I grabbed Meeka before she could find another puddle, and she went limp in my arms, hanging there like a furry sack of potatoes.

"Don't worry. She'll come back to play again. You've got a job to do." I figured she'd be a fun distraction for Elin so I could have a chat with her big sister.

Inside Unity, villagers and visitors alike roamed around looking happy and mellow.

"Yoga class finished two minutes ago," Jola stated from behind me. "Since it's so late in the day, this was a relaxation rather than rejuvenation session."

"Looks like it worked well. Is Runa Nygaard here?"

"She is. Elin too."

"Their mother is looking for them."

"Why? Does she have another task for Runa?" Jola slapped a hand over her mouth. "Sorry, that was uncalled for."

"But true?"

"Very much so. In between contractions, Freya was barking orders at the poor girl. 'Get me some ice chips.' 'Feed your sister.' 'Call Grandma and Grandpa and tell them what's going on.'" She shook her head. "It wasn't so much that she was making requests, but the tone of her voice. I don't know how to explain it, but it rubbed me the wrong way."

"A sort of expectation that Runa would do those things?"

"Like Freya is the queen and Runa the servant." Jola frowned. "Cybil can be that way with Lily Grace sometimes. Not that she treats her like a servant, but that she expects Lily Grace will do things her way and without question."

"And they wonder why she's thinking about leaving the village."

Jola nodded at a group coming from the meditation room in back. "Here's Runa. Should I go get Elin?"

"Not yet. I figured she could play with the furry one here while I talk with Runa for a few minutes. Is there someplace quiet I can sit with her?"

She took Meeka from my arms and immediately got a lick on the neck. "Love you, too, girl. You have very dirty paws, though."

"Sorry about that."

Jola shrugged. "I'll clean her up a bit before she plays with Elin. That was the last yoga class of the day. The clinic will stay open, but the spa is closing now. Take Runa back to the meditation room."

I thanked her and waited until the girl got close. She was laughing with some of the younger Chicago coven members and paused when she saw me.

"Your mother is looking for you," I stated.

Her head dropped forward. "So she sent the cops to drag me home?"

"No. Marie told me you left three hours ago, so I came after you on my own."

I twirled a finger, indicating she should return to the room she'd come from. The meditation room with the soaring cathedral ceiling and a huge butterfly mobile dangling from the peak was very relaxing. Runa headed straight for the trickling fountain in the far corner, Rosalyn's favorite spot in the room, and sat cross-legged on the floor.

"What's going on?" I sat next to her, mirroring her pose.

"I'm somewhere other than home?" She lifted a shoulder. "I was given the chance to do something different for a while? Elin too. Unless I take her to the playground, she only sees me all day long."

"In other words, you're bored?"

"Totally bored. My life is so routine. Toddlers have the attention span of a gnat. My job is to entertain Elin when she's awake and keep her from destroying the apartment. When she's sleeping, I study or clean up the messes she made before Freya gets home."

"Have you talked to your mom at all about getting a sitter? I mean, you're a kid yourself, no offense, and should be hanging out with friends."

She frowned. "No sense in saying anything. Freya makes it very clear that this is my job. Elin is my responsibility."

Why? Simply because she was the older sibling or was there something more to this? "Is Elin your daughter?"

Runa blinked at me. "Wow. Just lay it out there, don't you? No, she's my sister. Told you before, I'm breaking that 'secret lore' cycle. I don't know what I'm going to do yet, but I'm leaving the day I turn eighteen. If I can make it two more years."

"Are you running from someone?"

"No. No one's after us if that's what you mean. Not the law. None of Freya's *true loves*. Honestly, if I were to run, I'd run to my grandparents. I know for a fact they'd help us. Grandma tells me they will every time we see them."

"Tyra will be your responsibility now, too, won't she?"

"Of course she will. Freya is already calling for me when the kid is done on the boob." She held her hand high in the air and snapped her fingers as though trying to get someone's attention. "She doesn't even ask. Just snaps and holds her out to me. That's when Jola pulled me aside and told me to come over here for a while." She let out a heavy sigh. "Here at the spa, and the beautiful room at Pine Time, it's all been a nice little day trip, but nothing will change."

"Is there any reason your mother won't let your grandparents help?"

She shook her head. "Unless there's something she's not telling me, it's her stupid, stubborn pride. 'You're my girls. No one can take care of you better than me.' Guess that means I'm second best. What an honor."

"Maybe it's time to take your grandparents up on that offer. If the four of you can't move to their house, maybe they can pay for a sitter. How much sleep do you get?"

She shrugged. "Four or five hours a night. I'm fine."

I traced a finger beneath my eye and then pointed at hers. "Those dark circles tell me otherwise."

"You know what Freya will say? Same thing she always says whenever I bring it up. 'Plenty of mothers take care of their house and children without help.'" Her voice broke at the end.

"But you're not their mother." I was getting angry about this and needed to calm down. As much as I wanted to help, this wasn't my business. "Look, I understand a bit of what you're going through. I never had to watch a toddler, but my dad was gone a lot, so it was my job—"

And suddenly I understood why the Universe delivered the Nygaards to my doorstep. I'd forgotten about my issue list. Mom wasn't here simply for a visit. We weren't just supposed to hang out and catch up on the last nine months. At some point, I needed to convince her about the charm of Whispering Pines. But before I could do that, we had to fix what broke between us nearly eight years ago on the night Rosalyn was kidnapped.

"Jayne?" Runa was staring wide-eyed at me. "Are you okay? You're not having a stroke or something, are you? Should I get Jola?"

I blew out a slow breath. "No. I'm okay. I just figured something out."

"Yeah, I pretty much saw the lightbulb turn on."

I wanted to get home and talk to my mother. Hash out those events the way Rozzie and I did in October. But I needed to close this loop with Runa first.

"Can I offer my opinion?"

She replied with a half-shrug half-nod.

"I think you should call your grandparents. If they're willing to help, and your mother is too stubborn to ask, then for your sake and your sisters', you need to talk to them. You've got to make a change now or it will affect you for years to come. Trust me on this."

Runa squinted and stared deep into my eyes. "You really do understand, don't you?"

I cleared my throat of the lump of emotion suddenly clogging it. "Like I said, I didn't have to take care of a toddler. My job, from the time I was about nine, was to watch my little sister. She's five years younger than me. This went on even after I'd left for college. One night, I was angry at my mother for calling me home from school to 'babysit' a fifteen-year-old. I understand why now, my sister was a wild child, but because I was angry, I took my eyes off her, so to speak, and she got kidnapped. It took three days for the cops to find her."

"Holy crap. That's rough."

"It almost destroyed our relationship."

Almost on cue, Elin let out a screech and toddled at high speed across the room, Meeka running circles around her, to the waiting arms of her adoring big sister.

I smiled, my heart warming with memories. "Rozzie and I were that close. We are again now, but we lost each other for many years. Don't let that happen to you."

Meeka crawled into my lap, and I watched as Elin wrapped her little arms around Runa's neck. The look on Runa's face, one of absolute love and joy, was even more touching. The tears I suddenly fought with had nothing to do with them, though. I needed to get home. I didn't want to wait another day to start resolving the issues with my mom.

"Are you two ready to go back?" I asked.

Elin released the hug, stood in front of Runa, and placed her hands on Runa's cheeks. In a tone that declared the fate of the world rested on this, Elin said, "Ice cream." Except she pronounced it ice *queem*.

Runa's eyes shifted to me. With her cheeks squished together by toddler hands, she explained, "I promised her we could get ice cream before we went back."

Elin turned to me and pressed a finger to her lips. "Shh. Don't tell Mommy."

Tripp was making shrimp for dinner, but one scoop of ice cream wouldn't hurt my appetite.

"Let's go for a little walk through the woods," I told Elin. "I know a lady named Honey who makes the best ice cream in the world."

Her big blue eyes got even bigger and her cotton-candy-pink lips turned up in a smile. She nodded her head hard, causing her strawberry waves to bounce, and clapped her hands.

"Don't feel too bad for me." Runa took Elin's hand. "Not being able to spend time with her every day would be way worse."

Chapter 17

ELIN WAS SOUND ASLEEP BY the time we got back to the house. Runa thanked me for the heart-to-heart and promised she'd think about the things I'd told her.

"Can I help you with anything?" I asked as she pulled Elin out of the car and held her in her right arm. She flung a backpack with toddler supplies over her left shoulder, clutched two cloth grocery sacks in her left hand, and pushed the Volvo door shut with her foot.

"I'm good," she insisted.

Before she could clamp the bags between her teeth, or whatever she planned to do in order to dig her room key out of her back jeans pocket, I opened the front door for her.

"I'm going to check in with Freya and give this one a bath." She paused a few steps up to the second floor and added, "I'd better spend some time with my new sister. Never know what next week will bring. If Freya agrees to this plan, Grandma will never let Tyra go once she gets her hands on her. Gotta take advantage of the time while I've got it."

Feeling better about the Nygaard situation, I rounded the corner to the kitchen to find Mom and Tripp chatting up a storm about wine.

"Hello, Jayne," Mom greeted while placing flatware next to the three settings on the dinette table. "What's that smile on your face for? I take it you found the girls."

"I found them and had a good talk with Runa, the older one, and then ran them over to Treat Me Sweetly for some ice cream."

"You had ice cream for dinner?" Tripp dumped boiled pasta into a colander and steam billowed around him.

"I had one scoop. Call it an appetizer."

"Not the best choice," Mom scolded. "However, I did take your wine away, and you barely got any cheese or crackers."

I wandered into the kitchen area and over to Tripp. "She's acting weird. How much wine did she have?"

"Only one."

"Bottle?"

He made a *not funny* face. "One glass. And she's not acting weird. I think she's finally relaxing. The coven ladies went out to dinner. Freya isn't leaving her bed. River went to Morgan's. Rosalyn is off with Reed. And you were tracking down the girls. The house was practically empty."

"You used your charm on my mother while I was gone, didn't you?"

"We talked. She commented that this was the longest she'd been away from the spa in years, and the longest ever that didn't involve a conference of some kind."

He was right. Now that I thought about it, I couldn't remember her ever going on a vacation. She worked like a woman crazed while getting her day spa opened, worked even harder to establish its reputation once it was open, and kept that same pace to maintain its good standing.

I wanted to talk to her. Not only about the night Rosalyn went missing, but about her life too. Did she do anything other than work? Did she want to do anything else? Was it all to mask the pain of her failing marriage or was the spa truly her passion? I honestly didn't know. This wasn't the time for talking, though. The witches could return at any time. We needed a private place where we wouldn't get interrupted. Just the two of us. Not even Tripp or Rosalyn around. Right now, dinner was almost ready, so our talk would have to wait. While we devoured the delicious scampi, Mom told us about some changes she was planning to make at the spa.

"We're bringing in a nutritionist." She beamed over this news. "And possibly an acupuncturist."

Since the beginning, Melt Your Cares had only offered hair, skin, and nail services. This would be a great addition. I held up my water glass in a toast. "Treating the inside as well as the outside. Good for you."

She touched her glass to mine. "While you were gone, Tripp was telling me about what Unity offers. I've always wanted to try yoga, or maybe Tai Chi. We have a room that would be perfect for it."

"Uh-oh." I grinned. "Sounds like Whispering Pines is working its magic on you."

In a blink, the mood changed. Her expression became serious. Her posture even stiffened. Why did I say that? We could have had a perfectly nice discussion about sun salutations or tai chi postures, but I had to bring up the village and magic.

While forming the noodles on her plate into a nest, she said, "Since we're on the topic of business and I've got the two of you alone, we should discuss the financial status of Pine Time. It would be ideal for your father to be here, too, but who knows when or if the four of us will ever be together." She stabbed an asparagus spear with her fork. "You're halfway through your first year of business. Are you on track to make back the money we invested in renovating the house?"

That was the condition I'd agreed to. If we made back the renovation money within the first year, that would prove we could be profitable, and Pine Time could stay open. If not, Dad and Mom would put the house and land on the market. It was ambitious, but Tripp and I were sure we could succeed.

"Well," I began, my throat suddenly dry, "you know that winter is the slow time of year. Everyplace will be booked solid during the summer. Not only The Inn and Pine Time but all the rental cottages and the campground—"

"You're not answering my question," Mom interrupted. She had slipped into full business mode. "The village is prosperous. That's evident. I want to know how well Pine Time is doing."

Tripp stepped in. "We are fully booked starting with the weekend before Memorial Day weekend and all the way through mid-July. After that, we have bookings every week through Halloween but still have some availability."

Mom pursed her lips, reminding me of Flavia for a moment. "Some availability. That could mean anything from you have only one booking scheduled to you have only one room left to fill."

"During most weeks," Tripp replied, "it's the second option. Guests generally book with us for either a full week or a long weekend. Those days left in the middle of the week are harder to fill. We're trying a book three days get two days at half price deal. Or book four and get three at half. That has helped fill a few more weeks."

Mom nodded her approval. "Very innovative. Let's return to my initial question. I'll rephrase. Will you make back the money by Labor Day of this year?"

Tripp cleared his throat. "I believe we will, yes."

She turned to me. "Why does Tripp know this, and you don't?"

"It's not that I don't know, Mom. Tripp is far more involved with the guests and the daily goings-on around here since I also have law enforcement responsibilities. That doesn't mean I'm not involved with running the B&B. Unless there's something unusual going on, we check in with each other every night at dinner. He updates me on any new bookings or situations with guests or the property, and I tell him what's going on in the village."

"Unless there's something unusual going on," she repeated. "It seems that 'unusual' is the default around here. I've been here less than two days, and a girl has died. I can't understand why you would want to live in a place where that kind of thing happens so often."

She was balanced right on the edge. For every point of approval she had for Pine Time or Tripp, there was a point of contention for the village or me.

"People remember negative events before positive ones," I suggested, but my confidence was fading. "Unless that positive event is huge, like a significant birthday, a wedding, or the birth of a baby, which I'd like to point out also happened while you were here, those things get filed under same old, same old in our brains."

She tilted her head in a way that said she agreed with me on that one. Reluctantly, but she did agree.

"There is an unusual amount of death that happens here," I continued.

"Murder, Jayne," Mom corrected, her voice thick. "An unusual amount of *murder* happens in this small village." She paused, debating with something, and sighed. "You're divided between two full-time responsibilities, Pine Time and your sheriff's position. That's admirable, but I'm not sure you're cognizant of how much you rely on Tripp and Martin to ensure your success with both endeavors."

I didn't rely on them. I counted on them, sure, but that's because we were partners. Mom had Michael, her assistant manager. I had Tripp and Martin. We were all equally invested in our ventures. Okay, sure, I did divide my time, but that allowed me to do the two things I loved. A little selfish, maybe, but —

Do you? Jayne in my head cut in. *Do you love both jobs?*

"What it comes down to," Mom concluded, as I sat stunned by my own thoughts, "is that you can't serve two masters."

I was about to object and tell her I was fully capable of handling everything in my life. It was like having a job and a child. People around the world handled those two responsibilities every day. I'd been dealing just fine with both of mine for ten months. Voices filled the foyer before I could tell her that, however.

Marie, Calliope, Wanda, and Rosemary entered the great room, all of them talking at once. All the attention focused on Wanda. She saw me and stormed over to the dinette.

"Did you send your deputy after me?" Wanda was livid. "You're sitting here having a nice meal with your mother and boyfriend while your deputy does your dirty work?"

Good lord. What did Reed do?

I stood, feeling Mom's gaze burning into me as I did, and held my hands in front of me in a calm down gesture. "Wanda, I don't know what you're talking about. Why don't we have a seat in the great room, and you can tell me what happened?"

"I don't want to have a seat," she hissed. "The four of us went to dinner at the pub."

Calliope stepped forward. "Happy to say, the atmosphere was much more friendly this evening."

Behind her, Marie nodded in agreement.

"Afterward," Wanda continued, scowling at Calliope, "we went to the bookshop. I spent a lot of time in there today and told my friends about what a comforting place it is. We were browsing through the shelves when your deputy and your sister came in. Right there where everyone could hear, he says a coven member is dead and did I know anything about that."

Rosemary stepped forward at this point. "Not only did we have no idea one of our own had died, Deputy Reed made it obvious he felt Wanda was involved."

I was speechless. It almost sounded like she was accusing him of racial profiling. But I couldn't, in any conceivable situation, imagine Reed doing such a thing. At the same time, I had no reason to believe these four were lying to me.

"This incident was obviously very upsetting to you," I began. "I know an apology won't begin to make up for it, but I am very sorry—"

"You're right," Wanda blurted. "An apology will not make up for publicly humiliating me."

Marie touched Wanda's arm. "Let her speak. She's not asking you to dismiss what happened. Perhaps her explanation will help."

Reluctantly, Wanda crossed her arms and nodded for me to finish my statement.

"The only explanation I can give is that he's stressed." I stopped them before they could object. "I know, we all have stress, we all deal with a lot. He's been patrolling the village as well as handling the death investigation on his own."

The look on Wanda's face stopped me cold.

"Why," she demanded, "is he on his own? Aren't you the sheriff? What have you been doing?"

"I, um." Between Wanda's glare and the heat from my mother's stare, I felt like I was getting cut in two. "I've been taking care of things here. The Nygaard situation and—" I almost said visiting with my mom. "Deputy Reed isn't on his own. I didn't mean it like that. He found me at Hearth & Cauldron the moment he learned about the death, and I went to assist—"

"Assist?" Calliope asked with a scoffing laugh. "Call me

crazy, but I thought the deputy assisted the sheriff."

Everything I said tonight seemed to come out wrong. Or was it that everything I did was wrong? Even Meeka, sitting beneath the table waiting for one of us to drop a morsel she could gobble up, had turned her back on me.

"I'm sorry." It took all my energy to maintain the scraps of dignity I had left. "I'll fix this, I promise."

"Fix it?" Wanda glared down at me from her impressive and intimidating height. Her voice shook with rage. "Maewyn is dead. How can you fix that?"

"She can't undo what's been done," Mom offered, "but she can get back to work and get you some answers."

That was almost exactly what I was going to say. The words seemed to appease the foursome but coming from my mother's mouth rather than my own, they made me feel incompetent instead of in control. How had everything suddenly gone so far off the rails?

Chapter 18

FROM THE TIME ROSALYN WAS four years old until the night she was kidnapped, my job was to make sure she stayed safe, did her homework, got enough to eat, and took a bath before bed. I established a routine for us and eventually tasks got accomplished not because I made them happen but because Rosalyn automatically moved from one to the next. Snack, homework, dinner, play, bath, bed.

It occurred to me now that things getting accomplished around both Pine Time and Whispering Pines had nothing to do with me. Turned out, like with Rosalyn, all I'd done was set up the routine. The bed-and-breakfast and the village could function fine without me.

After Wanda and the others had gone upstairs, Mom, Tripp, and I cleared the table and cleaned up in silence. Well, I was silent, moping in my own little world. Mom and Tripp chatted about . . . something. I wasn't paying attention. We were almost done putting away the clean dishes when Rosalyn came home.

"I didn't expect you until later." Mom sounded instantly happier now that her younger daughter was back.

"Martin had a long day today," she explained, pulling off

her boots and tossing them in the general direction of her room. "He figures tomorrow will be just as bad."

Mom stared pointedly at me. The thing was, I didn't need any more input from her. I'd already made up my mind about how to handle this mess I'd created.

"You could cut the tension in here with a knife," Rosalyn chirped, trying to lighten the mood. "It's thick as pea soup."

Tripp laughed at her. "You're mixing metaphors. You cut tension with a knife, but fog is thick as pea soup. You don't cut soup."

"Po-tay-toe, po-tah-toe," Rosalyn responded. She came over to me and hooked an arm with mine. "Can I talk to you for a minute?"

I looked at Tripp. "Do you need any help first?"

"Nope. I'm going to prep for breakfast and then head up to the apartment and chill before bed."

Mom tossed her dish towel into the laundry basket in the pantry. "I'm going to call it a night as well. Think I'll check my emails, call your father, take a bath, and settle in with a book. I haven't taken time to read in years. Goodnight, all."

"Say hi to Daddy," Rosalyn called after her and dragged me into her room, snatching up her boots from where they'd landed along the way. Meeka slipped in ahead of us the second the door opened.

"What happened with Reed at the bookstore?" I asked before she could say a word.

"That's what I wanted to talk to you about. Hang on, I'm going to change into my jammies."

While she performed her bedtime ritual, I flopped down on her bed. Meeka jumped up and sat at my side.

"Are you done being mad at me?"

She laid her chin on my belly and let out a sigh. Then she army-crawled closer and snuggled into the crook of my arm.

I flipped onto my right side and pulled her in tight. She

went limp, letting me soothe myself with her warmth and doggie smell. With each breath, my blood pressure lowered, and a sense of calm settled in.

Twenty minutes later, Rosalyn reappeared in her pajamas with her face scrubbed clean of makeup.

"Did you remember to brush your teeth?" I teased, wishing suddenly that we could go back to the time when she was my responsibility. As much as I resented it, things were simpler then.

"Smell my breath." She exhaled in my face the way she used to do every night when I tucked her in. Minty freshness surrounded me. "What was going on out there? I thought Mom was starting to relax. Did you have a fight?"

"It wasn't really a fight."

"What did you say this time?"

I sat up, propped two of her pillows against the headboard, and sat cross-legged against them. "It's more what I did. Or didn't do."

"Okay." She copied my position with another set of pillows, and Meeka crawled between us. "What didn't you do?"

"Seems I'm not doing my job. Either of them." I gave her the recap on the conversation, and she listened without interrupting even once. That had to be a first.

"She's kind of right," she said when I was done. "Not that I think it matters."

I wasn't sure if I should be offended or heartened.

"What's your job here?" Roz asked.

"Sheriff and B&B owner."

"No. Why are you here? What were you brought here to do?"

That's right. Rozzie drank the Kool-Aid. She was fully in love with this place now and accepted my off-the-wall theory that the village, not the people but Whispering Pines itself, was making things happen around here.

"My job is to restore the village to what it used to be."

"Nope."

I let my head drop back. "Just tell me. I've got too many hats to wear."

"You told me you think the village is protecting you so you can fix what's wrong. That's different from restoring it. Restoration implies returning to the past, which isn't the right answer. We read Gran's journals, remember?"

"I remember."

"I don't think we want to go back. Things weren't so great here back then. Your job is to fix the problems and move the village forward."

"Not according to Cybil, Effie, and Sugar." I told her about their gripes at Hearth & Cauldron earlier.

Rosalyn swatted a hand. "Crabby old biddies, the lot of them. Like it or not, move forward we must, and Gran and the village decided you're the one to lead us there."

I frowned. "Gran?"

"Did you forget about the message she left for you?"

She meant the simple note Gran had tucked into the box of tablecloths she used during the Samhain celebration. I remembered every word.

My Darling Dearest,
Thank you for taking over.
Love and blessings, Gran

"Dearest" was her pet name for me. I hadn't forgotten, but I hadn't thought about the note in months.

"Or the message at the séance?" Rosalyn added.

Lily Grace had done a reading, of sorts, for us on Halloween night. The teen had been overwhelmed by spirit activity that night due to the thin veil between the worlds. She couldn't be in the rooms where the other tellers were conducting séances and stirring things up even more, so she tried to do a private one for Roz, Tripp, and me. It turned into a sort of half-séance, half-reading where instead of giving Lily Grace a message to deliver to us, it seemed Tripp's mom and Gran took over her body and spoke to us directly.

Again, I remembered every word of Gran's message to me. *My Darling Dearest, it's all yours now. I trust you. Do what you feel is best.*

"You remember, don't you?" Rosalyn raised a triumphant fist in the air. When I didn't react, she waved her fist in front of my face. That made me laugh.

"Do what you feel is best," I murmured. "So being the sheriff and B&B owner isn't important."

"Let's not go that far. You accepted the responsibility of both, after all."

I let my head flop toward my sister. "You're making my eye twitch."

"Think of it as being undercover. Your primary job is to save the universe, but the villagers can't know that, or they'd be all over you like peanut butter on toast." She frowned and shook her head. "That doesn't work. Peanut butter slides off hot toast. I've got to work on my metaphors. Anyway, you're more like the village manager. You've found folks to fill the roles and now you're making sure they're doing their jobs."

"Like what Reed said about enlisting the carnies' help."

"Like that. And yes, he told me about his idea."

"It's okay for me to float between roles," I reasoned, "because my true role is bigger than the others."

"For now."

My head flopped to the side again. "For now?"

"Well, yeah. Once you've conquered the Big Bad, you'll have to settle into one. Mom's right. You can't give one hundred percent to two full-time jobs."

I reached up and placed a sloppy kiss on her cheek. "You're kinda smart, you know."

She wiped her cheek and pushed back her shoulders. "I know. I've been waiting for you to catch up."

Feeling a little better about things now, I asked, "Was there something else you wanted to talk to me about?"

"Oh, yes." She shifted positions to face me, legs still in crisscross, Meeka now in her lap. "Martin needs help."

"There are a lot of topics that statement could apply to. In which way does he need help?"

She sighed. "He'll be furious if he knows I told you. He's not ready to take on the role of acting sheriff. If this death hadn't happened, he'd be fine. He's okay with patrolling and keeping the witches in line. He's not ready to lead a death investigation on his own, though."

Part of me winced at the position I'd unintentionally put him in. Another part of me cheered that he'd figured it out so quickly. There were days I wasn't even sure I could handle the job of sheriff. I knew the only way to get his newly graduated ego out of the way was to let him figure out his abilities on his own.

"I never dreamed there'd be a death for him to handle," I told her. "Wanda was irate over what he did at the bookstore. Wait, let's back up to that. What did happen?"

"We had dinner at Grapes, Grains, and Grub," Roz began. "Wanda and the others were there, and Martin told me he suspected one of them. He didn't say who and never gave me any details about the death."

"Nothing at all?"

"Only that a young woman had died and her body was found on the lake. In this village right now, that leaves it wide open. Anyway, they finished eating and left. Martin was distracted by then and needed to go home and get some sleep. So I paid the bill and we left. Outside, we found Wanda's group walking toward Biblichor. Martin said he had to talk with them about the death, so we followed them inside."

"And he confronted Wanda in front of the whole store," I stated. "That's what Wanda claimed."

"It wasn't quite that dramatic. He pulled the group to a quiet corner, told them that someone had died, and that he'd like to talk with them about it at the station in the morning."

I waited for more. "That's it?"

She held a hand up as though swearing an oath. "That's it. Wanda went ballistic, though."

"You've got to admit, her reaction was kind of understandable. I mean, breaking the news about Maewyn's death that way had to be shocking."

Roz tilted her head. "Maewyn? The loudmouthed one from last night?"

Something wasn't adding up. "He didn't tell you who died, but he must have told them. They knew it was her. Wanda named her."

Rosalyn thought back through the events and shook her head slowly. "No. I wasn't right next to them, but I was close enough to hear. He never said a name."

"Then how did the witches know it was her?" I mumbled mostly to myself.

"Figuring out those details is your job. Well, one of your jobs." She took one of my hands in hers. "Promise me you'll help him. He's really feeling lost and like he's going to screw up this investigation."

"Don't worry. I get it. Time for me to take over."

It wasn't time to save the Universe yet. It also wasn't time to cross Mom's name off my list. I had to catch a killer first.

Chapter 19

ROSALYN AND I WATCHED A movie after our chat, so it was late when I finally left her room. I tiptoed up the stairs to our apartment, crawled into bed, and almost shrieked when Tripp rolled toward me.

"Sorry to wake you," I whispered and gave him a quick kiss. "Go back to sleep."

"I've been waiting for you. Can't sleep until I know you're okay."

I couldn't love this man more if I tried. "You know my theory that the village brought us here for a reason? You, me, and River?"

"Yeah."

"Rosalyn says my real job here is to fix the village so it can move forward. My law enforcement and B&B roles are camouflage so the villagers don't get suspicious. Or something like that."

He hooked an arm around my waist and pulled me against him, spoon style. "Either I'm really tired or she's right because I can't disagree."

"Still, I'm taking over the investigation in the morning." I explained how Reed was having a hard time.

"Then we'd better get to sleep. We'll need to get up early in the morning." He yawned. "This week is good practice. I should start getting up early every day and make breakfast so I can get back in the habit." He paused and yawned again. "Maybe every other day."

"Right. You've got to ease into things like that." I snuggled in but slept fitfully. I dreamed I was Durga, the Hindu goddess of war and had seven arms like her. In my seven hands, I carried my badge, Glock, handcuffs, notepad and pen, latex gloves, camera, and walkie talkie. Instead of riding a tiger like she did, I rode a Westie. Equally fierce, but I had to carry her more often than she carried me.

In the morning, Tripp got up first and assembled a couple dozen individual oven-baked Denver omelets. They'd get baked closer to the seven thirty serving time, but he'd popped two in the oven right away for us. Over the winter months, he didn't make a formal breakfast unless we had guests in the house. We just grabbed coffee and whatever was easy. Sitting at the dinette together first thing in the morning, with the sunlight shining through the tree boughs, was such a peaceful way to start the day. I hadn't realized how much I'd missed our early morning breakfasts together. Afterward, Meeka and I got into uniform and went to the station. We hadn't been there ten minutes when Reed walked in.

"You must miss work," he called out as he hung his jacket over his desk chair. "Either that or you're really eager to get back to that whiteboard."

"Little of both, I think," I responded from my desk. "I'm ready when you are."

He poured himself a cup of coffee and then took his position in front of the board.

"Let's talk a minute first." I pointed at a chair.

He paled a little and perched on the edge of the seat. "What's up?"

"Wanda Bishop came back to the B&B after dinner last night and was upset about a confrontation she says the two of you had at Biblichor."

Reed's head dropped forward. "I could tell by the look on her face that it might turn into something like that. There wasn't a confrontation."

"I know. Rosalyn told me her version of events."

"I guess I could have pulled them all into the corner one by one. I didn't want to take that much of their time, though, so asked them all at once to come here this morning. I mentioned there was a death and asked if they'd come in to talk about it. That was it. No confrontation."

I glanced at the clock over my door. "It's a little past seven now. When are they coming?"

"Eight thirty. I told them to have breakfast and not rush."

"Unfortunately, they've had almost twelve hours to discuss what happened to Barnes."

"No," he shook his head. "I never gave a name. There's a rumor going around that something happened to Barnes because no one has seen her since dinner the other night. Iris is telling everyone she's under the weather." He laughed. "Naturally, all the green witches started asking for her symptoms so they can make her a concoction or tea."

Oddly, that made me feel better. Despite the obvious problem of someone disliking Maewyn enough to kill her, it was nice to know she had people that cared about her too.

"Regardless, they know." And by not denying it to Wanda and her group last night, I confirmed it for them. "Rosalyn told me something else. Don't get mad at her because she was only trying to be helpful."

He remained silent, waiting for the hammer to fall, so to speak.

"She says you're feeling overwhelmed. That if it was just patrolling the witches, you'd be fine, but the death investigation on top of that is too much."

He sat back in his chair. "Thank the Goddess. I hoped she'd say something."

"You used my sister?"

Shaking his head, he clarified, "I figured she wouldn't keep quiet and relied on her inclination to help. She didn't let me down."

"Why didn't you come to me? I told you to ask for help if you needed it."

He squirmed. "I didn't want to let *you* down."

I debated about giving him a motivational "you can handle it" pep talk and settled instead on, "Very touching. All right, you had your time as acting sheriff. I'm taking over."

"Works for me. Can we whiteboard now?" He stood to man the markers when I nodded and added, "Thanks for giving me the chance, boss."

"I'm glad to know you're comfortable working the crowd. That will take up most of our summer after all." I pointed to the board. "Okay, we've got victim, manner of death, and a few suspects. Let's discuss strangulation for a bit. What do we know about that?"

"Considering Barnes's death appears to be a manual strangulation, we can assume it wasn't premeditated."

"Good. Most likely a heat of the moment killing."

"The killer lost control," Reed mused. "This means we're looking for someone with strong hands."

"Maybe. Dr. Bundy said it only takes eleven pounds of pressure on the carotid arteries to cause someone to blackout."

"And then four to five minutes of continued pressure to cause death." He pointed at his neck. "Let's act this out. Pretend to choke me."

Figuring it was always good to get into the killer's mind as well as the victim's, I was willing to play along. I stood and placed my hands around his throat.

"Don't actually squeeze, please," he joked.

I counted out loud for ten seconds. "Okay, you're passed out. Drop to the ground."

As he did, he almost slid out of my hands. "If I was really doing this, I'd need to squeeze harder at this point to not lose my grip on you."

He lay on the ground, and I pretended to maintain pressure. "This angle, with my arms to the side, is awkward. I'd have to straddle you to make it easier. I won't though."

After only ninety seconds and not applying actual pressure, I announced, "My hands are cramping. The killer would have had an enormous amount of adrenaline flowing through them and likely wouldn't be tired yet."

Another ninety seconds.

"We're only at three minutes," I reported. "There's still a minimum of sixty seconds to go before death."

I released him then, technique understood.

"Dr. Bundy was right." Reed rubbed his throat. "The intensity of the rage going through the killer is unfathomable to me."

"That's what I was thinking. Who was angry enough at Barnes to maintain that?"

"Wanda Bishop is at the top of my list. That woman is full of anger."

"Which might be why she felt you were singling her out last night. But why would she be that angry at Barnes?" With no answer for that, we looked at the board. "You listed Skye Blue. Why?"

"Because of her reaction to Barnes's monologue at Triple G."

"What did you see that I didn't? She was calm and talked about the importance of not applying labels."

"Too calm. Sometimes those folks are volcanoes ready to explode."

"I disagree. Not about the volcano thing. Skye Blue's reaction isn't enough for me, but if you'd like to interview her, go ahead. Next name on the board, Amaya. Does she have a last name?"

"Most likely, but I haven't spoken with her yet and haven't heard one. I added her because of the way she confronted Barnes at the pub. She kept insisting she settle down and even told her to find another coven."

"They worked together. Or rather, Barnes worked at Amaya's occult shop." I explained how Barnes offended some of the customers and inspired others.

"Anger and frustration over harming her business could have been building over the months." Reed put a star by her name. "She's one to interview for sure."

"It's confusing, though. I sensed a bit of a love/hate thing between them. Amaya seemed torn about Barnes. She scared off some customers by always spouting her opinions but also brought in a lot of sales during their motivational women only nights. Not sure if she would have been angry enough to strangle someone, but yes, let's talk with her." I looked at the next name on the list. "Why Iris?"

"Because of her knowledge of Barnes's last actions."

"You mean the shoes and sweater in the hotel room?"

"Yeah. Who recognizes stuff like that?"

"Plenty of people. Not you, I take it. I didn't sense anything but concern from Iris, but if you want to press her more, that's fine."

"What about motive?" Reed asked, adding the word to the whiteboard.

I stood and paced. "Barnes was vocal and rubbed some people the wrong way."

"True, but is bugging people enough to induce murder?"

"Sure it is. Rage can lie dormant for years. Sometimes, the simplest thing can set it off."

Reed pointed at my desk. "May I use your computer?"

"Sure. What are you looking for?"

"We keep talking about anger. Most of the world seems angry about something right now, but few people commit murder. I'm looking for reasons for rage. That might help us come up with a possibility or two." He typed in the question, waited a few seconds, and then read, "Anger can act like a motivator."

I thought back to my time patrolling the streets of Madison. "I can't tell you how many domestic violence calls I responded to and heard the abuser say something like, 'She keeps pushing my buttons. I couldn't take it anymore.'"

"You think maybe Barnes was dating someone from the coven? Maybe they broke things off and it turned nasty." He liked that one well enough to return to the whiteboard and add it beneath *Motive*. Then he went back to the computer. "Causes of anger or rage are fear, frustration, pain . . . Emotional pain, too, like sadness."

"Fear," I repeated as my instincts tingled. "Fear of loss?"

"What are you thinking?"

"Barnes was so vocal about the coven changing its ways that both Amaya and Wanda told her to find another coven." I thought of Cybil, Effie, and Sugar. "What if other members were equally angry about her trying to change things? Change can equate to loss for plenty of people. I'm thinking of Rosemary in particular. She's been the High Priestess for fifteen years and referred to the coven as her baby."

Without commenting, Reed added *Fear of coven changing* beneath *Motive*.

"I like this anger path," I told him. "We still don't have much to work with, but when we talk with the coven members, we can ask about anyone who might seem angry."

Reed grew quiet then suggested, "What if we release the victim's identity? Word is out that there's been a death and that Barnes is missing. If we release her name, maybe that will bring people forward."

"And some are already sure it's her." I scanned the pluses and minuses of this plan and decided, "Go ahead. Release her name."

"But obviously nothing else."

Was he reminding me to keep quiet about key evidence? Like I'd forgotten that in the month and a half since the last death in this village. "Obviously."

"We're here," a barking voice announced from the main room. It had to be Wanda.

Reed turned the whiteboard around so anyone who passed by my door wouldn't see what we'd written. In the main room, we found the Circle of 3 Moons royalty, as I'd come to think of them: Wanda, Rosemary, Marie, Skye Blue, and Calliope.

"Thank you for coming," Reed greeted. "I'd like to first say that I understand my approach last night upset you. I sincerely apologize. That wasn't my intention."

"You told us Maewyn is dead," Skye Blue declared. "In a very public place. How could that be anything but distressing?"

"Again," Reed said, "I apologize."

I was thrilled that he'd followed his own advice and didn't point out that he hadn't told them it was Maewyn.

"We'd like to talk with each of you individually," I told them.

"Back to work, are you, Sheriff?" Wanda asked with plenty of sarcasm.

I smiled appeasingly and ignored her jab. "Who'd like to go first?"

Chapter 20

REED DRAGGED MY TWO GUEST chairs into the main room and placed them next to the two by his desk for the waiting women. Then, claiming they needed entertainment, he turned on some jazzy music. Really, it was to muffle our voices so we could leave the door open and keep an eye on them while we conducted interviews. Didn't want possible murder suspects roaming freely through the station.

Since we were only talking, not interrogating, I kept the setup a little more casual. Normally I'd put the suspect with their back to the door, which was unsettling, and positioned my chair a few inches away from them, which made them even more uncomfortable. Reed preferred to stand in the corner and hover like a nightclub bouncer. This time, I put the chairs in a triangle with a bit of breathing room between them.

Reed took the chair next to me. Meeka patrolled the main room, distracting the women further. Skye Blue came in with us first.

"For the record," I began, setting my voice recorder on my knee, "please state your full name."

"Skye Blue."

"Is Blue your last name or a middle name?"

Her shoulders pushed back as her chin lifted slightly. "My name is Skye Blue."

Kind of like Lily Grace. I was ninety-nine percent sure Grace was her last name, but no one ever called her Lily. Guess I could ask.

"How long have you been with the Circle of 3 Moons coven?"

She kicked off her bright red clogs, pulled her legs up into lotus pose on the chair, and positioned her floor-length black dress around them. "Good Goddess, has it been fifteen years?" She played with a Celtic knot pendant at her throat and considered that. "Yes, that's accurate. I joined 3 Moons shortly after Rosemary became the High Priestess."

"What is the coven's hierarchy?" Reed asked.

Skye Blue settled her hands in her lap as though she was meditating. "To join Circle of 3 Moons, you begin as an Initiate where you cast a wide net. You study and practice a bit of everything until you find your best fit. After you've shown an inclination to a specific calling, you become an Apprentice where you'll continue learning. Apprentices also help mentor Initiates."

Was this how the Whispering Pines coven worked? Again, I could ask.

"The third level," Skye Blue continued, "is what we call Sage. These are members who have dedicated years to a certain skill and are considered specialists. Fourth level, or Elder, is a member who has expert knowledge of the craft. They are equal in skill to a High Priestess or Priest but have not taken on the leadership role. Finally, the fifth level is the High Priestess and/or Priest. Circle of 3 Moons does not currently have a qualified fifth level male, so we operate without a High Priest."

Reed chuckled. "This always reminds me of Boy Scouts. Earn enough badges, advance in ranks, and then you're declared an Eagle. Or in taekwondo, there are nine degrees of black belt. After the fourth, you're a Master. After the seventh, you're a Grand Master. Some recognize a tenth, but you can't achieve it until you die."

This earned him a withering look from Skye Blue. It said the two weren't even close.

I cleared my throat and got us back on track. "Who fills these roles for the coven?"

The woman focused on Reed for another moment, then her gaze shifted to me. "As you're aware, Rosemary is our High Priestess. Wanda and I are Elders. Calliope, Marie, and others of our older members are Sages. Some of our younger members have advanced to the second or Apprentice level, but most of them are still Initiates."

"There's obvious animosity between some of the older and younger members," I noted.

Skye Blue released a heavy sigh. "Yes. Many of these girls are not dedicated to the craft. They simply like the idea of being a witch. They find it romantic or rebellious."

That's what Rosemary said the other night. Or rather, what she said Wanda said. Seems Wanda wasn't the only one who felt that way.

"These younger members," Reed began, "do they cause problems with the others?"

She scowled at him. "Why don't you ask what you really want to know?"

Reed stiffened. "Tell us about the problems Maewyn Barnes caused within the group."

Skye Blue nodded with approval this time. "You and your villagers got a good show two nights ago. Maewyn wasn't always that vocal, but she always wore her opinions for all to see. As far as she was concerned, Wicca was for women, and women don't need men." She held up a hand as though deflecting questions we hadn't asked. "I'm sure you get the point and there's no need for me to go further."

"That explains Maewyn," I stated. "What did the others think? Was she having any sway?"

Another heavy sigh. "Sadly, yes. Some of the younger members, and a handful of the older women, like the idea of a man-free zone."

"What about you and the other Elders?"

She gave me the same disapproving look she'd given Reed earlier. "What is Whispering Pines' motto?"

It took me a moment to realize she actually wanted me to answer. "All are welcome, and those in need may stay."

She waggled a long, thin finger at me. "That first part. All are welcome. That has been Circle of 3 Moons' motto since its inception. It is unthinkable to those of us who have been members for fifteen, twenty, thirty or more years for that to change."

Her volume and pace were rising, and her hands had clenched.

"You seem to be getting a little worked up, Skye Blue," I noted calmly.

She closed her eyes, pressed her lips together, and shook her head crisply as though denying the claim. My mother did the same thing when upset, but she usually hummed as well.

The Elder regained her composure. "We welcome the girls who join with the desire to learn. We're thrilled to see the increased interest in the religion and want nothing more than to teach Initiates. We also have no problem with other sects. All we ask is that they join those sects rather than try to change what's working with ours."

"And Maewyn Barnes refused to leave?" Reed asked.

"Maewyn was difficult in many ways. Rosemary, Wanda, and I talked with her numerous times about how to conduct herself."

"Did she comply?" I asked.

"At times, yes. Other times, she followed her own path." Her eyes shifted between Reed and me. "Your next question will surely be, if she was causing problems and had been warned about her actions, why didn't we remove her from the coven." Reed and I nodded. "There are extenuating reasons that I am not at liberty to reveal."

Reed leaned forward, elbows resting on knees. "By not revealing those reasons, you could be preventing us from finding Maewyn's killer."

"I understand that. But I assure you, Deputy, I have no idea who killed Maewyn." There was a good deal of emotion in her voice. For as frustrating and disruptive as Maewyn had been, Skye Blue seemed to have a soft spot for the girl.

I reached forward and touched her knee. "Anything you can tell us, no matter how insignificant it may seem to you, could help us find out who did this to her."

She nodded, her gaze cast down now. "I understand." But she refused to say anything more.

We thanked her for her time and dismissed her. Calliope came in next, and her statement was almost identical to Skye Blue's. She had more frustration and anger for Maewyn than compassion, however, and also claimed to not know who the killer could be.

Marie was third and explained the coven's hierarchy the same way Skye Blue did, but she also had a different perspective on the goings-on within it.

"Honestly, I come to the gatherings to worship. I'm happy to teach and guide those who request it, but I'm really a solitary witch."

"Solitary within a coven?" Reed asked lightly.

"Unusual, yes. I enjoy being with people for a while, and then I stay home until I feel the need for companionship again." She pondered this a moment. "I think this is why being a midwife is so appealing to me. I get to interact with a limited number of people for a finite period of time. Then I return home with the satisfaction of knowing I'd been helpful."

Second to last, Rosemary had surprisingly little to say. "Maewyn was far from everyone's favorite coven member, but she also wasn't hated. I don't know what more I can tell you."

"Oh, come on," I pushed. "You're the High Priestess. If anyone had a problem, they'd come to you, right?" She gave a single nod. "Then I'm betting you know more than you're telling us."

She grew quiet, so we waited her out.

"Maewyn had personal problems," she stated after nearly a minute. "She and her mother had a tumultuous relationship. I believe she joined Circle of 3 Moons to repair what was broken."

"And was she able to do that?" Reed asked. "In a coven the size of yours with women of various ages, she had plenty of maternal figures to choose from. Did she find a replacement?"

Rosemary smiled at him. "That would have been nice, wouldn't it? But no, to my knowledge, she did not find anyone to replace her mother."

"Who in your coven was angry enough with her to . . . kill her?" I asked, almost saying strangle instead of kill.

She sat forward. "What makes you think it was someone from my coven? And why do you believe they were angry?"

I chose my words carefully. "We won't get the autopsy results back for a day or two, but the medical examiner's cursory check at the scene showed the killer would have been quite angry."

Rosemary didn't flinch. "You're not telling me everything."

I held her gaze. "Neither are you."

After a lengthy pause, she stated, "Except for Maewyn, I have never witnessed angry outbursts between coven members, and can't know what a member's temperament is when they aren't in my presence. We may well have some very angry witches among us, but I cannot point them out for you."

I furrowed my brow. "Amaya comes off as angry and a bit confrontational." I tapped a pen to my chin, pretending to think for a moment, and then pointed it at her. "Wanda too."

Rosemary clenched her jaw and turned away.

"Feels like you might be protecting someone," Reed noted.

Another pause. "I care a great deal for every member of my coven. As you pointed out, my members come to me. They do so in confidence, which I will not break."

"What about those hobbyist members," I began, "who see Wicca as more of a social gathering rather than a religion?"

"We give everyone a fair chance. Many times, those who come for entertainment find a family instead." She shifted to the edge of her chair. "There's really nothing more I can tell you about Maewyn's death. Are we done? You still need to speak with Wanda, I realize, but we planned to go to the Barlow cottage today. This is a special day for us, and we would like to celebrate with those who understand the significance."

I forgot that today was Ostara. It was like bringing a Christian in and interrogating them on Easter. Not that crime waited for a convenient day.

"Are you still staying in the village until Sunday as you'd planned?" I asked. "Or, considering the tragedy, will you be leaving sooner?"

"We will stay through today," Rosemary confirmed. "The five of us may leave in the morning. We understand that you will expect us to pay for the unused nights."

When she left the room, I turned to Reed. "The clock is officially ticking."

He nodded. "We can't force them to stay. We need to figure out whodunnit today."

Wanda walked in, took the chair Rosemary had vacated, and the blood drained from my face. I'd seen her hands when she and the others first arrived at Pine Time but had forgotten about them. At that time, I thought she must be a green witch because her hands reminded me of Briar's. Wanda, our prime suspect, wasn't our killer. There was no way those twisted, arthritic fingers could have squeezed the life out of Maewyn Barnes.

Chapter 21

REGARDLESS OF WHETHER WANDA BISHOP was or wasn't our killer, we still needed to question her. I'd get Reed's take on things once the witches left, but my interest was now squarely on Rosemary. I wasn't sure she did it, but I was positive she was hiding information and might know who the killer was.

"How long have you been a member of Circle of 3 Moons?" I asked Wanda.

"Nearly twenty years." Her squared shoulders and raised chin told us she was very proud of this.

"You've known Rosemary that whole time?"

"We joined the coven at the same time, but she and I were friends long before that." She smiled, her crusty exterior cracking a bit. "We met at an art class when we were in our thirties. One of those mixer events. Not one for finding dates, neither of us were interested in that. This one was to find friends. Or simply to hang out with others for a while. There was no pressure to interact. Some just wanted to be around other people. In fact, a handful of students were content to sit alone at the back of the full room and work on their projects."

"That's when you became friends?"

"The first night." She smiled again, caught up in a memory. "We went out for drinks afterward, and in the thirty years since, not a day had passed that we haven't spoken."

"What do you do?" I asked. "For a living, I mean."

"I'm the executive office manager for a mid-size law firm. Rosemary works with Chicago-area residents looking for jobs or needing training for better positions."

I hadn't asked about Rosemary and couldn't help but notice that she didn't offer information on any of the other members. After so many years as friends that never missed a day talking to each other, had Wanda's anger and Rosemary's passion for the coven merged and resulted in Barnes's death?

"You obviously know," I stated, "that Maewyn is the coven member who died."

She looked at Reed. "I do. Your deputy told me."

Reed waited for me to give a nod. "Actually, I didn't. I pulled all five of you aside at the bookstore and told you a coven member was found dead. Then I asked if you all would come to the station this morning to answer some questions. And I directed all statements at the group, not only you."

Before she could argue with him, I stepped in. "My sister Rosalyn was there last night and overheard the conversation. She told me what she witnessed, and then when I got here this morning, without knowing that I'd spoken with her, Deputy Reed corroborated Rosalyn's statement almost exactly."

"Is there some reason," Reed began, "you felt I was targeting you?"

Wanda reverted to the angrier version of herself. "Do you mean am I feeling guilty about something? Did I kill Maewyn? I absolutely did not."

"Sheriff O'Shea and I both saw you at the pub the night Maewyn died. Where did you go after that?"

"I left about the same time you did. Around six. I wasn't ready to go back to the B&B so went to the bookstore instead.

India can confirm I was there. What a lovely person. She and I chatted about various genres until closing time."

"Which was eight o'clock," Reed supplied. "And then where did you go?"

"I returned to the bed-and-breakfast. You can verify that with Rosemary and Calliope."

I made a note to check with both India and Calliope. I no longer considered Rosemary's word credible.

"And after you returned," Reed pressed, "you stayed at Pine Time the entire night?"

Wanda's eyes narrowed. "You can verify my whereabouts with Rosemary."

"That response doesn't answer my question," Reed countered.

She was fidgeting in her chair, likely to storm out if he kept pushing her that way, so I stepped in. "Ms. Bishop, you've made it clear that you had nothing to do with Maewyn's death. Any thoughts on who might have killed her?"

She flung a hand toward the women waiting for her in the main room. "Are you only speaking with older coven members? While we may have been annoyed by the girl's behavior, plenty of the younger members, especially those truly interested in studying the religion and craft, were flat out embarrassed by her. Are any of them on your suspect list?"

"I assure you," Reed tapped his notebook as though offering proof, "we have plenty of people we plan to talk to."

"Do you have any suggestions for where we should start?" I asked in a gentler good-cop tone.

Wanda sniffed. "That Amaya girl seems angry at the world. I'd start with her." She stood then. "If you're done accusing me of something I didn't do and asking me questions I can't answer, I would like to get on with my day now."

"Of course." I walked with her into the main room. Reed

followed. "Thank you for your time, ladies. We know where to find you if we have any more questions."

That statement earned me a small smile from Marie, a snort from Calliope, and a scowl from the other three. As soon as they were gone, I grabbed my guest chairs and motioned for Reed to follow me into my office. While he paced, I spun the whiteboard around.

"What did that tell us?" I asked.

"We know those five are coven royalty. You were right about Skye Blue. I don't think she had anything to do with Barnes's death."

I agreed and drew a line through her name on the board.

"Calliope and Marie," Reed continued, "are also clear."

I circled Rosemary Chauderon's name and faced Reed. "Thoughts on her and Wanda?"

He blew out a breath. "Wanda didn't do it. Her hands are too twisted to have grasped the victim's neck for even the initial ten seconds let alone four to five minutes."

"She for sure didn't do it on her own. What if she and Rosemary were in it together?"

Reed considered this. "I don't know about that, boss."

"Chauderon and Bishop are sharing a room. Barnes died sometime in the middle of the night. They could have slipped out, done the deed, returned, and no one would have known."

He stared at the board. "Will your fancy security system tell you if they left?"

"Good question. It doesn't tell us who leaves, but does track who swipes in."

While Reed waited, I called Tripp and asked him to bring up the file from two nights ago.

"Thanks for checking." I hung up and shook my head. "The last time a door opened was when Amaya asked if it was okay that she smoke on the back patio because her roommates didn't want her to do so on the boathouse deck."

"What about Amaya?" Reed mused. "Wanda said we should talk to her."

"I'm not ruling her out, but the discussion I had with her about Barnes working for her happened before the death."

"You said she smoked on the back patio. Where did she go after that? Back to the boathouse or back into the village to hunt down her employee?"

"I hadn't considered that. We'll have to check with the others. The keycard system is only on the house. I could check the outdoor cameras to see if her car left." I put a star by Amaya's name on the board. "See why I'm so happy you're back?"

He blushed a little and his chest puffed.

I thought back to my discussion with Amaya that night. "If she'd had a gripe with her employee, I probably would have gotten a sense of that when we talked. Not only was she calm, she sounded like even though Barnes could be difficult, she appreciated her because she brought in a lot of sales."

"Unless she was planning ahead. Plant the idea that she was frustrated with her but grateful to have her as an employee. This gathering is the perfect opportunity if she was considering doing anything to her. All these coven members around, plenty of whom didn't like Barnes . . ."

"That would poke a hole in our crime of passion/rage theory."

"Maybe she planned to kill her another way."

"That fell apart, so she resorted to clamping her hands around Barnes's throat for four to five minutes?" Reed shook his head.

"It's not impossible."

I made a note of the option next to Amaya's name on the board and stood back to read everything we had there. I wasn't happy with any of it. There were far too many holes and unanswered questions. "While possible, neither the

Chauderon/Bishop or the Amaya options feel solid. We need to keep talking to people."

"I'll head over to The Inn. I'm not sure if there are any specific events planned for today so don't know how many will be there."

"A lot are gathering at the Barlow cottage. That's where Rosemary and her group are going. Think I'll go eavesdrop. In fact, I'll bring my mom and Rosalyn and leave the uniform at home. Uniforms put people on edge. Relaxed people tend to let things slip."

"Meet back here in" — he glanced at the clock — "two hours?"

It was almost eleven o'clock. "Let's make it three hours. It might take me an hour to convince my mom to come with me."

On the way home, my mind raced, and my frustration grew. I couldn't remember ever feeling as unsure about an investigation as I did about this one.

~~~

Mom stood in Pine Time's kitchen with her arms crossed. "Why on earth would I want to go over there?"

"Oh, come on, Mom," Rosalyn urged. "It's part of the equinox festivities. It'll be fun."

"And," I offered, grateful for my sister's backup, "you and Briar might be able to work through whatever this is between you."

She crossed her arms tighter and glared. "You're assuming that woman will even let me into her home."

"I'm sure she will. I know Briar."

We'd been arguing about whether Mom would or wouldn't be welcome for a few minutes when Tripp tapped me on the shoulder and handed me the house phone. "Here. Talk to Morgan."

Leave it to Tripp. We could debate this for another twenty minutes or I could talk to Morgan and get her approval.

"Of course you're all welcome," she assured after I told her about the plan and Mom's concern. "Even if Georgia chooses not to, I would like you to come and offer police presence. I hate the idea of a killer being in my home."

"Can you do a spell to reveal or something?" I teased and froze when I saw the look on Mom's face.

"I could, but that takes time, and there are people all over my cottage at the moment. Mama can't handle them all by herself."

"We'll keep it in mind for later. If Mom chooses to come, will you convince Briar to play nice?"

That made Mom smile.

"You know I can never guarantee anything with Mama, but I will do my best. I agree, a face-to-face discussion is ideal."

"All right. At least one of us will be there soon."

"Blessed be."

Mom opened her mouth to object, and I cut her off. "No one except you believes Dad and Briar had something going on. If anything had happened, trust me, Morgan would know. They were like siblings or best friends. Even the village's chief busybodies from when they were kids, Sugar and Honey, say there was never anything between them."

Rosalyn stood next to me. "Mom, you and Dad have been working so hard at a reconciliation. He would have come clean about something like that."

I nodded. "You've got to let this go. All that anger" — my mind flashed to the bruises on Maewyn's neck — "it's not good to hold on to that."

She stared between us and then asked Tripp, "What do you think? Be the tiebreaker."

"There are two of us," Rosalyn pointed out, "and one of you."

"I get two votes. One as mother and one as myself."

Rosalyn crossed her arms. "That stopped working on us twenty years ago."

"I agree with Jayne," Tripp replied. "And not because I live with her. You need to resolve this, Georgia. Whatever the truth is, you need to move past it. I saw Dillon and Briar together when he was here. They're very close, yes, but I know how a guy looks when he has feelings for a woman. Maybe there was something between them once, but it was a long time ago. I don't think anything is going on now."

"Don't assume," Rosalyn added, "that because of the Donovan thing he's lying about this too."

I blinked at my sister. "Wow. I'm glad you said that. Mom, she's right. I think he would have told you by now. Or one of the villagers would have either let something slip or flat out tattled on them. These people know everything about each other."

Mom walked to the windows and stared out at the lake. After a long moment, with her back to us, she mumbled, "I've never felt so ganged up on in my life."

Rosalyn went over and draped an arm over her shoulders. "We took a vote, and you lost. If we're wrong, you can let us know about it every chance you get."

Mom removed Rosalyn's arm. "Let's go get this over with before I change my mind."

While Roz put on her boots, I grabbed Meeka's leash because I knew she'd want to play with Pitch, and asked Tripp, "Are you coming? They're planting seeds."

He pointed at the second floor. "As much as I'd love some fresh herbs, we still have guests up there. And I've got stuff to do here."

My heart fell. I hated that he was always strapped to the house. He couldn't spend the entire summer that way. I, at least, could paddle around the lake in the kayak if I got up early. He was already up early and could only leave when our housekeepers were here. And it would be nice if the two of us could go on a date now and then that didn't mean sitting on the patio. We needed to come up with a plan.

I threw my arms around his neck and gave him a kiss. "I love you, you know."

"I do know. But it's nice to hear." He returned the kiss. "Good luck at the Barlows'. On both missions."

Chapter 22

I NEVER WOULD HAVE GUESSED so many people could fit in the little Barlow cottage. The most I'd ever seen at one time were five of us—Morgan, Briar, River, Tripp, and me. Right now, between the living room, kitchen, atrium, and garden patio, there had to be at least fifty villagers and coven members packed in. All of them had cardboard egg cartons filled with empty eggshell halves.

"This is a great, earth-friendly way of starting seeds," Morgan explained when Rosalyn asked why eggshells. "Much better than the plastic trays they use at garden centers. Making a cylinder out of strips of paper also works. In this case, the shells also serve as fertilizer and help keep beetles and slugs away."

We watched as people plucked shells from a two-foot-tall by two-foot-wide wicker basket in the kitchen. It was half full of eggshells and had probably been near overflowing not long ago.

"Once the shells are filled," Morgan continued, "put them in an egg carton, place the carton near a sunny window, and mist with water to keep the soil moist but not wet. Once the seed has sprouted and the soil outside has risen to the proper planting temperature, pop the shells into the ground."

"Where did you get so many shells?" Mom asked, peeking in the basket.

"We save them all year, as this is our preferred method for starting seeds. Laurel and Maeve had their kitchens save theirs over the last month or two as well for the Ostara festivities."

"Can we try?" Rosalyn asked, always eager to take part in anything Whispering Pines had to offer.

"Where would you plant them? You live in an apartment." Mom's eyes never stopped scanning the room. Whether observing the others or looking for Briar, I wasn't sure.

"You can start seeds for indoor plants this way as well," Morgan encouraged. "Come back to the atrium with me. We'll get you some shells and discuss what sort of sunlight your homes get."

I followed the three back to the Barlows' amazing atrium, a place where I spent many happy days this winter attempting to sketch the plants. I also tried to draw the architecture of the beautiful room with its high ceilings, inlaid tile floor, and windows on every wall as well as the ceiling. *Attempting* and *tried* being the keywords. I needed more practice on perspective.

Around the large wooden table that also served as Morgan and Briar's altar, people were sorting through seed packets, spooning dirt into eggshells, and dropping in seeds. Two extra tables had been set up for this process. All three were completely surrounded.

While Morgan discussed sunlight and plant preferences with Mom and Roz, I mingled among the crowd. I paused here and there to not only watch the planting but hopefully to pick up on comments related to Barnes. In the kitchen at the table that served as a cooking station, I heard a few.

"I heard she slit her wrists."

"She did not. She drowned."

"No, they found her on the lake not in the water," corrected a young woman with long black hair streaked with purple. "Someone's fishing hut fell through the ice yesterday. Whoever killed Mae probably thought she would too."

There was an explanation I hadn't considered. If that had worked, it would have been an easy way to get rid of the evidence. Her body wouldn't resurface until the water warmed up or some poor person snagged her while fishing. I continued my slow path around the table.

"Whatever happened," Purple Streak continued, "she had it coming. You can't mess with karma that way."

I blindly grabbed seed packets from the table, feigning interest in the contents while listening to the discussion.

"This coven was a peaceful, welcoming place before she came along," the witch with orange hair said.

"You've only been a member for two months," a barely five-foot-tall woman stated.

"Well, that's what I heard. The older members talk about how Rosemary has made it a priority for everyone to feel equal."

A man, one of the few in this coven, laughed. "That's what they tell you when you join. Really, though, it doesn't matter what the Initiates and Apprentices think. The Elders and Sages make the rules. You're equal as long as you agree with their vision."

The short woman shook her head. "You're wrong about the Sages. Plenty of them are very willing to help us newbies find our way. I've been working with Marie to define my path as a solitary witch. She told me they want to know you're serious about learning before they invest their time in you."

"Can't blame them for that," Orange Hair agreed. "I mean, some are only here for selfish reasons and have no actual interest in Wicca. Kegan Cleareye"—a few of them giggled at the name—"is only interested in photo ops for Instagram."

"Maewyn was causing division," Purple Streak insisted, returning them to the original topic. "Like I said, you shouldn't mess with karma. I'm not surprised something happened to her."

Other members throughout the cottage were saying pretty much the same thing. A few defended Barnes and her forward thinking, while far more agreed that something had needed to be done about her for weeks. Not death, though, they all agreed.

The Barlows would need to do a lot of smudging once everyone left to clear the negativity from their home.

I wandered outside to the patio next where Rosemary and the royals had settled into the sitting area beneath a small arbor that would be covered with wisteria in a few months. I loved sitting out here, enjoying a cup of tea and sugar cookies with Morgan and Briar. A rustic fence made of fallen tree branches enclosed and delineated the sitting area from the rest of the garden. It also provided easy cover for eavesdropping. No, investigating. Not eavesdropping. I was investigating a death.

Regardless of what I was doing, the royals were so focused on their discussion, none of them noticed me. I stood there for five minutes and none of them ever mentioned Barnes. In fact, the group seemed more lighthearted than I'd heard them. Even Wanda. Why had their moods changed so dramatically? All of them had been so serious at the station. Either none of them were responsible, the guilty party was really good at hiding her guilt, or they figured they were in the clear now that they'd spoken with Reed and me.

I watched as Pitch chased Meeka at the far end of the garden and listened for another minute. Getting nothing of value for the investigation, I made my way back to the atrium to see which plants Mom and Rosalyn had decided on. In the living room, Ariel, Kegan, Selina, Amaya, and Iris sat cross-legged on the floor. In a pentacle formation, I couldn't help but notice. Also, they were all dressed in shades of gray from dove to gunmetal. Must be the color of the day.

Brown craft paper lay spread out before them, and they each had their own cartons with eggshells and were talking non-stop while planting. Ariel and Selina sat with their heads together as they compared seed packets. Amaya laughed at something Iris said and bumped their shoulders together. Kegan was documenting the process by taking pictures more than doing actual planting.

Were any of them involved in Barnes's death? Had they been in on it together? They were all acting as though everything was fine despite their friend being dead. Maybe it wasn't an act. Maybe everything was fine now because the troublemaker was gone. No. Just like my earlier suggestion of Rosemary and Wanda being co-killers, that was really weak. As were all the options we'd come up with.

There was nothing for me to hide behind, like the rustic fence outside, so I stood in the doorway between the living room and kitchen with my back to the group and an ear cocked their direction. With so many people in the cottage, though, I couldn't hear a thing they were saying. I headed back to the atrium, making a mental note to pull them into the station later and talk with them.

Something you observed here is significant, Jayne in my head said.

That explains my feeling of being off-balance, I thought back at her. *I'm not sure if it's the five sitting on the floor or the five sitting on the patio.*

Do something else, she instructed. *Let your brain ponder this. If you ignore it for a while, sooner or later it will demand your attention with the answer.*

Hopefully sooner. That clock was still ticking.

In the atrium, Mom and Rosalyn stood at the altar table, with Morgan instructing them and others on how to plant their seeds with intent. Briar did the same for those at the other tables.

"What did you decide?" I asked them.

"Your mother," Morgan began with a pleased smile, "has decided to try herbs."

"Basil, oregano, and chives," Mom agreed. "I love chives in my scrambled eggs and on baked potatoes. The basil is for margherita pizza. Basil and oregano for marinara sauce. Morgan says I need a window that gets plenty of sun."

"That one in the dining room," I suggested.

"That's where I was thinking too." She sprinkled a pinch of tiny seeds that looked like black sesame seeds into her last eggshell. "That's a good place to start. The deck gets plenty of sun in the summer. Perhaps I'll move them out there when they're bigger. Kick them out of the nest, so to speak."

She seemed more excited than I thought she'd be about her to-be herbs.

"Her biggest problem will be to remember to water them," Rosalyn said.

"Speak for yourself." Mom brushed her hands together. "I'll make it part of my nightly routine. I'll mist them right before I get ready for bed."

"Good plan." I rested my chin on Rosalyn's shoulder and found what looked like little already sprouted plants in front of her. "Wow. You must have a little green witch in you."

"We decided I'm better off with a grown-up plant." She patted her baby plants and smiled proudly. "I'll have better luck taking care of these than watering seeds every day."

Couldn't argue with that. Rosalyn was easily distracted

even when not preparing for final exams and college graduation.

"These are spider plants." She held up what looked like a miniature version of a full-grown plant. It had long, skinny pale-green and white striped leaves. "All I have to do is keep them in water and wait for roots to grow. Then I transfer them to a pot. Even I can remember to put water in a glass once a week."

I pulled Morgan to the side to ask about Mom and Briar. "Have they spoken yet?"

"They've exchanged glances but nothing more. Everyone is almost done planting. We'll bless the seeds, then it will be time for people to leave, and they can have their chat." Morgan put her hands to her lower belly and made her baby-on-my-bladder face. "I'm glad we specified a window this year. Last year people came and went at their leisure throughout the day. What about you? Did you have any luck narrowing your suspect list?"

I tapped the back of my head. "Something is simmering back here, but it's taking its time to come to a boil. I have no idea why I'm using cooking metaphors. I must be hungry."

I told her about what I'd heard from the three groups.

"Patience," she advised. "You're getting closer."

"Everyone is ready," Briar informed her daughter. "Would you like to lead this blessing?"

"You can do the atrium group, Mama. I'll take those in the living room and kitchen out on the patio."

Briar stood where she could see all three tables at once. "Everyone, take a water bottle from the center of your table and hold it in both hands. Close your eyes and envision gold and green lights streaming from your hands into the water."

Mom glanced over her shoulder at me with a look that said, *Is she serious?*

I stepped over to her and whispered, "Do yourself a favor

and go with it. Pretend for two minutes that you believe in the power of the Universe."

She made a face as she grabbed a small spray bottle.

"The gold," Briar explained, "represents sunlight. The green, the sprouts your seeds will become." She waited a few seconds for everyone to do this. "Now, repeat after me. In this small seed, magic does live." She paused while the group repeated the words. "Vitality and strength this water gives." Pause. "Add sun and earth and it will grow." Pause. "Blessed Goddess, I will it so."

She had the group repeat this twice more, and then they misted their shells.

"Thank you all for sharing part of your Ostara with us," Briar concluded. "If you would, please tidy your stations and then we must ask you to leave. I'm old and Morgan's pregnant. It's naptime for both of us." There were chuckles and words of thanks all around as Briar went to Mom's side. "I understand we need to talk."

Chapter 23

WAITING FOR MOM TO RESPOND to Briar felt like we were living through the moment in the movie when the timer on the bomb ticks down to zero. The hero cut the wire. Did it work or were we all about to witness an explosion?

Adjusting and readjusting the eggshells in her carton, Mom replied, "That's my understanding as well. However, if you need to rest—"

Briar swatted a gnarled hand. "That was to get the others moving along. They'll be here all day otherwise."

A spot in my chest warmed when Mom smiled at that. We took a few minutes to help tidy the cottage, and then Briar prepared a large pot of tea. I moved the almost empty basket of shells to the atrium where Morgan and Briar would plant more flowers and herbs for their massive garden. They'd also bring some sprouts to Shoppe Mystique for others to buy for their gardens. I found River in the kitchen when I came back inside.

"Where were you?" I asked.

"Enjoying Ostara tea and a novel in the sunshine on the second-floor deck." He held up a saucer with a small mound of wet tea leaves. "I was instructed to save the dregs and distribute them around the base of a tree as an offering to the Goddess."

I couldn't decide if I was more surprised by him obediently saving used tea leaves or that the pasty-skinned man sat in the sun. "Did you plant seeds?"

He swallowed the last of the tea in his cup. "While my appreciation for gardeners is immense, I prefer to acquire my food in an already grown state." He glanced at the pregnant witch. "Please, do not mention that to Lady Morgan."

I mimed zipping my lips.

River took a large tray that held a pot of prepared tea, mugs, and a plate of cookies out to the patio and set it on the table. Then he placed a hand on Morgan's shoulder. "Unless there is something else you require, I will deposit my dregs next to the hawthorn out front and return to Pine Time."

I had to stifle a giggle at Mom's perplexed reaction to that.

Morgan touched his hand. "Thank you for your help today. Mama and I could have handled setting up the tables by ourselves."

"No need when I am available to assist," he replied and kissed her cheek.

"Come back for dinner?"

He bowed his head. "I shall."

Once he left, an uncomfortable silence fell over us. Mom was the first to speak. "I've been told, by numerous people, that I'm wrong about you and Dillon."

Rosalyn and I gasped and looked at each other, our eyes wide. Mom never admitted to being wrong about anything.

"We should have had this discussion years ago." Briar inhaled, steeling herself. "There's no point in beating around the bush. It's true, I have feelings for your husband."

Mom glared at me as though I'd lied.

"As a friend," Briar added firmly and with fondness. "I was five years old, I believe, when my mother moved us here. She and Lucy had become very good friends because of their shared belief in Wicca. Keven traveled a great deal, so Lucy was lonely. When she invited us to come for a visit, Mama said yes immediately. When she later invited us to move into that big beautiful house, we both said yes. Like Mama and Lucy, Dillon and I only had each other here."

"There were never romantic feelings?" Mom asked, clearly skeptical.

"Never."

Mom paused and then accused, "You knew his secret."

"He was not only my best friend, he was like a brother to me." Briar sat back, gazing at Mom over her teacup. "That didn't change when others moved here. After a while, all we had to do was look at each other to know what the other was thinking or that there was something we needed to talk about. I knew about Priscilla and Donovan, yes. Dillon swore me to secrecy. Like locking it away in a vault, we never even mentioned it for years. After he met you, however, I told him every chance I got that he needed to tell you."

Morgan touched Mom's arm on the table. "Perhaps this will help. For as far back in the Barlow history as you care to go, you will find only a line of very strong, independent women. Every one of them had one child, a daughter, and not one of them ever married."

"None of them," Briar clarified, "let their child's father stay in her life. Until now."

"River?" Mom guessed.

"River," Morgan agreed and added, "I have no intention of marrying him. His request to remain was . . . unexpected. Every other man has gone on his way, unaware of the child he created. River refuses to walk away from his daughter."

A smile played at Morgan's lips, and I couldn't help but stare at the third finger of her left hand. I thought of that gorgeous black opal ring in River's room at Pine Time. She may not intend to marry, but once again it seemed he had different plans.

"The point of all this being," Briar stated, "I am not the modern witch my daughter is. I never once wanted a man leaving his socks on the floor or expecting anything from me."

Mom cleared her throat. "Morgan's father — "

"Is not Dillon," Briar insisted.

"What?" Rosalyn and I blurted in unison.

"That's insane." Rosalyn crossed her arms and stared past me at Morgan. Searching for a family resemblance?

I understood paranoia better than anyone, but Mom thinking Dad was Morgan's father took it to a whole new level.

"We'll prove it with a blood test," Briar offered, "if it will ease your mind. There was exactly one girl in this village he had feelings for."

"Priscilla," Mom supplied.

Briar's voice softened. "He was heartbroken when she died. As we all were. Along with the manner of Priscilla's death, Lucy demanded that Dillon also keep Donovan a secret." She shook her head. "That wasn't hard for him. Donovan was nothing but a constant reminder of Priscilla."

"He never got over her," Rosalyn crooned and placed her hands over her heart, surely thinking of some sappy romantic movie.

"It's not that he never got over her," I insisted and turned toward Mom. "Priscilla was his first love. His *teenage* love."

Mom shook her head and held up a hand to quiet me. "It's never been the love he lost that bothered me. We all have lost loves." She glanced between Briar and Morgan. "Well, most of us do. It's the love that he never got to have that's been eating at me."

"Like siblings," Briar repeated with finality. "We never wanted more. I don't know what else to say."

Mom gave her a genuine smile. "I believe you. And something has become clear to me. It hasn't been you eating at me all this time, Briar." She turned to Morgan. "It was you."

Morgan accepted the accusation with grace. "You were afraid there was another child he never told you about."

"Funny what broken trust will lead to." Mom inhaled, looking a little lighter with this breath. "If you're willing to do a blood test, that's proof enough for me."

And with that, the air was cleared. I guess Mom simply needed to express her concerns and look into the eyes of the woman she thought might have been Dad's lover. There was still a good deal of tension and while anything was possible, Mom and Briar would likely never be friends. Since Ostara, like much of Wicca, was about new beginnings, I was fine letting this resolution be simple.

While Mom and Briar had one last private conversation on the patio, the three of us went inside.

"It's the *When Harry Met Sally* theory," Rosalyn declared. When I gaped open-mouthed at her, she explained, "That thing about men and women not being able to be friends."

I shook my head. "It's possible we've been spending too much time together. I was thinking that same thing earlier."

Roz linked an arm with mine and laid her head on my shoulder. "I could never spend too much time with you."

Morgan smiled. "English has only the one word to express love, but other languages have multiple words which makes sense as there are multiple kinds of love. There is, of course, the love for a soul mate. But that's not the same as the love one feels for a child." She put a hand to her belly and then reached out to touch Rosalyn's hand on my arm. "Or the love for a sibling. Or a friend."

"Or chocolate," I added.

"Or romantic movies," Roz teased.

Mom and Briar came in a few minutes later. An awkwardness hovered around them, but the awful tension was mostly gone.

"I don't want to rush things if you've got more to

discuss," I told them, "but I need to get back over to the station."

"Do what you need to do," Mom insisted. "You have a murderer to catch."

"We need you to do one thing before you go, Georgia." Briar went to a drawer in the kitchen and pulled out a pen, two small pieces of paper, and a length of string. She placed the items in Mom's hands and wrapped hers around them. "I'd like you to take a few moments to think loving thoughts about Dillon, yourself, and your marriage. Then write his name on one paper and yours on the other."

"You're going to do a spell," I guessed, "aren't you?"

Briar bowed her head in agreement. "A simple one to strengthen their marriage."

Mom arched a dubious eyebrow, but she played along.

When she'd finished writing, Briar instructed, "Place one page on top of the other, roll them into a scroll, and tie them together with the twine." As Mom followed the directive, Briar chanted, "With pure intent, bind these two. Let their love begin anew."

A chill ran up my back, and I thought of the binding ceremony Morgan, Briar, and River performed for Tripp and me. While sitting face to face in the center of a circle of stones, we expressed our love for each other. Then we tied a string around each other's left wrists. The strings broke off after a few weeks, on the same day funny enough, so we tied them together and put them in a hatbox covered in beautiful floral fabric we found in the attic. We decided it would be our memory box, and the strings were the first of many items we'd place inside during our life together.

Briar took the small scroll from Mom. "Morgan and I will perform a ceremony to further bless your union." She glanced at me. "Go on now. Rid the village of that killer."

Chapter 24

AS I PULLED INTO MY parking spot behind the station, Mom announced, "I could do with something to eat. How about the two of you? Can I buy my girls lunch?"

"I could eat," Rosalyn agreed. "How about The Inn?"

"I can always eat. I need to talk with Reed first. You guys go on over and get a table. I'll be there as fast as I can."

They wandered around the building to the Fairy Path, and I went inside to find my deputy. Reed looked up from his computer as I walked in and then followed me into my office.

My mind had been spinning in the background during our discussion on the Barlows' patio. The answer was in there, but it refused to float to the top. I stared at the scattered whiteboard and let my eyes roam from top to bottom, hoping the missing piece would pop out at me.

"Did you learn anything new?" I asked Reed.

He took a wide stance and hooked his thumbs in his back jeans pockets. "I talked with a bunch of the coven members. Opinions were divided in three. Some thought Barnes was causing unnecessary problems. Others thought she was bringing up valid points. Still others were focused on studying Wicca and claim they didn't pay any attention to her."

I thought of Purple Streak and her group. "That's pretty much what one group at the Barlows' said. Someone suggested the killer might have put Barnes's body out on the ice in hopes that it would fall through."

Reed nodded, approving of this theory. "The thickness of ice is really hard to tell from the surface. You're the Factoid Queen. Here's something for you to add to your trivia database. While there might be puddles on the surface, that doesn't necessarily mean the ice is melting, and the temperature doesn't have to be warm for it to melt. Primarily, ice melts from the bottom." He held one hand flat, representing a frozen lake, and placed the other perpendicular against it so the fingers were dangling beneath. "Sort of like a magnifying glass, the sun's rays shoot through the ice, warm the water beneath it, and melt it from there."

"It's not possible then to tell how much of the ice has melted without drilling a hole or measuring somehow."

"Right. If the killer heard about Verne's shanty going through—"

"And noticed that Brady's hut was leaning, they likely thought it would be next."

"But Brady builds everything that way." Reed leaned comically to the right. "He swears he can eyeball everything, but he needs glasses and refuses to get them."

"Either way, the ice was too thick for that plan to work." I grabbed a blue marker from the whiteboard tray and added *Killer thought Barnes would break through ice* on the right side of the board. "We've got more options for why. Are we any closer to our who?"

Reed shook his head. "Like I said, it was an even divide. And no one I spoke to had any guesses on who might have done this."

"We're letting the number of people who didn't like Barnes distract us." I removed the cap from the marker and drew a line beneath *fear of coven changing* beneath *Motive*. "Who is protecting the coven?"

"Any of the members who've been with it for a while."

"I don't think so. There are plenty of covens. Like moving to a new home or changing jobs, it's uncomfortable for a while, but if a member was unhappy with the direction the coven was going, they'd move to a new coven before resorting to murder."

"That might be true for the newer members, the Initiates or Apprentices. It would take more than the threat of change for the Sages and Elders to leave."

Fair point. "Okay, I think we have too many options. We need to narrow our focus."

"Agreed. We need to look at those who have invested the most into making the coven what it is."

I circled Wanda's and Rosemary's names and drew a line between them. "These two seem joined at the hip."

"We rejected them earlier because the security system showed they didn't leave Pine Time."

"Yes, but if we're looking for who invested the most in the coven, that would be Rosemary. What if she left, killed Barnes, and Wanda let her back in?"

Reed considered that, then shrugged. "Maybe. Who else?"

As I stared at the board, Iris's name stood out to me. Using a red marker instead of the blue, I circled it.

"I mentioned her earlier," Reed noted, "and you said no. What changed your mind?"

"I'm not sure. When I first met them at Sundry, I asked who would be staying at Pine Time. When Barnes heard that Wanda Bishop would be there, she demanded that Amaya trade rooms with her."

"Amaya was supposed to room with Iris Mohan at The Inn." He squinted as though trying to see what I saw. "I'm not getting the connection."

234 | SHAWN MCGUIRE

"I don't know what it is, but I saw Iris, Amaya, Ariel, Kegan, and Selina at the Barlows' and something about them has been bugging me ever since. It's a feeling more than anything concrete." A tingling instincts feeling, which meant I shouldn't discount it.

"Since we both have a gut feeling about Iris, I say we pursue it."

"I agree." I drew a triangle on the board with Maewyn Barnes's name at the peak, Amaya's on the right corner, and Iris Mohan's on the left. My stomach growled. Not only was I distracted by too many suspects, I was hungry. "My mother and sister are waiting for me at The Inn. I'm going to grab a quick lunch with them."

"All right. I'll talk to some of the chattier coven members and try to get something solid that will help us include or eliminate Iris Mohan."

"Good. We've got a plan." I tapped the pen on the circled names: Rosemary Chauderon, Wanda Bishop, and Iris Mohan. "Keep it narrow. Focus on these three. If we end up eliminating them, we'll start over."

Reed walked with Meeka and me to The Inn. There, he went in search of interviewees, and I headed for the dining room where Mom and Roz were sitting at the table in the corner to the right of the fireplace.

"Sylvie knows this is your preferred spot," Rosalyn told me when I took the chair in the corner. "I know that's your preferred seat."

"Did you order?" I asked as Meeka crawled beneath the table.

On cue, Sylvie appeared. "Now that you're all here, what would you like?"

Mom ordered French onion soup and a side salad. Rosalyn, a vegetarian stir fry plate. I got a double cheeseburger with bacon and extra fries.

"Jayne." Mom scowled. "That kind of eating will catch up with you."

"And when that time comes, I'll worry about it." I grinned big at her.

Sylvie delivered iced tea all around, placed a small basket of bread on the table, and handed me a parchment bag with biscuits for Meeka. When she left, Mom asked, "How's the investigation coming? Any leads?"

I nodded and looked pointedly at Rosalyn while chewing the buttered roll I'd shoved in my mouth. When Roz frowned in confusion, I jerked my head toward Mom.

"Oh, got it." Rosalyn cleared her throat. "She'll tell us but imagine a bubble of silence surrounding the table. The information cannot under any circumstances leave the bubble."

"All right," Mom agreed, as though the warning was unnecessary. "Is that really what all the head bobs and arching eyebrows meant?"

"Scary, isn't it?" I winked at Rosalyn, leaned toward them, and softly said, "We're looking at either Rosemary Chauderon or Wanda Bishop. Maybe both. We've also got our eye on Barnes's roommate here at The Inn. The problem is, we don't have anything solid enough on any of them to make an accusation, so that's our focus."

I held a biscuit beneath the table for my K-9, told them about the Barnes breaking through the ice theory, and that the killer was likely someone strong. I didn't, of course, mention the strangling. This led to a discussion about occupations that required physical strength that lasted until our food arrived.

"Do any of those career options fit what you've learned?" Mom had taken a genuine interest in this investigation.

I dunked three fries into the blob of ketchup on my plate. "I only know the occupations of four coven members. Rosemary works with social services, Wanda is an executive office manager, Iris works at a tattoo parlor, and Amaya owns an occult shop."

Rosalyn frowned. "None of those require physical strength. Except maybe Amaya to move things around her store."

I took a bite of my burger and spotted Ruby walking across the dining room toward me.

"Hello, O'Sheas," she sang out in greeting. "Sorry to interrupt, but I saw you sitting here and remembered I had a message for you."

I pointed at myself and through burger-filled cheeks asked, "Me?"

"Yes." Ruby scowled at my manners, so Mom didn't have to. "The egg maker returned."

I swallowed and wiped my mouth with my napkin. "The death egg?"

Mom sat up straight as Rosalyn repeated, "The death egg?"

"I didn't catch her name," Ruby continued. "Sorry. She was quite distinctive, though."

She held her hands about three inches away from her head to indicate big hair. I immediately assumed Wanda.

"She had dreadlocks," Ruby specified.

Not big hair. Lots of hair.

"She asked who took it, and I didn't want to out you." Ruby looked skyward. "Goddess forgive me, I lied. I told her I didn't know and that someone must have stolen it. I tried to get her to explain its significance by telling her how beautiful I thought it was, but she wouldn't say a thing."

I bit back a grin. Everyone thought they were a detective.

"Thanks, Ruby. That helps a lot."

She nodded and pushed her shoulders back, happy to have helped with the investigation.

"You were right," Rosalyn whispered. "Rosemary has dreadlocks."

"Indeed, she does." I nodded toward their lunches. "Finish eating. I'm going to call over to Pine Time and see if Rosemary is there."

If she wasn't, Reed and I would have to canvas the village and track her down.

Chapter 25

WE ARRIVED BACK AT PINE Time, and I breathed a little sigh of thanks to find Rosemary's Prius in the driveway right next to Wanda's Audi.

"Can we do anything to help?" Rosalyn asked and literally cracked her knuckles.

I burst out laughing. "Are you volunteering to be my bodyguard?"

According to the deep line of confusion that formed on her forehead, the knuckle cracking was a well-timed coincidence.

"Oh, good heavens." Mom reached out and smoothed the line. "Don't make that face. Those lines will stick."

Meanwhile, Meeka, who had been sequestered to a blanket on the backseat of Mom's car, made a beeline for the front yard as soon as I set her free, and went straight for a puddle. Again. Maybe Aunty Roz would be willing to give her this bath.

This day was one-part death investigation, one-part comedy routine.

"I'm fine," I told Rosalyn. "I'm going to bring Rosemary to the office and chat with her there."

Inside, the aroma of baking cookies hit me immediately, and I noticed Marie looking content, curled up in a chair in the sitting room with a book and mug of tea.

"The coven doesn't have anything going on?" I asked, pausing in the doorway.

She placed a finger between the pages to mark her spot. "Not until later tonight. Rosemary wants to have a gathering to remember Maewyn. Wanda will arrange for her cremation after we get back to Chicago."

Confused, I sat on the loveseat across from her and asked, "Wouldn't Maewyn's family make those arrangements?"

Marie sighed and closed her eyes. "Oh, dear Goddess. You don't know. Then again, there's no reason you would."

"Know what? Marie, if this will help find Maewyn's killer, I need you to tell me what you know."

She took a ribbon from the side table next to her and used it to mark her page. "Wanda is Maewyn's mother."

It was a good thing I was sitting, or I would have fallen over. I thought of sitting in the car outside Sundry with Tripp. We watched the coven members gather and noted the distinct division of younger on one side and older on the other. They appeared to be arguing more than talking. Tripp commented that Wanda and Maewyn looked like mother and daughter.

I pulled my voice recorder from its cargo pocket. "Do you mind?"

"Feel free. I have nothing to hide from you, Sheriff."

"For the recording, would you state your full name and contact information in case I need to follow up with you?"

She did and before I could ask the first question, Marie started telling me the story in her enchanting accent. "When Maewyn was very young, six or seven years old, Wanda and her husband went through a nasty divorce. Her husband didn't approve of Wanda exposing Maewyn to Wicca, and Wanda didn't have the money to fight him. She lost custody and was only allowed short visits on Mother's Day, her birthday, and Yule if Maewyn and her father were in town. Which, big surprise, they rarely were."

No wonder Wanda was so crabby. "Does anyone else know that they're mother and daughter? In the coven, I mean."

"I don't know who Maewyn would have told. Wanda told Rosemary of course, and me, Calliope, and Skye Blue. Possibly one or two of the other Elders, but as you may have deduced, the five of us are very close. The only reason Skye Blue didn't stay over here with us is because she is using these days to work with a Sage who is about to become an Elder."

"I saw Wanda and Maewyn together a couple times. There is a resemblance, but they barely acknowledged each other."

"You can probably imagine what it would be like to live through your teenage years with so little contact with your mother."

"Better than you could possibly know."

Marie tilted her head in question.

I waved it off. "Please continue."

"Maewyn's father's actions were horrible. Keeping her from the woman who loved her so much because of religious preference." She shook her head. "It wasn't as though he didn't know Wanda was Wiccan when they married. Wanda insists she never put religious expectations on the girl. She believes, as we all do, that religion is a choice. Ironic how Maewyn chose Wicca in the end."

"Perhaps not so much ironic as an attempt to be closer to her mother."

She pondered that. "You're probably right. For years, she ignored Wanda's attempts at reconciliation. By the time she was eighteen and free to make her own choices, which also meant seeing through her father's lies, they started to connect again."

"How did they end up in the same coven?"

Marie smiled. "Rosemary."

And just like that, I felt my prime suspect slipping away from me. "What did she do?"

"It was rather roundabout. Let me back up a little. Maewyn's father died a few months after her eighteenth birthday. Maewyn's relationship with him had always been strained at best. She was diagnosed with Oppositional Defiant Disorder as a child, and while the symptoms eased as she grew older, they never fully resolved. Physical tantrums turned into the type of verbal outburst you witnessed at the pub. She left his home during her senior year in high school and stayed with whichever friend had space on their couch. Unfortunately, her temper and disregard for house rules meant she moved a lot. She graduated high school but didn't go to college or learn a trade."

"Rosemary works for social services," I remembered.

Marie pointed at me in a *you got it* way.

"Didn't it click with Rosemary that this girl was Wanda's daughter?"

She shook her head. "Maewyn was going by Mae at the time. Since their last names were different, it didn't connect with Rosemary. Amaya had been a member of 3 Moons for six months and was looking for help in her shop. Rosemary sent Maewyn there. At some point, Maewyn noticed Amaya's Triple Moon Goddess tattoo" — Marie absently touched a spot above her left breast indicating its location — "and asked where she got it."

"Amaya sent her to Iris's parlor." I knew the story from here. "Iris and Maewyn became friends. Eventually Iris told Maewyn about her religion and invited her to come to a coven gathering."

"Oh," Marie put her hands over her heart, "if you could have seen the look on Wanda's face when Maewyn walked in that first time. The five of us already knew the details behind Wanda's divorce and that she had a daughter. I'm not sure if we were more shocked by her initial appearance at our coven or that she came back a second time. When she asked to join 3 Moons, Wanda was elated. She was sure that meant Maewyn wanted to reconcile their relationship."

"And that didn't go so well?"

She shook her head and frowned. "Maewyn had good days when she and Wanda would go to dinner and spend hours talking. Then something would set the girl off and no one could get through to her. You witnessed a perfect example of that at the pub the other night."

I sat back in the loveseat, my mind spinning. Despite the security system technicalities, which only meant someone would have had to let her back in to avoid swiping her card, I was certain Rosemary was the killer. Especially after what Ruby said about the death egg's creator having dreadlocks.

"You thought Wanda was responsible for Maewyn's death," Marie guessed.

"For reasons I can't reveal, we believed it was Rosemary."

Marie's dark brows arched with surprise, then she nodded. "And do you still?"

I sat forward again. "You've been very honest with me, Marie. Is there a reason I shouldn't believe it?"

"Rosemary knew how badly Wanda wanted to reconcile with her daughter and did everything possible to help with that. They are as close as two people can be and not be twins or a couple."

"I hear you, and I wish that could be enough, but I need something solid." I needed proof both to exclude and to make an arrest. "Deputy Reed and I at first thought Wanda was the killer because of how angry she seemed toward Maewyn. We no longer believe that. Then we decided it was Rosemary and even considered the possibility of it being both of them. Can you offer me anything that will prove or disprove our suspicions?"

"I think so. After the scene with Maewyn at the pub, Wanda wanted a little time alone to gather her thoughts before dealing with Rosemary. Rosemary has a tendency to latch on to a problem and not let go until it's resolved. Wanda went to the bookstore, says she stayed there until it closed at eight, and was back here around eight-twenty. She was ready to talk and wanted to come up with a firm plan to help Maewyn — therapy, medication, hospitalization. Whatever was necessary. The four of us gathered in The Side room, since it's the bigger of the two, where we comforted and counseled her until two in the morning. I came downstairs to get us some tea once, but otherwise, none of us left the room. Ask all three of them individually, they'll give you the same version of events."

With that, I had no more questions. Was it possible Rosemary left the house after they finished talking? Sure. But where would Maewyn have been between four in the afternoon when she left Triple G and after two in the morning when Rosemary tracked her down, strangled her, and dumped her body on the lake? That pushed our theory past the plausible point.

After I'd switched off the voice recorder, Marie said, "I'm sorry to take away your suspect."

"It's frustrating to go back to the starting line, but the important thing is you've told me the truth. Thank you for talking with me. I am curious, why didn't you tell us any of this when we spoke this morning?"

"You asked if I knew who killed Maewyn," she stated simply. "I have no idea who might have done it. If I'd known you suspected either Wanda or Rosemary, I would have told you then."

I nodded. "I'll let you return to your book."

At the end of the hall, I found the four Nygaards coming

down the stairs, Freya very slowly and grimacing with each step.

"Are you going somewhere?" I winced and clenched my nether regions as I watched Freya's descent.

"Freya is going stir crazy in that room," Runa explained. "We thought we'd go get something to eat."

"Ice queem!" Elin squealed and jumped up and down.

"Or maybe lunch first," Runa corrected. "Of course, it's closer to suppertime." She bent, baby Tyra's carrier in hand, and poked Elin's tummy with her free hand. "Are we going to have lunch or supper?"

Elin put her little hands in the air. "Me don't know."

Runa debated this while tapping first Elin's nose then her chin then her tummy again, making her giggle. "I know. Lunch and supper is *lupper*. We'll get lupper first and then ice cream."

"Lupper!" Elin squealed and scampered off to the door.

Freya finally reached the last step and sighed. "Or perhaps I will decide. I am the mother."

Runa rolled her eyes in a *yeah, right* expression.

"You'll need to walk to get anywhere." Which could take forever based on Freya's current speed. I analyzed a mental map of the village. "You could park at Unity and ask to borrow a wheelchair. I'm sure they'd be fine with that."

"Good plan." Runa stood, took two steps toward the door, and then came back to me. "Speaking of Unity, that reminds me, I wanted to tell you I think I've decided on a career path. For now, at least."

"Really? That's great. What?"

"I'm thinking of becoming a massage therapist." She rolled her head lazily side to side. "I can't believe how much better I feel after that massage yesterday. A girl named Iris was there for the yoga class and we were talking about it. She explained that it's not all done with the hands. The therapists use their forearms and elbows too. That explains a lot. The lady who massaged me wasn't very big, but she was crazy strong." She shrugged. "Anyway, something for me to consider. I like the idea of helping people feel better. See you later, Sheriff."

They left the house, and I remained rooted to my spot. Iris did chair massage to help calm down her nervous tattoo and piercing clients. She also wore her hair in dreadlocks. And suddenly I understood why the group of five sitting on the floor at the Barlows' cottage bothered me so much. It wasn't the group, it was Iris.

Chapter 26

LIKE A LIGHT SWITCH HAD been flipped, I could see it clearly now. She'd had a scarf in ombre shades of gray around her neck at the Barlows' this morning. That must have been what my brain picked up on but didn't fully register. It blended with the other gray clothing so didn't stand out. She wore a brightly colored geometric-print scarf yesterday. She was staring at her phone and playing with the scarf's fringe while I searched her room at The Inn. I couldn't remember her wearing one at Grapes, Grains, and Grub the night Barnes died, but I hadn't met her yet. If I had to guess, I'd say it was the blood-orange colored one that had been wrapped around Barnes's neck.

I rushed to the office down the hall. Meeka, who'd squeezed inside as the Nygaards left, sensed my heightened emotions and followed me. Closing the door, I pulled my walkie talkie from my waist. "Sheriff O'Shea for Deputy Reed."

While I waited for him to respond, I glanced down at Meeka. She appeared to have self-cleaned by dragging her belly through a dry patch of grass. A trick Tripp had been working on with her, which got rid of the worst of the mud, but she was still a mess. I tapped one of her filthy paws with the toe of my boot. "You better not have gotten mud all over, or Arden will kick your furry butt."

As though understanding, she held up a paw. I took a look. Clean on the bottom but dried mud clung to the fur between her toes.

I ruffled her ears. "Not bad, but you're still getting a bath tonight."

She dropped to the floor with a huffy sigh.

"Stay out of the puddles, then." I called for Reed again.

Ten seconds later, "Deputy Reed here. I was finishing up with someone."

"Are you near a phone?"

"I'm at The Inn."

"Call me at the B&B."

It felt like an hour had passed before the phone rang. "Reed?"

"Yeah. You sound a little frantic. What's up?"

"It's not Rosemary, and it's not Wanda. Iris is the killer."

"Iris? How did you come to that conclusion?"

I gave him the quick version of Marie's statement. Then I told him what Runa had said about looking into massage therapy and how that connected to Iris. "And I figured out what was bothering me earlier. Do you recall seeing Iris wearing a scarf?"

The line went quiet and then, "I do. She was wearing one when I spoke with her the first time. Red and orange triangles or something. A lot like the scarf around Barnes's neck."

"Exactly. The biggest damn clue of all right there in our faces the entire time and neither of us saw it."

"She's here at The Inn. I was about to talk with her again. Should I bring her to the station?"

"Yes, I'll be right there." I nudged my K-9. "Let's go, muddy one. We've got a tattoo artist to interview."

I was pulling up to the intersection of my driveway and the highway when Reed's voice came over the talkie. With my left foot on the brake and my right on the gas to keep the SUV from stalling, I grabbed my talkie and answered, "Sheriff here."

"Did you leave the house? Can I call?"

"No, I'm in my car."

"Secure station."

That was our signal to click up five channels so no one else would hear us. Or so we hoped. Never a guarantee with walkie talkies, so we gave minimal information.

I'd barely switched over when he stated, "She's not here. All her stuff is gone."

"How long? You said she was there before. Did you actually see her?"

"I did. I screwed up. I saw her in the dining room with some of the others and told her I wanted to talk with her."

"You spooked her."

"Majorly screwed up."

"It's done. Let it go. Any idea how long ago she left?"

"Emery says he checked her out within the last ten minutes."

The map of Whispering Pines filled my head again. How far could she walk in ten minutes? My mind traced a path east from The Inn, the fastest way out of the village, and an image of Maewyn Barnes's keyring — three keys and two charms — appeared in my mind like a premonition.

"I think I know where she might be. Head on over to the station. Stay on this channel. I'll call when I have confirmation."

My Cherokee didn't have lights or a siren. They were rarely necessary in the village, but they'd sure be handy now. That was one more check mark in the Get a New Vehicle column. Staying alert to anyone walking near the road or trying to cross it, I raced to the far side of the village. I entered the east side parking lot as the backup lights on an older model pine-green Camry came on. I blocked her in, got out of my vehicle, and stood behind the open door.

"Iris, turn off the engine, roll down your window, and show me your hands." I waited three seconds and repeated the order for her to lower her window at a higher volume. Slowly, the window went down. "Turn off the engine and show me your hands."

Praying I wouldn't need to pull it, my hand hovered near the Glock at my side. Thankfully, she followed my command, and both hands came out of the window, fingers splayed wide.

"Open the door from the outside." When she did, I ordered, "Slowly, get out of the vehicle. Keep your hands where I can see them. Do it now."

Again, she followed instructions without hesitation. She also never once asked what was going on. She knew.

Once she was out of the vehicle, I ordered, "Walk backwards to me with your hands where I can see them." When she was a few feet away from me, I told her to stop and get to her knees. "Iris Mohan, I'm arresting you for the death of Maewyn Barnes."

A minute later, I had her cuffed and belted into the back of the Cherokee.

~~~

Reed was sitting on a corner of his desk and facing the back door when we got there.

"There's a voice message from Dr. Bundy," he reported. "He doesn't have autopsy results yet but wants us to call."

"This case is as much yours as mine," I told him while removing the cuffs and placing Mohan into a cell. "Listen in on your extension."

After a minute of small talk with Joan, Dr. Bundy's secretary, she sent me through to him.

"I know you're working on a deadline," Dr. B greeted when he picked up. "I've got something that might be of interest."

"You're just in time, Doc," I told him. "We were about to interview our presumed killer. What have you got?"

"It's nothing earth-shattering. An extra detail, I guess you could say."

"Never know what might be important," Reed commented.

"That's new," the medical examiner mused. "I've got both of you on the line. Anyway, I was about to start the autopsy and found more bruising when we removed the victim's clothing. You recall the scarf around her neck?"

I nodded and said, "Vividly."

"I only pulled it down a little at the scene. When we took it off her, we found distinct ligature marks."

"The scarf was used to strangle her," Reed supplied.

"That's our assumption. We can't tell which came first, but the safe guess is that the suspect applied pressure to the victim's carotid with their hands first, causing the victim to lose consciousness. When they released their grip, the victim revived. Do you remember what I told you about how long it takes to strangle someone to death?"

"Four to five minutes." My stomach reacted at the memory of pretending to strangle Reed.

"Correct. After the victim revived, I'm guessing the scarf was then used, for lack of a better phrase, to complete the job."

I saw the scene play out before me. Mohan came across Barnes, and a fight ensued. Mohan became irate for whatever reason, wrapped her hands around Barnes's neck, and it played out as Dr. Bundy described. That explained the red marks I saw on Mohan's hands below each pinkie finger. She said they were from using a rowing machine too aggressively. They were actually friction marks from the scarf. Why? What had pushed seemingly even-tempered Iris Mohan into a rage?

"I also," Dr. Bundy began, snapping me out of the vision, "found a large bruise in the middle of the victim's upper back."

"Upper back?" Reed repeated.

"Any idea what might have caused it?" I asked.

"Again, I'm guessing, but possibly a knee."

"A knee? How would—" But it came clear before I could finish the question. Barnes was face down on the ground. Mohan wrapped the scarf around her neck, pulled it taut, and created more tension by pushing on Barnes's back with her knee.

"You've got the picture, don't you?" the ME asked.

"I do indeed. And I understand why these kinds of deaths upset you so much." I took a breath, clearing the disturbing image from my mind. "Thanks for this, Doc. It gives us a direction to follow when we interview the suspect."

"Remember, this is all speculation," he cautioned. "I'll verify what I can during the autopsy and send the results ASAP."

"Understood."

Reed appeared in my doorway a few seconds later. "The pieces are all falling together. Now to put them all together."

"Exactly. Want to run the interview?"

He stiffened and shoved his hands in his pockets. A clear sign that he was uncomfortable with this option. "I've already messed things up."

"You didn't mess things up. We've got her in custody and, unless we're way off base, about to book her on murder charges." He still didn't look convinced. "All right, I'll lead, you pipe up with questions when you have them. And sit next to me like you did earlier."

While I positioned the chairs in the interview room, Reed retrieved Mohan from the cell. As the three of us took our seats, Meeka sat in the corner where Reed usually stood to observe.

I turned on the voice recorder and set it on my knee. We went through the give your name and address details for the recording, and then I began. "We've brought you in for the murder of Maewyn Barnes."

Mohan didn't react. She sat with her hands folded in her lap, her focus on the ground in front of her.

"When we spoke yesterday," I continued, "you told me you believed Ms. Barnes went for a walk to cool down after dinner two nights ago. What were you doing at that time?"

In an even reporting-the-facts sort of way, she replied, "I left the pub with some of the other coven members at about six fifteen. We stopped in Shoppe Mystique for half an hour and then went to The Inn."

Time and place. No other details. Her words sounded rehearsed. I could see her pacing in her room, going over and over her statement as though memorizing lines for a performance.

"You saw Maewyn leaving The Inn around quarter to seven. Correct?"

She nodded. Eyes still lowered.

"Then what?" Reed asked.

"I followed her." She paused then added, "I went up to our room first. That's when I saw she had changed clothes. Then I followed her."

"You felt it was significant that she'd changed?" he clarified.

Mohan plucked at the hem of her slouchy gray sweater but still didn't look up. "I did. I told the sheriff before that Mae liked to walk when she was angry. She wore a light-weight hoodie and ballerina flats to dinner. When I saw them by the desk and noticed that her walking boots were gone, I knew she had to be really mad about what had happened at the pub."

He gave a nod. "All right. Please continue."

In the same even, practiced way, she explained, "Everyone saw her leave the pub at four-something."

"And you didn't see her again," I interrupted, "until six forty-five. What do you suppose she did for almost two and a half hours?"

She shifted in her chair but still refused to look up. "I don't know. I assume she either walked around the village or hung out in the room. Regardless, like I said, I saw her leaving The Inn and knew she must be mad so went after her."

Mohan's sequence of events had shifted slightly. That was the problem with rehearsing. Unexpected questions made you lose your place in the script. It also presented me with the opportunity to confuse her a little.

"Hang on," I interrupted again. "I want to make sure we've got this right. You followed her before or after you went up to the room and saw that she had changed clothes? Because you said you saw her shoes and sweater in the room and that made you think she was angry. Then you said you saw her walking and assumed she was doing what she normally did when she got angry."

"Right." Mohan hesitated a few seconds, sorting through my statements. "It was after. I saw her clothes were there and that her boots were gone and figured that meant she was walking."

"But you already knew she was walking," I stated, "because you saw her outside The Inn."

She sighed, a frustrated sound. "You're confusing my words. Yes, I saw her outside The Inn, then saw she had changed clothes and that her boots were missing. That's when I figured she was on one of her cooldown walks, so I grabbed a heavier sweater for myself, dropped off my bag, and went to find her."

She exhaled. Pleased to have gotten back on track with her prepared statement?

"No one offered to go with you?" Reed asked. "In my experience, girls go places in packs."

She scowled at him. "There were a bunch of coven members hanging out in the lobby by the fireplace. A couple of them offered, but I told them I wanted to walk alone."

"Why did you follow her?" I asked. "Why not just let her walk until she cooled off?"

She lifted a shoulder in a slight shrug. "Guess I was worried about her. I wanted to see if she was okay."

I didn't buy that for one moment. The big question was, had she planned to kill her all along or was it a heat of the moment situation?

"You were concerned about her because of her blow up at Grapes, Grains, and Grub?" I restated.

"Right."

I made a confused humming sound. The one Gran used on Roz and me when she knew we were fibbing about which of us ate all the brownies. "You knew how upset she was when she left. Why didn't you follow her out of the pub? Why wait more than two hours to check on her?"

Finally, Mohan looked up, revealing dark, emotionless eyes. "She did stuff like that all the time. If she didn't get her way, she'd throw a tantrum. She could be such a child."

"Then why go after her at all?" Reed asked.

Before she could respond, I added, "How was it rooming with her?"

She hesitated again, unprepared for the purposeful change of subject. "Not pleasant. She was obsessive about her stuff. I couldn't touch anything. If I did, she'd pitch a fit."

I nodded, feigning empathy. "You were initially supposed

to room with Amaya, correct?"

The shift in demeanor was dramatic. Her eyes softened, and the dark expression lightened. Like the clouds had split, and the sun shined through. "We'd been planning it for weeks. As soon as Rosemary announced the trip, we signed up." The clouds closed up again. "Mae didn't like that."

Reed and I shared a glance. We were finally going to get the motive.

"She didn't like that you and Amaya were going to room together?" Reed clarified.

"She hated it."

"Why is that?" I asked.

Mohan wouldn't answer, so we waited her out. Finally, she hissed, "She was jealous."

"Of what?" I pushed.

"Of how close we'd become."

I glanced at the recorder, verifying it was still running. "Close friends? Or is it more than that?"

She locked eyes with me. "What makes you say that?"

She wasn't attempting to deny anything. It was more like she wanted to know how I'd come to that conclusion.

"Because the moment we said Amaya's name, you did a one-eighty. You went from visibly angry to almost giddy." I waited to see if she'd respond. When she didn't, I asked, "Are you and Amaya a couple? Was this a love triangle gone bad?"

"No. Well, yes, Amaya and I are dating. Mae wasn't in the picture that way." She couldn't seem to stop the grin that took over her face. "It's only been a month. We haven't told anyone in the coven. Amaya wasn't ready for that. She's taken a lot of crap from people about her lifestyle. She moved from one side of Chicago to the other in the hopes of keeping her personal life separate from her business life. She was scared the harassment would start again and someone would trash her shop like they did last time." Mohan frowned, hurting for her girlfriend. "Mae only knew because she caught us kissing in the back room of Amaya's shop." She blew out a breath and shook her head. "You thought the performance at the pub was bad. That was nothing compared to the tantrum she threw that night."

"Maewyn wanted to keep you and Amaya apart?" Reed asked.

Mohan nodded. "From the start, she didn't even like us talking at coven gatherings. A couple months after she joined, she said one of us had to find a new coven. When Amaya suggested maybe she should be the one to go, that's when the real trouble started."

"When you all got here," I began, "Maewyn wanted Amaya to switch rooms. That didn't have anything to do with Wanda, did it?"

"No. And for the record, we know they're mother and daughter. Mae told us one night when she was feeling especially rebellious. Wanda wanted to keep it quiet so they could work on their issues in private. Like that would work. Ask Mae to keep a secret, any secret, and it's pretty much a guarantee she'll tell everyone."

I believed that. I believed everything she'd said about Barnes.

Reed slid to the edge of his chair, his knees almost touching hers. "You weren't really worried about her when you followed her that night, were you?"

For thirty seconds, the only sound we heard was the ticking of the clock on the wall in my office.

"No. I wanted to confront her about leaving us alone." She put her hands to her face. Stalling for time or stopping herself from saying too much? "I don't know where Amaya and I are going with this. It might last another week, or it might go for a lifetime. Mae was trying to kill us before we even got off the ground."

"Interesting choice of words," I noted. "What happened when you caught up with her?"

Tears slid slowly and steadily down Mohan's cheeks as she spoke, but her voice stayed rock solid. "I found her at the docks. She was just standing there, staring up at the moon." She sopped up the tears with her sleeve. "It was the calmest I'd ever seen her. She could never stand still. If she wasn't pacing in a circle, she was bouncing up and down or swaying side to side. She heard me coming before I even said a thing."

"You had an argument," I offered when she grew quiet again. "Who started it?"

She laughed. "Depends on who you ask. She'd say I did by being there. She made some juvenile 'where's your girlfriend' comment, and I asked why she couldn't leave us alone. That started a tirade about how she was friends with Amaya first, even though Amaya and I had been in the coven together for months before Mae came around. We said a bunch of really immature things to each other, and then she threatened Amaya."

"What was the threat?" Reed asked.

She hesitated before saying, "She said that if we didn't stop seeing each other and one of us leave the coven within the next twenty-four hours, she would tell everyone about us. We could have dealt with her telling the coven members. They don't think twice about stuff like that. But then she said she'd tell every single customer who came into the shop, put up flyers on the light poles in the shop's neighborhood, and spread it all over social media."

"And how did you respond to the threat?" I pushed.

Her tears stopped, and her expression turned flat. "I lunged at her. I didn't plan it. There was nothing premeditated. I followed her to talk to her and ended up with my hands around her throat. I thought she was dead, but a couple seconds after I let her go, she came to. I knew she'd follow through with all her threats as well as accuse me of trying to kill her. I couldn't let Amaya go through that. So I knocked her to the ground and jumped on her back. I don't remember wrapping my scarf around her neck, but I did. I pulled until she quit struggling. Then I kept pulling. I'm not even sure for how long."

"Four to five minutes," I murmured. At her confused look, I explained, "That's how long it takes to kill someone via strangulation."

Reed asked, "How did she end up on the ice?"

"I thought she'd break through. We were at the coffee shop yesterday morning and some locals were talking about a fishing hut that went through a patch of thin ice. I saw that one, the leaning one, and figured it would be gone by morning. I dragged her out there and put her next to it." She shrugged, devoid of emotion. "Guess the ice there wasn't that thin yet."

"One last question." I retrieved the death egg from the evidence locker. Her answer wouldn't really matter to the case, but it would satisfy my curiosity. "Did you make this?"

Her face brightened. "I did. Isn't it cool?"

"That depends. Is the symbolism behind it purposeful?"

She frowned. "What do you mean?"

I explained the colors and the sawtooth pattern.

"The colors were unintentional. I just like black and beige together. The saw pattern, yeah. That Ruby lady had an idea sheet. The meaning was on there. Guess I was getting out my frustrations over Mae." She tilted her head to the side. "Why? What did you think it meant?"

There was no point in discussing it further. Since we had nothing else to ask her, Reed brought her back to the cell, and I called Deputy Atkins at the county sheriff's office to come pick her up. Then Reed said he'd handle the paperwork.

"You're volunteering to do paperwork?" What kind of

brainwashing technique did they use on him at the academy?

He hung his head. "I messed up a lot of things on this case."

"You didn't mess up anything. Your only questionable move was announcing to Mohan that we wanted to talk to her." I pointed at the cell. "We've got her and a full confession."

"Do you want to do it then?"

"God, no. I hate paperwork. I just don't want you adding guilt to an already miserable job. I'll have a report to add to the file, so let me know when you're done."

He gave a salute. "You can go if you want. I'll give Atkins everything he needs."

"I should go tell Rosemary and the others what happened."

He brightened a little. "This works out well. I'd rather do paperwork than reveal that kind of news."

I paused before leaving and thought about stopping by the cell and asking Mohan if she had any messages for her coven members. That would only serve to make her feel better, though, not them. Wanda and Amaya wouldn't get the chance to express their thoughts to her. Well, maybe at the sentencing phase of the trial or at a prison visitation if they felt it was necessary. I believed that Mohan's actions were a heat-of-the-moment thing, but that didn't change the fact that she was a murderer. I also believed that those left behind shouldn't have to suffer anything else being thrust upon them.

"Meeka." I let out a sharp whistle, and she appeared in my office doorway, tail wagging. "Let's go home, girl."

Chapter 27

WHO DID I TELL FIRST? High Priestess Rosemary because it was a coven member who had died during a coven event? She could break the news to everyone. Or should I tell Wanda because the victim was her daughter? The decision was made for me because they were glued to each other's sides in the sitting room at Pine Time. They both looked up at me. Wanda's eyes were red from crying, and she appeared shrunken with grief. Rosemary looked heartbroken for her friend.

"We caught the killer," I announced. "I'll tell the others if you'd like me to."

"I'll do that," Rosemary declared without hesitation. She took a deep, centering breath. "Please, give us the details."

"Amaya should be here," Wanda stated. "Not only was she Maewyn's boss, they were friends. Iris, too, but she's over at The Inn, and I don't want to wait for her to get here."

Doing my best to not react to Iris's name, I told them I'd get Amaya from the boathouse.

"Can't we come too?" Kegan asked, meaning herself, Ariel, and Selina.

Why? To get a photographic record of people's shock and

grief? "No, sorry. Wanda only requested Amaya."

She pouted and flopped onto the pulled-out sofa sleeper. While Amaya slid on her shoes, I couldn't help but notice that they had trashed the apartment. Nothing was broken as far as I could tell, but clothes, shoes, and Wiccan items were everywhere. I made a mental note that four adults might be too many in this space.

Amaya walked silently next to me as we crossed the yard. What was she thinking? Did she have any clue what her girlfriend had done? How would she react when she learned the truth?

Wanda and Rosemary met us in the great room.

"Since there's just the three of you," I told them, "let's go into the office where we'll have privacy. It'll be a little snug, but this shouldn't take long."

Before I could stop her, Meeka darted in and slid under the desk. No worries, I could use the moral support. Amaya took the guest chair closest to the wall, Rosemary the one next to it. I gave my desk chair to Wanda and leaned against the credenza.

"The final autopsy results will take a while," I began, "but Iris Mohan has confessed to killing Maewyn."

Wanda and Rosemary gasped. Amaya muttered, "No, no, no."

"She says they had an argument," I explained, "and things got very heated." I waited, prepared for one of them to ask for details. But none of them looked at me, and no one spoke. As gently as I could, I added, "I'm sure you have questions. I'll answer what I can, and the medical examiner will—"

Without a word, a visibly distraught Wanda got up and left the room.

Rosemary stood. "I'd better go with her. Can I speak with you later, Sheriff?"

She left before I could say yes.

"They fought about Iris and me, didn't they?" Amaya asked once I'd closed the door again.

"That's what Iris said in her statement." I returned my chair to its spot behind the desk and sat in the one next to her.

"Maewyn was irrational about us. I think she truly believed she had exclusive rights to each of us as friends. When she caught us in the back room that day, something in her snapped. It scared me. Her problem wasn't a mental one, I know that, but it was like something inside her switched off. It was like another loss in her already loss-filled life, and she couldn't deal with it." She looked up at me with tears in her eyes. "If you would have told me Maewyn killed Iris, I wouldn't be surprised. I didn't see this coming."

"I only know what she told me in her confession. I can't tell you everything, but I will say she claimed she was defending you."

"She was afraid Maewyn was going to tell people about us." She pushed her shoulders back and adjusted her ever-present headwrap. "I'm not ashamed of who or what I am. And if I had been ready to declare that I was in love with Iris, I would've fought any battle. But we just started dating. We didn't know each other well enough yet to make any kind of declaration." She twisted a ring around and around her finger. "Is our relationship going to come out?"

I shrugged. "I can't say. It will depend on whether she pleads guilty to everything and goes straight to sentencing or if she goes to trial."

"We never went out in public together as a couple, so as far as I know, Maewyn was the only one who knew about us." She stared at her hands. "Guess I have a decision to make. Do I keep it to myself or let the truth out?"

"You know not coming forward will lead to rumors."

"I know."

"It's your choice, but I suggest you at least tell Wanda. A mother deserves to know why her child died."

She nodded. "Do you have any other rooms available? I'm not sure I can stay with those three tonight. All they'll want to do is talk about this, and I'm not ready for that."

"Every room is booked until tomorrow. The best I can do is offer a couch in the great room."

She shifted to the edge of her chair, then stood. "Think I'll go for a walk. Gotta clear my head."

I directed her up the driveway and to the campground on the west side. "Traffic can get tricky along the highway with the curves. You can safely wander around the campground all you want."

She mumbled her thanks and left. Once I was sure the coast was clear, I made my way to the kitchen. I could hear the sounds of someone in there and hoped it was Tripp because I needed a hug. Fortunately, it was him.

"Hey." He smiled when he saw me, but it quickly morphed into a frown. "Oh, you look like you've gone nine rounds." He wrapped his arms around me. "I take it you caught the killer."

I nodded and mumbled into his chest, "Iris Mohan."

"Not sure I know who she is."

"Dreadlocks. Tattoos everywhere."

He shook his head.

"I'll explain later. The short version is it was the story of new love that ended badly."

He kissed the top of my head. "I made those white chocolate macadamia cookies. Would you like some?"

"You told me I'm not supposed to self-medicate with food."

"You're not self-medicating." He took the cookie jar out of the pantry. "I'm offering comfort."

"Well, in that case, I'll take six."

Midway through my comfort snack, Mom came into the kitchen.

"Are you done?" She slid onto the barstool next to me. "Did you crack the case?"

She was in a good mood. "I did. And as long as everyone else behaves themselves, I can spend two whole days with my mom and sister. What would you like to do?"

She took a cookie from the jar and a napkin from the basket next to it. As was her habit, she broke the cookie into bite-size pieces that she could pop into her mouth and not smear her lipstick. "I'd like to see your she loft."

I choked on a crumb. "You what?"

"Your father went on and on about this area you set up for yourself. He sounded very impressed, and I'd like to see what all the fuss is about."

Not even close to what I'd expected her to say. "I thought maybe you'd want to go to the bookstore or the other shops in the village."

She swatted at me in a distinctly Rosalyn way. "We'll do that tomorrow. Or maybe Saturday. For now, she loft."

"All right. Finish your cookie and I'll show you."

Chapter 28

I HELD MY BREATH AS we crested the top of the staircase. Mom was always so . . . particular? Persnickety? Exacting in her choices? Whatever the word, what would she think of my loft? I loved it and adored its rustic ambiance. But now, as I stood back and looked at the details while she inspected my space, all the flaws stood out like they'd been highlighted in neon orange. The floorboards were scuffed, and the lighting too dim. The walls were bare. Spiderwebs hung from the exposed rafters. The furnishings I'd chosen from Gran's things felt like treasures from the past at the time. Now they looked like beat-up castoffs.

Mom wandered with her hands clasped in front of her chest as though afraid to touch anything. She paused to scrutinize the beige chaise lounge, small round side table, and floor lamp with a Tiffany-style shade. The trio rested on an Oriental rug in shades of blue that filled the center of the space. Next, she drifted to the bookshelf beneath the windows that looked out at the lake. I'd used the case not only for books and art supplies but also as a beverage center. On top, a large silver tray held an electric kettle and an assortment of tea and powdered drinks.

"It's a little chilly up here," she commented.

I turned on a space heater near the foot of the chaise. "That's why I brought this up here. Tripp is going to re-insulate the walls and ceiling."

"Don't let him cover up those beams." She gazed up at the ceiling.

Not at all what I thought she'd say. "You like the exposed rafters?"

"Oh, yes. They add a great deal of character." With hands still over her heart, she turned to me. "This is lovely, Jayne. Any woman would be envious of your space. I am."

A gentle breeze could have knocked me over. "Really?"

"Why do you sound so surprised? You've surrounded yourself with items that have history and bring you joy. It's so much more personal than buying new furnishings and accessories with no meaning attached to them."

"Well, the space heater and tea kettle are new."

"Only two new items. Very economical. I told you before, every woman needs her own space even if it's simply a chair in a corner. We take on a lot, too much at times, and forget to take care of ourselves."

She crossed to the far corner and lifted the edge of the cloth covering the wooden table there. Beneath it was the Triple Moon Goddess symbol Gran had burned into the wood.

"I thought so. This was her altar, wasn't it?"

Mom's voice held a tone I couldn't quite identify. She was speaking of my grandmother, the woman who had almost destroyed her marriage with a single comment. She didn't sound angry, though. Tired, maybe.

"It was," I confirmed. "The armoire still holds all her things. It didn't feel right to take any of it out of here."

She reached out to the armoire door on the far wall, touched it lightly, and pulled her hand back. "May I?"

"Yeah, sure."

Behind the doors of the stately dark-stained piece were Gran's robes, candles, altar cloths, incense, and other Wiccan items.

"I wish we would have spoken before she died," Mom said so softly I almost didn't hear the comment.

"You and Gran? What would you have talked about?"

She tossed a glance over her shoulder at me. "I think you know. There are few things worse than leaving words unsaid."

This was the second time in as many days where she'd let herself be vulnerable. "It's not too late to talk to her."

She laughed. "Of course it is."

"It's not. I know you don't agree with a lot of the beliefs here, but there's one thing about Wicca that I've come to love." She turned, curious. "There's always time for a fresh start. It's okay to learn from our mistakes and try again."

She blinked and swallowed. "What do you suggest?"

"Talk to her." I held my hands out to encompass the entire loft. "Here among her things, in the space that was hers first, is the perfect place. And there's no time like now."

Her fingers played together, and she looked somewhere between nervous and terrified. She sat on the edge of the chaise, then she scooted all the way back and propped her feet up. When I turned to leave and give her privacy, she reached for me.

"Don't go. This won't take long. And it's okay for you to hear. Important, even, that you do."

"All right." I took a light-blue candle from the armoire, set it on the table next to her, and lit it. "You may remember that blue was her favorite color."

"How could I forget?"

"Use the candle as a focal point."

She cleared her throat as I sat by her feet. "Just talk?"

I smiled and nodded. "Just talk. She'll hear you."

It felt like a lifetime had passed when she finally said, "Lucy, I know you meant well. For years, I thought you revealed Dillon's secret to unburden yourself. I now understand that the bigger reason was to take the weight off his shoulders." She inhaled shakily and exhaled. "Your delivery method wasn't the greatest, but I believe your intent was sincere. And I've learned over the past few days that intent is a big deal with you Wiccans." She smiled as though sharing a laugh with Gran. "We all make mistakes, and I forgive you. Dillon does, too, although he probably already told you that. He may have also told you that we're working on repairing our marriage." She reached for my hand, and I slid it into hers. "We've all missed out. We've all wasted far too many years being angry. I ask"—her voice broke—"I ask that you forgive me too. My hurt and anger resulted in you losing out on years with your son and granddaughters. I'm sorry I didn't realize this sooner." Her voice faded away, and she looked at me like an uncertain little girl. "How was that?"

I blinked at the tears stinging my eyes, and my voice wouldn't rise above a whisper. "That was perfect, Mom." I slid closer and wrapped her in a hug. After a few tender seconds, I felt her playing with my hair. Seriously? "Are you inspecting my ends?"

"So many splits! Did you shampoo it this morning?"

Moment broken, I pulled away. "Yes. I haven't gotten it cut in months, but I wash it every day. Usually."

"I wasn't criticizing." She stood. "Stay here, I'll be right back."

While she was off doing whatever she was doing, I started two mugs of tea.

"Bet you never thought you'd hear those words, did you, Gran?" The candle flame flickered wildly as I pressed the button on the kettle. "Or maybe you always knew you would."

I thought of the near twenty years since the feud began. The almost eight years since Rosalyn was kidnapped. The year and a half since I quit my job with the Madison Police Department. The ten months since I moved to the village. We were all circling back together now, and for whatever reason, this was how our lives were meant to play out. The Universe had strange ways.

By the time the tea was ready, Mom had returned with an old-fashioned train case. The kind of small, hard-sided tote women used to carry their beauty supplies while traveling.

"What's that?" I asked.

"Cape, water bottle, combs, clips, scissors." She looked around at the furniture we'd stored at the other end of the loft, found an old dining room chair, and set it on the hardwood a foot or so from the rug. "This will work."

"For what?"

She stared at me for a beat. "Isn't it obvious? I'm going to give you a haircut."

"You what? Do you even cut hair anymore?"

"There are a few clients who still request my services. And unless you'd like a new style, all I have to do is trim the ends."

"A trim is fine." I handed her a mug. "This is for you."

"Thank you." She took a sip. "Very tasty."

"Morgan's Chill Out blend. My favorite."

Before I lost my nerve, I blurted, "We need to talk about when Rosalyn was kidnapped."

She paused, cup almost to her lips, and sat on the chaise lounge. She patted the cushion, indicating I should join her. "Why do you feel we need to talk about it?"

"Because you blame me."

She blinked and straightened. "Blame you? Why on earth would I blame you?"

Confusion started edging out the guilt I'd been holding on

to for eight years. "Because it was my job to watch her that night."

Mom drank from the mug and then held it in her lap, hands clasped around it. "All three of us were so angry then. Weren't we? Rosalyn felt ignored because I spent so much time setting up the spa. You were a college freshman, finally experiencing freedom, and I kept calling you back. I wanted your father to be home." She stared at her hands, then cleared her throat. "I needed help. Even before I took on a new business, I was alone with a house and two teenage girls. I was too proud to ask family or friends, so I chose you." She smiled but looked embarrassed. "You always took responsibility for Rosalyn."

Took it? Did I? I'd always thought they forced it on me. Either way, I admitted through a throat so tight I could barely breathe let alone speak, "I wasn't responsible that night."

"I shouldn't have asked you." She looked me in the eye and placed a hand on my back. "I was operating on autopilot. There was so much to do. My former boss had warned me about how much it would take to run my own place. She even cautioned me against it. All I could think was, what would happen if Dillon never came home? How would I support you girls? So I put all of my focus into the spa." Her voice caught. "Unfortunately, that meant I didn't have much left for you two." Her hand, still on my back, rubbed in small circles. "I never blamed you for Rosalyn going missing, Jayne. I blamed myself. She was my daughter, my responsibility, and I passed her off."

Now, shock kept me from speaking. I had no idea.

"My guilt was horrible," she continued. "When we realized she was gone, all I could think was that we needed to find her. Once she was back, all I could think was that I needed to make up for not paying enough attention to her." Deep lines normally camouflaged by a mask of makeup appeared beneath her eyes. "Once again, I could only divide my attention so far. That meant you ended up in the background."

"I understand what you're saying, Mom, but this isn't all on you." I couldn't make her accept my confession, but I needed to say the words. "You're right. I was angry. At you, yes, but even more at Dad. He should have been there with us. Because he wasn't, I took it out on you." Different sides of the same coin. "I was angry and took my eyes off Rosalyn that night. You asked me to do a job, and I failed."

Her hand moved from my back to my cheek for a moment. "We've both been carrying the blame for far too long. Like I just told your grandmother, I'm sorry we never talked about it. I think when time passes for too long on something like that, it's easy to believe that it's over and done. Best to let the past stay in the past."

I nodded. Like with the secrets in this village, unresolved issues fester and infect. "Better out than in, as Gramps used to say." We both laughed at that. Gramps could be a little crude sometimes. "I'm sorry, too, Mom."

Having spoken our truths, we let it go at that. I moved to the waiting dining room chair. Mom draped the cape around me and sprayed my hair with water from the bottle. As she combed, I closed my eyes and felt first my shoulders and then my whole body relax. Why was it so comforting to have someone play with your hair? And in this case, my mom taking care of me this way brought up a new wave of unexpected emotions. Insecurity over the choices I'd made over the past eighteen months. Uncertainty that came with wondering daily if I was up for the tasks ahead of me. Desperate loneliness had been replaced with my dear new friends here and was finally refilling with the family I'd lost touch with. Tears trailed down my cheeks. When I reached from beneath the cape to wipe them away, she asked, "Are you crying?"

"No." I cleared my throat. "It's water from my hair."

She stepped in front of me, tears brimming in her eyes too. "I didn't wet it that much."

"Why are you crying?"

"Look down." She stepped back, pushed my head forward, twisted most of my hair up, and clipped it out of the way. "You said before that me opening the day spa took courage." She ran the scissors against my back as she made the first cuts, causing a shiver to race through me. "What you've done here also took courage. A big part of why I came was to see you. It's been far too long. The reason I was so intent on you solving this crime, however, was that I wanted to see you in your element. I needed to know this is the right place for you. You can look up now."

As she combed out the next layer of hair, I found that once again words wouldn't come, so I sat silently and waited for her to say more.

"When your father came home after his last visit here, we went out to dinner. He talked non-stop about how you saved a villager trapped in a fishing shack and how you found out who had run that poor woman off the road. If you could have seen the look of pride on his face when he talked about you."

I closed my eyes, letting my emotions swirl.

"I'm sorry Maewyn died, but I now understand what you're capable of. I'm very proud of you and can see that Whispering Pines is absolutely the right place for you. And Tripp is the right person for you to be here with." She stepped in front of me again, and this time wiped my tears for me. "I like him very much. And Martin seems like a fine young man." After a short pause, she added, "Thank you for taking me to the Barlows' cottage today. I didn't realize that the third reason I came here was to clear away my own ghosts."

"Do you feel better after talking to Briar?"

"I do. I won't request a paternity test, but in the unlikely chance that Morgan is your half-sister, I can live with that."

"Great. Thanks a lot, Mom. Now I'm always going to wonder."

She snipped my dried, splitting ends and sighed. "Welcome to my world."

Chapter 29

FRIDAY MORNING WAS BOTH A somber time and an exciting one. Somber because all the coven members who had been staying at Pine Time checked out. Amaya took me up on the offer of the couch for the night and barely spoke to anyone at breakfast.

"I'm not ready yet," she told me in confidence while helping me clear the dishes from the dining room table.

"For a day or two, no one will question it," I replied. "Everyone, regardless of how close they were to Maewyn or Iris, is in a bit of shock. I wouldn't let your silence go on for too long, though."

She thanked me for my advice and went to the boathouse to collect her things.

Next, Wanda came down the stairs with her luggage. Rosemary, Marie, and Calliope close behind. She trudged straight to the front door, then stopped, and came back. Tripp stood behind me, and her gaze shifted between us.

"Thank you for your hospitality. You have a beautiful home." Then she looked at only me. "I won't say thank you for what you did because it doesn't feel right, but I appreciate your efforts in uncovering the truth."

Before I could reply, she left.

"I'm going to follow her and make sure she doesn't take off without us." Calliope paused in the doorway and called, *"Gracias por todo."*

"How's Wanda doing this morning?" Tripp asked Rosemary.

"The shock is wearing off. Anger is setting in." She let out a slow breath. "They were so close to getting Maewyn the help she needed. That's the saddest part. Other than the obvious."

"I imagine," I began, "this will affect the coven as well."

"Despite our fair share of drama, we are a family." Rosemary pondered that for a moment. "I suppose the drama makes us even more of a family. We'll go through a mourning period. Goddess only knows what will happen after that. We'll take it as it comes, though." She placed her palms together. "Thank you for everything. Blessed be, both of you."

Marie gave a wave from the front door, and I called her back.

"I wanted to thank you again for all that you did. For helping out with Freya, and for telling me about Maewyn and Wanda. I'm so glad you were here."

"We think we're in charge," she replied, "but the Universe often dictates the path we follow. I was here because I was meant to be."

"Not to be insensitive," Tripp murmured once they'd all left, "but the house feels lighter."

We heard two distinctive cries coming from the staircase then.

"Elin doesn't want to leave." Runa held tight to the screaming toddler's hand as she made her way very slowly down the stairs. "I made the mistake of telling her she gets to share a room with Tyra when we get home. She liked sharing with me these last two nights."

"And why is the baby crying?" I asked and immediately realized what a stupid question that was.

"Who knows?" Freya grumbled, also moving slowly but a bit faster than yesterday. "We're still getting to know her."

"You're the one who named her after thunder or war or whatever Tyra means." Runa picked Elin up, carried her the rest of the way, and plunked her on the landing at the bottom of the stairs.

Elin screeched and climbed back up a few steps. "Me do it!"

"I said lighter, not quieter," Tripp insisted when I glanced at him.

"Go with Mommy," Runa told Elin and handed Tyra in her carrier to Freya. "I need to talk to Jayne for a minute." When they'd left the house, Runa wrapped her arms around me. "Thanks for the talk. The one at Unity, I mean. After Elin was asleep last night, Mom and I had a good long heart-to-heart. I told her I can't do this anymore and that it wasn't fair for her to expect me to. She agreed to call Grandma and Grandpa. I couldn't believe it."

"That's great." I squeezed her tight before letting her go. "Send us an email sometime and let us know how things are going."

She promised she would and went after her family.

Tripp sighed. "Now, it's quiet too."

"Reed is running the station today and will call if there are any problems. Mom and Rosalyn want to go shopping. Want to come into the village with us? I'll help you with the dishes first."

"Sounds good to me. Not the shopping part. They'll have a game of some kind on at Triple G. And beer."

I pouted. "That sounds better than shopping."

We cleaned the kitchen, waited until Arden and Holly showed up to take care of the house and boathouse, then headed for the village commons. Rosalyn stocked up on more coffee from Ye Olde Bean Grinder.

"To get me through the last push to graduation," she claimed.

"I can't believe," I told Mom, "you've been here for two days and haven't had any of Violet's coffee yet."

"This is what they serve at The Inn. I had some there." She drank from the cup in her hand. "This, however, is quite possibly the best cinnamon dolce latte I've ever had. Not too sweet and the coffee blend is perfect."

"Told you." Rosalyn sipped from her own convoluted concoction and sighed happily.

"That's because I make my flavoring instead of buying premade stuff," Violet explained, placing Rosalyn's ground beans on the counter.

"Good thing we still have another day," Mom mused. "Think I'll come back tomorrow and try one of Jayne's mochas."

Shoppe Mystique was full, but nowhere near as crowded as I'd seen it in the past. Any of the Chicago coven members still in the village were looking for crystals and talismans and other memorabilia to remember their time here.

A tap on my shoulder made me jump.

"I'm so glad you're here." Morgan led me toward the reading room at the back of the store. "There's something I wanted to talk to you about."

I settled into my preferred spot on the worn velvet settee and watched all the shoppers in the room vacate it. "Funny how we always get this room to ourselves."

Morgan smiled her witchy grin, winked, and lowered with a groan onto the other end. "I won't take much of your time. Nice to see you out with Georgia and Rosalyn." She tilted her head. "Did you get your hair cut?"

"Mom did it for me."

"From the smile on your face, I'd say there was more to it than a cut."

"I'll tell you about it later. So what's going on?"

She let out a sigh that sounded equal parts tired and emotional. "I've decided to make some additional changes to go along with the obvious ones coming to my life. I'll be stepping down as High Priestess of our coven."

"Wow. Does it take up that much of your time?"

"It's not that. Everything considered, this is the perfect time for someone new to step up."

I got a sinking feeling in my gut. "Why are you telling me this?"

"Because I'm going to recommend to the coven that Reeva take over."

I stared at her. "Are you purposely causing trouble? Is it the hormones? Is the baby infusing you with wickedness?"

She ignored my protest. "Flavia will retaliate, but Reeva is the best choice. She's the third strongest witch in the coven. Mama being first." She gave me an apologetic smile. "I thought you'd want to know ahead of time."

"Like that will help. When exactly are you bringing the wrath of Flavia down on the unsuspecting villagers?"

"At the next month's esbat gathering."

"Oh goody. Something to look forward to."

Back in the main room, we found Mom inspecting Morgan's handmade cosmetics and face creams. She held up a jar. "The labels say all natural ingredients."

"Herbs from my garden," Morgan explained. "Honey and beeswax from Beckett. Anything that doesn't come from Whispering Pines comes from organic distributors I know personally."

Businesswoman Mom came out. Glad to see I wasn't the only one living with multiple versions of myself.

"And if I like them," she said, tapping the full basket hanging off her arm, "how long would it take to get inventory for my store?"

Morgan considered the question. "Normally these products are only available here. But since we're *family*, I could be convinced to make an exception."

At the emphasis on the word *family* and the accompanying wink, Mom gasped and then squinted at her. "Jayne's right. You are a witch."

Later that night, Rosalyn had a date with Reed, and Mom went to her room somewhat early to call Dad. That meant Tripp and I had time alone. With Meeka, who sat on my feet when we stretched out on our sofa.

I sighed as he rubbed my shoulders. "It feels like a week since it was just the two of us."

"You're so tense, babe. Time to relax now."

I told him what Morgan said about Reeva taking over as High Priestess.

"Wow. Well, try to relax anyway. It'll all work out. How are you doing after everything that happened with Maewyn?"

"This one is different for me." I angled my neck so he could get at a particularly stubborn knot.

"What are you struggling with? Iris committed murder."

"I'm not dismissing Iris's actions. That's not it." I explained the mechanics behind strangling a person to death. "What makes an otherwise normal, calm person do such a thing? Are any of us capable of something like that if pushed far enough? Or is there something unique to someone like Iris that brings on that kind of rage?"

After a few seconds he asked, "Am I supposed to answer that?"

"No." I twisted out of his hands, which also twisted my feet out from beneath Meeka. She yapped at me and trotted off to her cushion by our bed. "There's something else I want to talk with you about."

"Uh-oh."

"This will benefit you."

He grinned and gave me his sultriest look.

I laughed. "Not that. At least not right now. I don't want you to spend the summer chained to this house like a father with a baby."

"That pretty much goes with the B&B territory, babe."

"My point is it doesn't have to. We could get you some help. I don't imagine you want to let go of making breakfast."

He shook his head. "No. I really enjoy the cooking part."

"We could hire a babysitter, so to speak. Maybe Arden or Holly would want to pick up a couple extra hours in the afternoon so you can go do your own thing. Hiking or kayaking or whatever."

"It would be exactly like hiring a sitter. This place is like our baby."

That explained the look on his face. Like an emotional parent dropping off their child at daycare for the first time.

"We don't have to decide now. Think about it, though."

"What I'd like is to run this place with you." He pulled me onto his lap. "Just the two of us. And Arden and Holly."

Across the room, Meeka sneezed.

"And the furry one." He looked seriously at me. "Could you ever see that happening?"

"Stepping down from being sheriff?" My throat constricted, and my heart started racing. I was probably making the same handing-over-my-baby face he did. "Not right now. Not until I've completed whatever I was brought here to do."

He smiled. "You didn't say no. I'll put a checkmark in the win column."

We sat in silence for a few minutes and stared out at the treetops. Me in his lap, his arms tight around me making me feel comfortable and secure.

"Why do I feel like things are about to change?"

"Because a lot just did. You and your mom made a big breakthrough."

"That's true. We did."

"Only one thing left on your list, right?"

I nodded and settled back into him. "Fix the village and help it move forward. Who knows how long that will take."

"Don't care. Neither should you. We're here for the duration, no matter what that means, and it's not like we're leaving once you've completed your task. Serenity will take over Whispering Pines, and we'll settle in to a new normal."

"A normal life. Now there's a problem to have."

I let myself get lost in his kisses and wandering hands. When things got steamy, he picked me up and carried me to bed for more. For the moment, life was perfect.

Suspense and fantasy author Shawn McGuire loves creating characters and places her fans want to return to again and again. She started writing after seeing the first Star Wars movie (that's episode IV) as a kid. She couldn't wait for the next installment to come out so wrote her own. Sadly, those notebooks are long lost, but her desire to tell a tale is as strong now as it was then. She lives in Wisconsin near the beautiful Mississippi River and when not writing or reading, she might be baking, crafting, going for a long walk, or nibbling really dark chocolate.

Made in the USA
Monee, IL
09 May 2023